'Jane Caro has pulled it off again. You are drawn into a fascinating, original mystery thriller, but you're soon caring as fiercely as Jane about the issues of injustice and prejudice that she has smuggled in under your nose. *Lyrebird* satisfies as a story and also as an eloquent and impassioned appeal for how much better our world could be.'
MALCOLM KNOX, author of THE FIRST FRIEND

PRAISE FOR
THE MOTHER

'*The Mother* is a gripping, insightful and compelling book about a family grappling with the issue of coercive control. Jane Caro's deep research, wisdom and compassion are evident on every page. The characters are beautifully drawn and extremely real. Truly, I could not put this book down. It will spark fierce debate about how we should punish perpetrators, and support victim–survivors. I gasped out loud at some of the plot twists, and wept at the end. Every Australian should read this book. Choose this for your next book club, and talk about it with your family and friends.' **TRACEY SPICER, journalist and author of THE GOOD GIRL STRIPPED BARE**

'Chillingly authentic, dark and exhilarating, a domestic revenge tale for any mother who's ever wondered how far she would go to protect her children.' **JUANITA PHILLIPS, journalist**

'How refreshing to read something so human and honest and so firmly entrenched in the perspective of women subjected to abuse and coercive control. To feel what those women have felt. To gain insight into their experience. And especially, not to have their sufferings blunted or Hollywood-ised. *The Mother* is devastating, frightening and heartbreaking, but also compassionate and empowering. It felt so convincing and real. With incisive clarity and insight, Caro shows how pressure builds on those who are oppressed and fearful. A deeply moving portrait of the shattering emotional impact of abuse on women and their families.' **KAREN VIGGERS, author of SIDELINES**

'In her passionate and compelling novel, Jane Caro tells the vivid and heart-stopping tale of a young family in danger and the mother who will do anything to save them. I couldn't put it down. Passionate, vivid and unsettling, this heart-stopping tale of a family in turmoil had me transfixed.' **SUZANNE LEAL, author of THE WATCHFUL WIFE**

'A feminist thriller that layers intrigue, darkness, insight and motherly love to create an addictive read. What I love most about this work is that it starts with a seemingly ordinary family scenario, but Jane's writing builds and builds suspense to a shattering crescendo.' **GINGER GORMAN, author of TROLL HUNTING**

'A gripping read that explores the complexity of family relationships and asks the ultimate question: how far would you go to protect your kids?' **DEE MADIGAN, writer and creative director**

'I know a great deal about abusive relationships and, still, my sense of foreboding was so strong from so early in the book that I had to get up from the table and pace the house to walk off the adrenaline. Jane Caro has beautifully captured the slow burn towards greater control, and the confusion of outsiders about the real mechanics of the relationship till it's so far gone. Jane's descriptions of coercive control and domestic violence felt very realistic to me, particularly the exhaustion of relatives over endless court battles and a life you didn't choose, where you are constantly looking over your shoulder, even in your own home.' **ANNABELLE DANIEL, CEO Women's Community Shelters**

'A clever domestic noir with a plot that keeps you guessing . . . The shocks come thick and fast, as love, loss and empathy combine with explosive effect. Most of all, these are people we can all recognise. Thought-provoking reading.' **AUSTRALIAN WOMEN'S WEEKLY**

'A confronting yet important read that tackles themes of domestic violence and coercive control . . . Caro once again demonstrates her brilliance as both a writer and social commentator, using this timely thriller to send a powerful message to readers.' **BETTER READING**

'A gripping tale.' **MAMAMIA**

'An extremely powerful read that I recommend without question.' **MRS B'S BOOK REVIEWS**

Jane Caro AM is a Walkley award–winning Australian columnist, author, novelist, feminist, public education activist and social commentator. She was awarded the B&T Women in Media Lifetime Achievement Award in 2023. Once upon a time, she was a multi-award-winning advertising copywriter and an academic. These days, she is a full-time writer, novelist, speaker, MC and TV, radio and media pundit. She has published thirteen books, including the bestselling novel *The Mother*. *Lyrebird* is her second novel for adults.

LYREBIRD
JANE CARO

ALLEN&UNWIN
SYDNEY·MELBOURNE·AUCKLAND·LONDON

This is a work of fiction. Names, characters, places and incidents are products of the author's imagination or are used fictitiously. Any resemblance to actual events, locales or persons, living or dead, is entirely coincidental.

First published in 2025

Copyright © Jane Caro 2025

All rights reserved. No part of this book may be reproduced or transmitted in any form or by any means, electronic or mechanical, including photocopying, recording or by any information storage and retrieval system, without prior permission in writing from the publisher. The Australian *Copyright Act 1968* (the Act) allows a maximum of one chapter or 10 per cent of this book, whichever is the greater, to be photocopied by any educational institution for its educational purposes provided that the educational institution (or body that administers it) has given a remuneration notice to the Copyright Agency (Australia) under the Act.

Allen & Unwin
Cammeraygal Country
83 Alexander Street
Crows Nest NSW 2065
Australia
Phone: (61 2) 8425 0100
Email: info@allenandunwin.com
Web: www.allenandunwin.com

Allen & Unwin acknowledges the Traditional Owners of the Country on which we live and work. We pay our respects to all Aboriginal and Torres Strait Islander Elders, past and present.

 A catalogue record for this book is available from the National Library of Australia

ISBN 978 1 76147 153 7

Set in 12/18.5 pt Adobe Caslon Pro by Bookhouse, Sydney
Printed and bound in Australia by the Opus Group

10 9 8 7 6

 The paper in this book is FSC® certified. FSC® promotes environmentally responsible, socially beneficial and economically viable management of the world's forests.

THIS BOOK IS DEDICATED TO EVERYONE WHO IS
DOING WHAT THEY CAN TO COMBAT CLIMATE CHANGE.
IT IS WRITTEN IN THE HOPE THAT MORE OF US WILL
JOIN THIS EXISTENTIAL FIGHT.

PROLOGUE

Thank God the ibuprofen had kicked in. The head she had woken up with that morning would not have coped with the dirt road. She hadn't been able to see the potholes in the dappled light so she'd bashed and bumped her way along the crumbling dirt road to the summit. Forget her head, had her compact four-wheel drive coped with it? It had made a horrible crunching noise as it bottomed out, and there was no mobile phone reception to call for help once she'd entered the forest.

Ibuprofen or not, she felt like shit. How many hours had she slept? Three, four at the most? And how many drinks had she downed at the Bar on the Hill? The last couple of hours before she'd staggered home to her flat were a blur. *Note to self, Jessica Weston: no more than three drinks in one night.* It was a vow she had made and broken many times. There was a bloke who had pestered her, she remembered, and she'd been irritated when he wouldn't take no for an answer, but he must have done eventually given she'd woken up alone.

She'd been out for the count when the alarm rang at 6.30 a.m. When she'd collapsed on her bed the night before, she had forgotten to turn the bloody thing off. She'd set it yesterday afternoon, so she'd wake up in time for her field trip into the Barringtons. *My sober self getting the jump on my drunk self,* she thought. *Bloody birds, I hope they appreciate the efforts I am making to aid their survival.*

The branches of the hide were digging into her back. She folded her rain jacket into a cushion and leant against it. It helped—a little. Fortunately, field work wasn't particularly taxing. It could be exciting if she caught a rare bird in her lens, but in the meantime, all she had to do was let the camera positioned just outside the entrance to the hide do its job. She was well prepared for a long wait. She had a blister pack of painkillers, a packet of sandwiches, lollies, some chocolate biscuits, a thermos of hot coffee and nothing to do but wait.

The day was warm for July, and the forest alive with birdsong. Despite her hangover, it was lovely to be completely alone in this beautiful place. Alone except for the abundant wildlife. She closed her eyes and listened to the ecstatic sounds of the forest. At least, that's how it always sounded to her—as if the world was bursting with joy. Yes, she knew nature was red in tooth and claw, but every time she went out into the bush she felt this bliss. This was how the world was meant to be, and she was going to do everything she could to keep it that way. But she was increasingly worried about the birds; that was why she had studied ornithology and was now researching her PhD at Newcastle Uni, where she also worked as a tutor.

The track she'd followed to get to the hide wound through the rainforest to Burraga Swamp, the highest hanging peat bog in the southern hemisphere. The forest was still beautiful, but Jessica's expert eye saw the deterioration that had followed the cuts to the National Parks and Wildlife Service budget. Tracks were no longer cleared regularly, for one thing. Weeds were encroaching, and if trees fell and blocked the path—and they fell all the time—they often weren't moved for months, meaning walkers had to find another way around, trampling more of the forest's undergrowth.

A rustle in said undergrowth caught her attention. The camera was still recording and Jessica wondered what she might catch on video. She was counting and recording the birds, of course, but she also had her eyes and ears open for illegal commercial logging or locals felling the odd red cedar or white mahogany for fence posts. She sat forward, on the alert, but the rustle stopped just as suddenly as it had started and she assumed whatever had caused it had moved away. She looked at her watch; not yet 10 a.m. She'd have at least four hours of good strong daylight. The birds were always more numerous and more vocal in the sun. With a bit of luck, she might even see a lyrebird. Recording one of those doing its spectacular mating dance was number one on her bucket list.

She settled back against her makeshift cushion once more and passed the time by testing her ability to identify each bird from its song: the chortling of fairy wrens, the long notes of whipbirds with their staccato ending, the harsh cries of yellow-tailed black cockatoos. Scrub wrens, shrike-thrushes, willie wagtails, grey fantails, magpies, butcherbirds, lyrebirds . . .

Jessica's eyes snapped open. She must have drifted into sleep. The sun was much higher in the sky, and she needed to pee. She straightened her stiff legs and crawled out of the hide. It was a relief to stand up and stretch. She headed back towards a fallen cedar she'd had to clamber over earlier and crouched behind it, slightly off the path, so she would be out of sight in the unlikely event another human came this way. She pulled down her shorts and squatted, positioning her butt at the top of a small rise so her wee would run downhill and away from her feet, as her mother had taught her. As always, the thought of her mother caused Jessica a pang. She still missed her.

She was rebuttoning her shorts when a sound froze her blood.

A woman. A woman screaming in pure terror. Screaming and sobbing—begging—out here, in this desolate place. Jessica's instinct was to turn and run to the car and get the hell out. But she could not abandon the woman. Even if she was unable to help her, at least she could be a witness. She knew she must go towards the sound. 'Just do what is right,' her mother had always said to her, and so she did.

Her heart pounded so loudly she thought whoever was up ahead must be able to hear it, but she crept through the undergrowth, avoiding the path and hoping against hope that the dappled light and her khaki work gear would conceal her approach. The screaming was closer now. Jessica dropped to her stomach and commando-crawled through the tree ferns towards the sound. Rigid with terror, she dropped into a small ditch, then slowly lifted her head.

What she saw almost made her cry with relief. There was no woman screaming, no brute towering over her with a weapon in hand. What she saw was a superb lyrebird, a male, beginning its mating dance and song. Head thrown back, beak wide, tail feathers open and shaking, the bird was mimicking the sounds of human terror, the way she had heard other lyrebirds mimic chainsaws, car alarms and every other bird in the forest.

Her legs felt a bit wobbly as she stood. She hoped she was capturing this on film. Bugger, she shouldn't have left the hide; that was always the time when the best shit happened. Quickly and quietly, Jessica returned to her shelter and checked the camera. Its recording light glowed steadily. And, she reassured herself, the sound recorder she had around her neck as backup had been on the whole time.

By now, the bird had begun mimicking a kookaburra. Then, warming to its task, it began to run through its repertoire: whipbirds, the whirr and buzz of bowerbirds and the screech of cockatoos, reproduced so accurately that if she'd had her eyes closed she would have sworn she was surrounded by them all. As the momentum of its calls increased, so did the bird's dance. He stamped and scratched then flicked his lyrates wide, revealing the dark filamentous feathers underneath. As he turned—searching, Jessica knew, for a shaft of sunlight—he mimicked other sounds: a chainsaw, a car engine starting and a radio being tuned. His dance intensifying, his feathers stiff with excitement, he suddenly flipped his tail over his head as he turned slowly. The dark filamentous feathers disappeared, replaced by their brilliant white underside flashing as they caught the sun. As the bird's feathers reflected the light into every corner of the leafy clearing, he began to mimic the woman again, and the note of pure terror he hit made Jessica gasp. *It's just a bird*, she reminded herself. *It's not really happening.*

The bird displayed for almost twelve minutes, but in vain. Jessica caught a glimpse of a female in the undergrowth, but apparently she was not impressed enough to approach as she scurried away. (*Like me last night*, Jessica thought.) His display unsuccessful, the male ended his dance, winding it down slowly, making sure he had got all his feathers back into place. His parting calls were in the sobbing woman's terrified voice—'*Ayúdame, ayúdame*'—then he disappeared into the forest.

Jessica sat for a moment, turning off the camera to preserve its battery. What an incredible experience. It wasn't until she began to replay what she had recorded, to double-check the camera had worked, that it dawned on her. Lyrebirds were mimics. They didn't create the sounds they made, only repeated what they had heard. Had the bird actually listened to some poor woman begging for her life? Surely not. Maybe it had heard a recording, someone playing something on their CD player or radio. There must be another explanation. Jessica looked around uneasily. The bush that had seemed so benign and beautiful only minutes before now seemed sinister.

TWENTY YEARS LATER

ONE

Megan had just flopped down on the sofa, a cup of tea in front of her and the TV remote in her hand, when she heard a car pull up in her driveway. *Who could this be?* She wasn't expecting visitors; Jason had moved away to Melbourne and no one else was likely to drop by. She sipped her tea as she pulled back the front curtain. It was a police car. Four decades in the police force meant she wasn't fazed—interested, but not fazed.

As the two cops got out of the car, she recognised Phil Arlott. She'd worked with him in Maitland for years. They'd been friends, though she hadn't seen much of him since she'd retired. As much her fault as his. She'd meant to get in touch but just never got around to it. However, this wasn't a social visit; Phil's much younger sidekick was in uniform. Megan had been a civilian for at least a year. They wouldn't call on her for an unpaid parking fine or speeding ticket, and those were the only infractions she could imagine she'd committed. And she'd spoken to Jason on the phone only a few minutes ago so knew he and all the family were fine. No, this must be business. She felt a surge. Megan had not been enjoying retirement as much as she had thought she would.

She opened her front door before the visitors had a chance to ring the bell. 'Senior Sergeant Arlott! Long time, no see. To what do I owe the pleasure?'

'Lovely to see you too, Sarge . . . I mean Megan.'

She smiled at the slip of the tongue.

'This is Constable Samira Kumar.' Phil gestured towards the young woman beside him.

'Pleased to meet you, Ms Blaxland. You're a legend at the station.'

'A legend? That's code for old, isn't it?'

Kumar looked mortified and Megan felt sorry.

'Don't take anything Megan says seriously,' Phil told her. 'She's old school. Always taking the piss.'

'Enough with the old, okay?' Megan quipped.

The awkward moment had passed. Phil was a dinosaur, but the nicer kind.

Megan stepped back and held the door open so they could enter.

'I'm assuming this isn't a social call,' she said.

The two police officers sat. Megan settled herself in the chair opposite and took another sip from the cup she was still holding.

'Tea?' she asked, gesturing at the pot. She was old school about that too. Proper leaf tea, correctly brewed in a pre-warmed pot.

The two on the couch politely declined.

'We've found a body,' Phil said abruptly. 'Up near Burraga Swamp.'

Megan put her tea down and gave her former colleague a long look.

'Lisa—I mean Inspector George—told us to come and let you know. In fact, she was wondering if you'd consider being seconded to the investigation for a few months. She thinks—we all think—it's your cold case.'

Megan's heart leapt. There was nothing she'd like better. She was bored and lonely in retirement, wondering how on earth she was going to fill each day. But this was more; this was vindication. She and that student—Jessica Weston—had been right all along. Nevertheless, she kept her face expressionless. 'What makes you think it's the lyrebird case?'

'Where it was found, and forensics reckon from the state of decomposition that it's been there about twenty years.'

'A woman's body?'

'Yeah.'

'Why didn't Inspector George come and ask me herself?'

Phil shrugged. 'You know Li— the Inspector; she's a stickler.'

'Bloody good copper. Always knew she'd go far.'

'Anyway, what do you reckon? We'd all love to see you back. And you've only been gone a year.'

'A year on 28 August.' A fortnight ago, Megan realised.

'Things haven't changed much.'

'Not sure that's any kind of recommendation.'

'And it's your case,' Phil added. 'You know it and nobody else does.'

It was true. The lyrebird case was her first as a wet-behind-the-ears detective constable, and the mockery she'd copped over it had been a big factor in why she had let it go cold. She'd been forty then, old for a new detective. It had taken her years to qualify, trying to juggle parenting Jason with being a cop on the beat and studying. Her age had made her more sensitive to criticism. She'd absorbed the idea that she was a slow learner. Stupid, she thought now; she should have stuck to her guns. But this bizarre case had nagged at her over the years, and she didn't like loose ends. That's what had made her such a good detective. She'd risen to the rank of senior sergeant—Phil's rank now—but she hadn't made inspector because, unlike Lisa, she'd do what it took to solve a case, even if it sometimes meant bending the rules. And she was champing at the bit to finally solve this one.

It was more than just a second chance or vindication, though. She had a responsibility. Back then she'd allowed herself to be persuaded that a lyrebird's song was no kind of evidence on which to spend precious police resources. There'd been no body, and no one who could have been the woman the bird was mimicking on the tape had been reported missing. They'd got no calls when they'd played the screaming lyrebird to the media, apart from a few lyrebird fanciers asking where they could get a copy.

The investigation came to a dead end. Apart from Jessica's video, there was no evidence that a crime had even been committed. But she'd believed the young woman when she'd told her that lyrebirds don't make up their songs. Megan had taken Jessica seriously as an expert in her field, while her colleagues, mostly blokes, had seen only a flaky uni student who probably drank too much and seemed like a fucking tree-hugger, high on whacky tobaccy—as she remembered them calling it—or magic mushrooms. Megan could hear their taunts now. If she could solve the mystery, crack it after all these years . . . but she mustn't get ahead of herself.

'If you're up for it, we could take you to view the remains and the crime scene now.' Phil inclined his head towards his car.

'Are you going to pay me?' It wouldn't do to seem too eager. Police culture—at Maitland, anyway—was all about appearing laconic.

'Consultant's fees.'

Much better than a copper's pay, they all knew that.

'In that case, count me in.'

—

The road to the Upper Allyn was even worse than Megan remembered. More patches than road, potholes formed in potholes. She was bouncing around in the back seat like a sack of potatoes and her sixty-year-old bones were protesting.

'Sorry.' Kumar was behind the wheel. 'Sometimes there are so many they're impossible to avoid.'

'No worries,' Megan said. And she wasn't just being polite. She was surprised at how pleased she was to be back on the job, even if only for a short time. She was even impatient to see the remains. 'Who found the body?'

'There was a landslip after the heavy rain earlier in the week,' Phil said. 'It revealed the grave.'

'Yeah, but who noticed? Not many dog walkers and joggers out here.'

They had not passed another car since they'd entered the forest.

'A couple of park rangers. They don't visit often these days, apparently. But after heavy rain, they do try to make sure that there's nothing dangerous on the trails. Fear of being sued, I suppose. There are walkers and twitchers who still come up here, and campers especially on weekends. Anyway, the rangers came up first thing this morning and found her. Used their radio to call it in.'

'Are they still on site?'

'Yep.'

'Good. Who else is up there?'

'Forensics and a copper from East Gresford. No one else about.'

Constable Kumar had not taken her eyes off the road as they climbed ever higher into the Tops. Just as well; beyond the edge was a drop of hundreds of feet. They were in a police four-wheel drive but, even so, the wheels kept slipping on the wet clay. Kumar was taking it very slow.

'There will be tomorrow, though,' Phil went on. 'This place is packed with campers and caravanners every weekend. Has been ever since Covid.'

'Any media?'

'Not yet, but I reckon once the rangers get back to town the place will be crawling with them. Nothing they like better than a juicy murder.'

Nothing I like better, thought Megan, with a pang of shame.

'Forensics will have taken the body by then, surely?'

Phil turned to look at her. 'Yeah, they're just waiting for you to see it first.'

He grinned and Megan gave him a look. They'd known all along she'd say yes.

When they pulled into the Burraga Swamp car park, just past the turn-off to Mount Allyn, Megan was struck by how neglected it looked. The signs identifying the walk and the destination had rotted. The once-clear print naming the swamp, giving a few facts about the length and degree of difficulty of the walk, had become so obscured with mould and decay as to be indecipherable. *What an awful place to be buried*, Megan thought.

The ground was still muddy and Megan was relieved she'd brought her gumboots. The track—if you could still call it that—was overgrown and much harder going than it had been the last time she'd set foot in this place. Great swathes of nettles and other weeds had grown across the forest floor.

'Hello, Sarge.'

The Gresford copper who was lifting the police tape looked familiar to Megan.

'Josh Baker, remember?'

She did, but only vaguely. She hadn't had much cause to come up this way for ages. 'Of course! Nice to see you again.'

'And you. I thought you'd retired?'

'Should you be letting me in without a badge?'

'Will he vouch for you?' Baker gestured at Phil.

'Nope,' Phil said. 'Loose cannon, like always.'

Megan rolled her eyes, but the banter felt good.

'Here, put these on.'

Protective bootees; of course. Kumar also handed her a pair of gloves.

'Have you taken a statement?' Megan asked Baker, inclining her head towards the two park rangers who were standing off to one side.

'Yep.'

'Go and have a quick word, Constable,' Megan said to Kumar. As Kumar hurried away Megan could almost feel her relief. She could understand why a newbie might not want to see the body. To Baker she said, 'It's best if someone directly involved in the investigation also has a word with them.'

'I'd like to be involved, if possible. I was first on the scene, and I am a local.'

He had a point. 'I'll let you know,' Megan said. 'In the meantime . . .' She gestured in the direction of the tent forensics had erected to cover the remains and began to stride towards it, surprised at how impatient she was to get started. Like Kumar, she'd always hated viewing the corpse. She must have toughened up in her old age. Or maybe boredom had outweighed squeamishness.

'It's Scotty,' Phil said, falling into step beside her.

'Jackpot!'

Megan loved Scotty, trusted the forensic officer's knowledge and judgement absolutely. No one was more experienced. And

Scotty was a friend. They'd met up a few times since Megan had retired.

'I thought you'd be pleased.'

He'd pulled some strings for her, Megan realised. 'Thanks, mate. I owe you.'

Inside the white tent Scotty was crouched down taking photos of the remains. Megan could see a wet and muddy skeleton, the greenish white of the bones shocking against the thick black soil. She had an impulse to cover the body with a blanket. How cold and lonely it must have been out here, lying mouldering in the grave for two long decades and, given the complete blank they'd drawn when trying to find a possible murder victim, no one even noticing you were gone.

'Nice to have you back, Sarge.' It was typical of Scotty to address Megan by her rank. The other woman understood how important it was to her.

'Nice to be back, even under these circumstances.'

'Don't give me that.'

Scotty knew her too well, but Megan's pleasure at being back on the job was tempered by her pity for the corpse, so slight, so vulnerable, so enigmatic.

'Well, it's good to be useful.'

She and Phil stood in silence, surveying the scene. Megan could see where the land had slipped away, revealing the skeletal remains. Otherwise, there was nothing obvious. Twenty years is a long time for a crime scene.

'What have you got?' she asked the forensics officer.

'Female. Late twenties, early thirties maybe. Small. Given the state of the remains, I'd say she's been here at least twenty years. But that's only a guess at this stage, of course.'

Scotty's guesses were generally right.

'Cause of death?'

'Hard to tell. I haven't found a bullet hole or a stoved-in skull or anything nice and obvious. Signs of old injuries, however. I suspect she lived a hard life.'

'And a short one.'

No one responded.

'Killed here?'

'Difficult to tell after all this time.'

A flock of yellow-tailed black cockatoos took flight, screeching at one another. Their cries sounded desolate. The birds reminded Megan of the ornithology student who'd set off the original investigation. She turned to Phil, but before she could speak Scotty drew her attention back to the woman in the open grave.

'There is this . . .'

Scotty was pointing to the skeleton's left leg. Most of the clothing had rotted in the mud, only a few wisps clung to its torso. All of the skeleton's hair had gone too. Scotty was carefully brushing away more of the soil to reveal a shoe.

'She was wearing runners. I can't find the other one, but this one is cheap—plastic, polyester and nylon. That's why it survived, I guess. No doubt they made them by the millions, and that'll make finding an owner like a needle in a haystack. But this might yield more info—it wasn't sold with the shoe, that's for sure. Made by hand, I reckon.'

Scotty was pointing to the shoelace. It was distinctive, even after decades in the ground. Filthy though it was, the strands making up the braid looked like they might once have been brightly coloured.

Megan nodded. 'It's something to go on. I don't want her to stay a Jane Doe.' She turned back to Phil. 'I guess we'd better tell that student who first reported the lyrebird.'

Scotty rose from her haunches and stretched her back. Maybe age was catching up with her too.

'You think this is connected with that lyrebird case?' she asked.

Scotty had been Megan's sounding board back then. They'd both been younger and idealistic, and two of the only women with any seniority.

'The location is right and the body has been in the ground the appropriate amount of time,' Megan said.

'Do you still have the student's contact details?' Phil looked sceptical.

'I've got them,' Megan said. 'Her name is Jessica Weston.'

TWO

'I hate you!'

Sheridan slammed her bedroom door so hard Jessica thought the old plaster ceiling might come crashing down. She almost wished it would. Jessica was just as angry as her fifteen-year-old, but she was the mother, so she kept a lid on the hot lava of her rage.

'Well, I don't like you very much at the moment either!'

Jessica walked back to the kitchen. She'd known being a single parent would be hard, but did it have to be this hard? Jessica and Sheridan had been everything in the world to one another after she and Steve had decided to call it quits. They'd parted amicably enough and shared the parenting, although Jessica had done most of the heavy lifting. She hadn't minded. She loved her daughter ferociously. She still did, even though a couple of years ago her sweet and biddable child had been replaced by a foul-mouthed, selfish harridan. Fighting with her daughter reminded her of her relationship with her own mother.

Maybe that was part of what enraged her so much. She'd lost her mother just after she'd graduated high school—killed in a car accident. There'd been so much she'd missed out on. Maybe she expected too much of her teenage daughter, wanting her to fill the hole her own mother had left.

During Covid, Jessica had been a bit smug about what a good job she had done of parenting. The two of them had jogged along quite well, despite being almost constantly in one another's company. They'd had a few battles about schoolwork and eating properly—if Sheridan had had her way it would have been Uber Eats every night—but compared to the stories Jessica had heard from friends, Sheridan had been a dream. Jessica was paying for her complacency now. Sunny Sheridan had become a handful, straining at the leash, desperate to do things that Jessica did not think remotely appropriate for a girl of fifteen. But Sheridan didn't look fifteen. Maybe that was the problem. She was tall and willowy. With make-up and her hair done, she could pass for twenty-five. And it seemed as if she thought she was twenty-five. Any rule, any restriction, was treated as a human rights issue. Sheridan's sense of injustice was finely honed, and she could argue black was white until Jessica gave up in frustration. This latest fight had been about Sheridan's curfew—9.30 p.m. was quite late enough at her age—and Sheridan's wheedling about there being no school tomorrow as it was Friday cut no ice with her. Jessica knew she was an anxious mother. She did not trust that things would turn out all right. Her mother's death was part of that, of course, but not all of it. That lyrebird's horrible screaming continued to haunt her twenty years later. She dreamt of it still, and sometimes the screams were in Sheridan's voice. She knew it was all in her head, that she was being ridiculous, but that didn't stop her feeling frightened.

Saying no takes so much more energy than saying yes, Jessica thought as she reached into the fridge for the chardonnay. 'Sheridan's driven me to drink,' she said out loud, and poured herself a generous slug. Just the one, she told herself, just the one.

Jessica Weston was not used to coping with defiance. She was an associate professor now. No one knew more about the superb lyrebird, and her speciality had become even more noteworthy since the 2019 bushfires. Between a third and half of the birds' forest habitats had burnt and the birds' classification had gone from 'common' to 'threatened'. This had resulted in even more invitations to international conferences, symposiums on conservation, summits on the environment and earnest debates about the effects of climate change on wildlife. And it had been a smart move to make such a performer her special subject. People were fascinated and entertained by lyrebirds. The film archives she had built up of the bird's spectacular mating ritual was in high demand. There was one film she never played, however.

Jessica sat down in front of the TV. She still had time to catch the end of the ABC news. She'd just turned it on when Sheridan came to stand in front of her, looking mulish.

'Can I have money for a cab?'

'What?'

'It's not like you'll be in a fit state to pick me up.' Her daughter pointed at the giant glass of wine.

Jessica opened her wallet and handed her daughter a fifty-dollar note.

'Make sure you text me the taxi number when you get in it at nine fifteen.'

Sheridan snatched the money. 'It's hardly worth going!'

'If you are not home on the dot of nine thirty you'll be grounded for a week. Got it?'

Sheridan rolled her eyes as she turned towards the front door.

'And for every ten minutes you're late you'll cop another week.'

But Sheridan had gone.

Jessica took a large gulp of wine.

'I shouldn't let her get to me,' she said to her glass.

Then she heard the front door open and Sheridan's feet pounding down the hall. She ran up to Jessica and leant in to give her a kiss.

'I don't know why I'm such a bitch,' her daughter said. Then she was gone again.

Jessica was left open-mouthed. Before she had a chance to make sense of her daughter's behaviour, her phone lit up. Was it Sheridan again? Surely not. She looked at the caller ID. Not Sheridan. The call was from someone Jessica had not heard from for a few years. Someone she liked. Just what she needed: a cheerful chat. Their friendship had been the only good thing to come out of the lyrebird incident.

'Megan! How lovely to hear from you!' She had her confident associate professor voice on.

'Hello, Jessica. It's lovely to hear your voice too.'

'How's Guido?' she asked.

There was a pause before Megan answered. 'He died.'

'Oh God! I'm so sorry.' Jessica was mortified that she had not kept in contact. How could she have let her friend go through all that alone? The memory of her own loneliness when her mother had been killed made her feel even worse.

'Yeah, it was tough.'

Silence. Jessica could hear Megan's breath. It sounded steady and calm. Jessica wondered whether she should say anything about losing her mum, but before she could Megan said, 'Look, I'm sorry to interrupt your evening, but I'm afraid this is not a social call.'

'What's up?' Jessica asked.

'We've found a body up at Burraga Swamp.'

Jessica sagged back into the couch, winded. She felt like a puppet whose strings had been cut.

'At last,' she said, when she could speak.

'That's what I thought too.'

'A woman?'

'Yes, and forensics think she's been there about twenty years.'

Hot tears pricked Jessica's eyes. She had not been delusional or gullible or stoned or any of the other horrible things people had claimed. She had been right. She bit her lip hard to stop herself from crying.

'Anyway, they've asked me to come out of retirement and take charge of the investigation, and I want to revisit the old evidence—your video and the recording. I was wondering if you could pop into the station on Monday morning so we could go through it together?'

Retirement? Jessica had not realised.

'I have a lecture first thing Monday, but I could be there about eleven.'

'Eleven is fine. Ask for me at the desk. Senior Sergeant Blaxland. They've given me my old rank back for the duration.'

'I didn't realise you'd left.'

'I retired after Guido died. I just didn't have any juice left for the job.'

'But now you do?'

'Now I do.'

THREE

When Jessica arrived at Maitland police station the following Monday, promptly at 11 a.m., Megan was in the foyer. The detective was heavier than when Jessica had last seen her, and her short, thick hair was now entirely grey, but her manner was still just as friendly and the blue eyes that crinkled when she smiled were still just as shrewd. *It's why she's such a good copper*, Jessica thought. *You can tell there's a human behind the badge.*

'Thank you for coming,' Megan said. 'I really appreciate it.'

'Try and stop me,' Jessica replied. 'I feel responsible for that woman, whoever she is.'

Megan nodded. She did too.

Jessica gestured to the satchel slung over shoulder. 'I brought my computer with the film and audio uploaded.'

'Thanks, but I've got them ready on the equipment in the comms room. Follow me.'

As they walked down the corridor Megan said, 'How's Sheridan?'

'A pain in the arse.'

'She was a very cute toddler.'

'Yeah, her looks deceived us all back then.'

She wasn't being quite fair. Sheridan had come home on the dot of 9.30 p.m. And Jessica had drunk only a single glass of wine—they had both done what they had said they would for once.

Megan gave a sympathetic laugh. 'Jason had his moments at that age. He's married with two of his own now.'

'I'm sorry about Guido.'

Jessica thought she saw Megan wince slightly as she paused to open a door. 'It was over a year ago now, but I still miss him.'

Jessica put a hand on Megan's arm and Megan covered it briefly with her own.

'Anyway,' she said, 'do you want a tea? I've just brewed a pot.'

Jessica nodded; Megan made the best tea.

Megan gestured towards the chair in front of the computer screen. 'Play it a couple of times. See if you notice anything you didn't notice before.'

'That's okay.' Jessica was suddenly filled with reluctance. 'I'll wait till you get back.'

'I'll just be a jiffy.'

Alone in the comms room, Jessica stared at the computer screen; her video was cued up. There was the lyrebird, frozen with its beak wide and its head thrown back. She could see the swelling in the bird's throat lit up by the shaft of sunlight he'd needed to highlight his display. He was spotlit, a stark contrast against the dark, dense forest. Jessica shuddered. Terrible things had gone on in those shadows and she was about to relive them—in her imagination, at least. Did she want to know what had happened? Did she want to solve this mystery? Yes, she realised, she did. Knowing—however bad the knowledge might be—was better than not knowing.

Megan returned with the tea. 'Ready?'

Jessica nodded and the detective pressed play.

She thought she had steeled herself, but when the lyrebird began screaming she gasped and choked on her tea, spluttering it all over the desk.

'God, sorry—I'm so sorry!'

Megan grabbed some tissues from a nearby box and began mopping up the mess. 'No need to apologise. I'd forgotten how shocking it was.'

'We're hearing the last moments of her life.'

Megan nodded grimly.

'Did you notice anything different? Did anything stand out?'

'Nothing new, just the Spanish words.'

Ayúdame, ayúdame.

The words meant 'help me' in Spanish; Jessica remembered that from the original investigation.

'Do you think she—the victim, I mean—was Spanish?' she asked.

'Maybe, but Spanish is spoken in a lot of countries in South and Central America. The Philippines too.'

'Right.'

'Anything else?'

'I'm sorry. I was so overwhelmed I didn't really notice anything but the bird. Play it over and I'll pay more attention.'

Jessica took a deep breath. She never wanted to see or hear that video again, but she owed it to that poor dead woman. So she concentrated hard, watching for anything that seemed odd or different. They went through it a few times, but to no avail.

'I'm sorry. The bird is displaying and dancing just as I'd expect, and as I remember. And the forest looks, well, like the forest. Apart from the screaming, it's a perfectly normal clip of a superb lyrebird performing his mating dance—unsuccessfully in this case.'

'How do you know that?'

'You can't see it on the tape, but a female did come to check him out. She mustn't have been impressed, as she went away.'

'Anything else you can recall that was outside the scope of your camera or your cassette recorder? Anything at all?'

Jessica racked her brain but nothing occurred to her. 'Not that I can think of,' she said, feeling useless.

'No, that's fair enough, but I do have to ask. Did you see anyone else that day? On the track? On the road? In the forest?'

'Christ! It's twenty years ago. I don't think so. In fact, I remember how scared I was when I realised that whatever the bird had heard he must have heard around there. I tried to persuade myself that he must have heard a film soundtrack or something—you know, on a CD player—but I didn't really believe it. Then I kept reminding myself that I hadn't passed another car once I entered the state forest, and that I'd only seen one after I hit the dirt road.'

Megan was rifling through the file.

'A car?' she said. 'That's right. We looked into it at the time.'

'And?'

'Dead end. Just a local buying eggs from the chicken farm up the road. He didn't even go into the forest.'

Jessica shook her head ruefully. 'I was badly hungover that day. I fell asleep not long before the bird did its thing. I've told you everything I know. I'm sorry I can't help you.'

'Don't apologise. Without your footage we'd have nothing to go on.'

Jessica took that as her cue to leave. She picked up her bag.

'There is one more thing,' Megan said as she reached for the mouse.

Jessica turned back to the screen, and Megan clicked on a picture of a filthy, half-rotted running shoe.

'Do you recognise this?'

Jessica shook her head. 'Was . . . was she wearing it?'

'Yeah.' Megan's voice was flat. 'What about this?'

Megan clicked to another photo, a braided shoelace. A small section had been cleaned so you could see the colours of the strands were red, yellow and green.

Jessica shook her head again. 'Are you trying DNA?'

'Scotty's on the case, but no result so far.'

'Helen Scott? She's great. She gives guest lectures at the uni on forensics occasionally. I've sat in on some of them.'

Megan nodded. 'Only the best for Jane Doe. I think we all feel a bit guilty about her.'

'Excuse me, Professor Weston, could you hang on a second?'

Jessica was walking through the police station towards the exit. She was still going over the day she had seen the lyrebird, trying to recall anything she might have forgotten. She was so preoccupied she almost ran into the bloke coming the other way.

'Sorry.'

'Professor Weston?'

She looked up to see a tall and burly man in his sixties. He didn't look familiar.

'We've met before,' he told her. 'Twenty years ago. My name's Arlott, Phil Arlott. I'll be working with Senior Sergeant Blaxland on the case.'

'Great,' Jessica said. 'I'm glad it's been reopened; I feel so bad about the woman lying there in the forest for so long.'

'We all do.'

'If I can be of any assistance, don't hesitate to ask—but I don't know how much more help I can be.'

The big man smiled.

'You'll be a help, all right. Particularly once we've caught the bastard and he goes to trial. And we will catch him.'

'He's had a hell of a head start.'

The big copper blushed. It made him seem boyish and suddenly he did look a bit familiar.

'Yeah,' he said. 'Sorry about that.' As if it was his fault.

She watched him walk on down the corridor, puzzled about why he had stopped her at all.

As she drove back to the university, Jessica's mind returned again to that day in Burraga Swamp. She remembered the state she had been in the last time she'd driven to Maitland police station. She'd been so panicked she'd forgotten her hangover. She'd driven as if the hounds of hell were at her heels, constantly checking her rear-view mirror as she hurtled along the steep and winding dirt road, convinced she'd see a car looming up behind her. It'd be easy for a large four-wheel drive to push her little RAV off the edge. She did not calm down even when she pulled into the car park at the police station.

Jessica felt anger at the memory of her terrified younger self. None of the blokes on the front desk had taken her seriously and yet her fear had not been irrational. Had the murderer been watching her in the bush that day? He could have been. There was no telling how long before she'd recorded the lyrebird that the creature had heard the screams. It could have been a month before she arrived or an hour.

'I want to report a murder,' she'd said.

One of the young cops looked up at her from behind the screen protecting him from the public. He raised an eyebrow. 'Can you give me more details?'

'It's all on here.' Jessica lobbed her video camera onto the desk.

Both his eyebrows shot up. 'You filmed the murder?'

'No, no—I filmed a lyrebird mimicking the screams of the victim.'

The cop glanced over at his colleagues and she saw the face he pulled. It was an I've-got-a-live-one-here face. Nevertheless, he followed protocol and fetched Megan Blaxland. Jessica hadn't known it at the time, but Megan was a new detective, so she got all the nutjobs, losers and cranks. She hadn't yet earnt any favours from the uniforms on the desk.

As the woman detective led her to an interview room, she'd overheard the cop behind the screen say, 'I've heard it all now.'

'She's pissed, I reckon. I could smell the alcohol from here.' The second cop—Arlott, Jessica realised suddenly as she stopped at a traffic light—hadn't even bothered to lower his voice. No wonder he'd apologised to her today.

Megan had been courteous and taken her seriously. She'd watched the video and listened to the tape, including the bit where Jessica went to pee. They'd both laughed at that, and Jessica had relaxed momentarily—until the screaming began.

'Those screams are hair-raising,' the woman detective had said. 'But is that all the evidence you've got?'

And that was the issue. A bird mimicking a woman's screams wasn't enough. Megan had done her best. She'd promised to follow every lead, not that there was anything else. Jessica hadn't missed the sotto voce bird squawks the cops had made as she had left the station that afternoon twenty years ago.

A few months later Megan had come to her flat to tell her the investigation had hit a dead end. It was kind of her, Jessica realised now. She could have just rung or sent a form letter.

'We'll keep it on file,' Megan had assured her. 'The case is still open.'

Jessica thought about the screams.

'But birds don't make things up,' she'd protested. 'A woman was killed out there and you're just ignoring her!'

Megan had looked stricken. 'But we have no more leads. No evidence beyond your recordings. We've been up to the site, done a thorough search and found nothing.'

Can't have been that thorough, thought Jessica now as she turned into the university gates. Jane Doe was there all the time.

'And maybe it wasn't murder,' Megan had added. 'We get called out for domestics more than any other crime. Women screaming is the soundtrack of our lives. Maybe some bloke thumped his wife while they were out walking or something.'

'You don't really believe that.'

'Or maybe your bird heard some kids mucking about.'

'Spanish-speaking kids? And the voice didn't sound like a kid, you know that.'

It was clear Megan was parroting what the blokes had said to her. Like Jessica, she surely knew the terror that bird had mimicked wasn't due to a slap or even a punch. It was someone in fear for their life. And maybe it was DV, but that didn't mean it wasn't murder. But at the time, Jessica could see now, Megan was new, junior and a woman. She'd had no clout back then.

Jessica walked towards her building. Twenty years ago, the case had been too hard and the cops had not wanted to be bothered. She was glad they felt guilty now.

Jessica and Megan had struck up a friendship in the aftermath. Just the occasional drink or a coffee, but they'd stayed in touch. Until Guido got sick, Jessica realised. Megan hadn't told her about that. And she hadn't asked.

—

Megan spent the afternoon reviewing the press release the police media unit had sent her about the discovery of the body. It featured a photo of the shoe and its distinctive shoelace. It would do. She looked up from the computer as Phil Arlott walked by.

'Phil! Got a sec?'

'Sure.'

'What do you think about seconding Josh Baker to the investigation?"

'Josh Baker?'

'Yeah. It'd be good to have a local on the team; he seems to know the lay of the land and all the locals.'

'Not that there are many to know.'

'Few hundred between Maitland and the forest, I would guess. Mostly farmers.'

'A few of them Pitt Street farmers.'

'Still worth knowing about,' Megan said.

'Do you think one of them might have done it?'

'Too early to tell, but local knowledge would help someone who was looking for a remote burial site.'

Phil was hovering.

'Have a look at this.' She angled the computer screen towards him. 'Do you think we'll get a bite?'

'Worth a try.'

Still staring at the shoe, Phil said, 'Do you remember that weird fence we passed on the way back from the crime scene?'

Megan did remember. 'The one that was hung with hundreds of pairs of shoes?'

'Yeah. Boot Hill it's called. Kumar found a report on it by NBN. Apparently it was set up decades ago as a laugh by some locals and then tourists started to add to it. It's a local landmark now. Bit of a coincidence, though.'

'And that's all it might be. But worth looking into.'

'That's what I thought. Our only clue is a shoe and its twin is missing.'

'Are you thinking the killer might have taken it?' Megan asked. 'Like a trophy?'

'Scotty reckons there's no evidence that an animal took it after the body was buried.' Phil was rubbing his chin. It was a familiar gesture, oddly comforting.

'She might have lost it in the struggle,' Megan suggested.

'Yes. That's possible. But we haven't found it.'

'Serial killers do take trophies, I suppose, but we've only found one body.'

'I still think it's worth a look.' Phil turned to go, then he stopped. 'Oh, are you mentioning the lyrebird in the press release?'

'No, not yet. I don't want a media frenzy.'

'We didn't get one last time.'

'Yeah, but we didn't have a body then. I'd like to hold it back till we really need it.'

Phil was still hovering. Did he fancy a drink or something? On a Monday night? Megan was on the verge of asking him when her phone rang. When she looked up, Phil had gone.

—

Megan was tired when she opened her front door that evening, but it was a different kind of tired. She was physically weary but more mentally energised than she had been for ages, maybe since Guido had died. She looked at his framed picture as she put her keys in the ceramic dish her youngest grandchild had made. Lopsided and garishly coloured, it had pride of place on the sideboard beside the front door. She smiled at it, then felt a pang. This was a grandchild Guido had hardly met.

'Evening, love,' she said to the photo. 'I've had a good day.'

Was it awful to get pleasure from murder? Because Scotty was right: Megan liked working a homicide. It was satisfying to bring killers to justice. Except when it was heartbreaking. Murder was a peculiar crime. Bad guys committed murder, of course—gang members, organised crime figures, domestic violence perpetrators and coercive controllers. But ordinary people did too. A lot of murders were one-offs. Someone pushed to the edge, doing something they never dreamt they'd do. Megan had seen and heard some terrible things in her time. Most coppers had. *It's what makes us gruff,* Megan thought as she opened the fridge.

She hadn't done the grocery shopping she'd planned to do last Friday but she had eggs. They'd have to do. A boiled egg and toast soldiers—comfort food, perfect. She put the water on the hob.

What if this is a serial killer? she mused. It was unlikely. As she had pointed out to Phil, they'd only found one victim in twenty years. She'd never come across a multiple murderer in all her years on the force. *It would be satisfying to catch one of those*, she thought. You'd really feel like you were saving lives. Mind you, if this was a serial killer and they found more bodies, that'd make those twenty wasted years feel even worse.

She flicked on the ABC news, keen to see if the press release had borne fruit. She'd done an on-camera interview on the street outside the station late in the afternoon, asking people to get in touch if they knew anything.

During her scratch meal, washed down with a cup of tea, Megan was rewarded. It was late in the run-down—the lead stories were about the war in Ukraine, the horrors of Gaza, melting sea ice and wildfires in Hawaii—but the report showed the shoe and the lace full screen and included a close-up of her face asking for information. That bit made her wince. *I look so old!* she thought. Then she opened her laptop and went to her social media feed to see if any other outlets had picked up the press release.

They had. The *Newcastle Herald*, the *SMH* and a few local papers had posted stories. Megan scrolled through the comments. Not many so far. One caught her eye, a comment about the shoelace.

Looks like French knitting.

Megan remembered Jason going through a craze for doing that when he was six or seven. The shoelace wasn't French knitting, more of a braid, but could a child have made it? Was Jane Doe a mother? If she was, why had no one reported her missing? Scotty had not discovered any matches so far in her DNA search. If it hadn't been for the bones lying in the morgue, she'd have thought the lyrebird had imitated a ghost.

In the months after Guido had died, she'd see his ghost sometimes, sitting in his chair. She looked over at it now, but it was empty. She hadn't seen him for months. Megan sighed. She'd always known the apparition was not real, but his presence had comforted her. She could pretend for a moment that everything was as it had been and that Guido had not died, coughing his lungs out, drowning in his own bodily fluids, swearing in Italian.

She'd stayed beside him through it all. Every ghastly intervention. Every miserable hour. She'd held his hand as he'd wheezed his way to death. She'd lain dry-eyed on his chest when he had finally stopped struggling for breath. She'd only shed tears when Jason had arrived; his grief had released her own.

Maybe I've had PTSD, she thought, *and that's why everything lost its flavour, even my job. Maybe that's why I drifted into retirement. Or maybe it was just grief.* Megan closed her computer and yawned.

'Night, love,' she said to the empty chair. She might not be able to see Guido's ghost these days but that didn't mean he wasn't there. She put her teacup in the sink, then went down the hall to the bedroom they used to share.

FOUR

Bridie Turner didn't often catch the ABC news. She was usually still at work or propping up a bar somewhere. At twenty-six she was still far too young, in her opinion, to be watching the news nightly. She had been a beautiful, well-behaved and studious child who was popular at her expensive private school, but not so popular it interfered with her studies. She'd graduated from uni with first-class honours. She'd done everything her parents expected of her, but now Bridie considered the debt was paid and she could be herself—whoever that was.

She had a good job at a big ad agency and a clutch of girlfriends she'd hung out with since primary school. She didn't have a boyfriend. She'd never had a boyfriend. Sometimes she worried that she did not like boys. She didn't know much about them. She had no brothers—no siblings at all. She had only attended girls' schools and her father had left home when she was six.

Her mother, the hyper-successful businesswoman, philanthropist and serial board director Amanda Turner, was always hinting that it was time to find the right kind of man. She had done it again just a few nights ago, when they'd met for drinks at the Caterpillar Club. Nobody met their mother at a club as hip as the Caterpillar except Bridie, and that was because Amanda chose the venue. Amanda always knew exactly where to be seen.

'You're looking gorgeous as usual, darling. I can't understand why men aren't queuing up.'

'I hardly know any men,' Bridie reminded her. 'If you'd wanted me to meet boys, you should have sent me to a co-ed school.'

'Don't be absurd. Sydney Uni was co-ed last time I looked. That's where you go to meet eligible men.'

'Like Dad?'

Ouch. Bridie's father was the only black mark in Amanda's otherwise superlative CV.

Amanda sipped her martini and kept her cool.

Daughters always knew their mother's sore spots, and Bridie was no exception. Bridie remembered Amanda's almost surgical ability to wound her own mother, a woman now so lost in the depths of dementia it no longer mattered. *Well*, thought Bridie, *like mother, like daughter.* She knew Amanda paid for an expensive aged-care facility and had set up an automatic order of flowers every week. Duty done. Bridie suspected her mother tried not to think about the woman who had given birth to her, just as she tried not to think about the man she had once been married to. When her mother couldn't avoid it—after all, they shared a child—she did what her therapist had told her to do—Bridie had heard more than she'd ever cared to about her mother's various therapies over the years—and reframed her relationship with her first husband in a positive light. After all, as she often said, without him she would not have Bridie.

Bridie knew Amanda adored her. But it was almost a burden to be so often under the penetrating gaze of her mother's sharp eyes. Amanda was proud of her daughter. Bridie knew that. She often told her how much she loved the way the young woman—the young woman she had made—looked, sounded and behaved. In Amanda's eyes she was perfect, except for the man thing, and even that, she was sure, was just a matter of time. Yet somehow, even in the midst of all the pride and compliments, there was always a sting in the tail and Bridie responded in kind. Infuriatingly, Amanda rationalised any negative reaction as just a phase that her daughter would leave behind as she grew and matured and found a good man. Bridie watched her mother warily, as the older woman took another sip of her excellent gin martini.

'You are much smarter than I am, darling. You will never allow yourself to be fooled by a pretty face and athletic prowess.'

Bridie agreed with her mother that she would never be seduced by a sexy jock. Not because she was somehow wiser about men than her mother had been, but because she was impervious to them. Amanda, on the other hand, was never without a male friend. They came and went so quickly that Bridie found it hard to keep up.

'How's Nathan?' she asked.

'William. Nathan's in recovery.'

'From what? You?'

'Don't be like that. It doesn't suit you. Is that why there are no members of the opposite sex on your radar?'

'If there were, I'd beat a hasty retreat.'

Maybe I'm gay, Bridie thought, sipping her own dirty martini. Trouble was, she was equally impervious to female charms. Perhaps she was just a cold-hearted bitch.

Despite how dismal those Friday night drinks had been, sitting on her couch now, alone with the TV, Bridie would have happily traded the remote for another round of ritzy cocktails with her mother. She was only here, at home in her immaculate flat—Amanda paid the cleaners who kept it pristine—because the client had pulled the pin on the campaign she was meant to be working on tonight. She'd suggested the team go for a drink instead, but it was a Monday night, and they all had husbands, wives, kids, cats to go home to. Reluctantly, sulkily, she had headed home at what she considered a ridiculously early hour.

Finally, finding nothing else on, she flicked on the news. They were just finishing a story about the never-ending war in Ukraine. It was a conflict she knew little about. *I* am *cold-hearted*, she thought, as the reporter listed the number of children killed in the latest drone attack. She took out her phone and checked her messages. There weren't any, not even from her mother. She started scrolling through Insta. It seemed to be all about melting sea ice. A lot of her friends were becoming activists. She knew how important climate change was. Like Amanda, who sat on the board of some climate organisation or other (Bridie never could remember the name), she donated regularly. She didn't have any time, but she did have money and, as her mother said, we all do what we can.

The news moved to a story about a woman's body having been found some place Bridie had never heard of. Like everyone else, Bridie loved a gritty British crime show. She was just thinking about changing the channel to BritBox when a picture flashed onto the screen.

It was a running shoe, a cheap running shoe that had seen much better days. It was laced with a colourful length of braid, made from plastic twine.

'If you recognise this shoe or its laces,' the reporter was saying, 'please call the number on the screen or Crime Stoppers. Police will treat all information received as confidential.'

Bridie dropped the remote and picked up her phone. She took a photo of the number just before a woman's face filled the screen, Senior Sergeant somebody or other.

'We are still trying to identify the body and need help from the public,' the detective said. 'If you recognise either of these items, please let us know. This unidentified person has been buried for two decades. Someone must know something.'

Gloria? *Gloria? Buried?* Bridie's heart lurched. Surely not! But that was one of the braided shoelaces Bridie had made for her. She'd have recognised it anywhere.

—

Bridie was five years old again, tongue between her teeth as she concentrated on plaiting the brightly coloured plastic strands the way her yaya—her nanny—had shown her. She was crying as she worked, tears dripping off her chin and snot running from her nose. They were tears of grief and tears of anger. She knew Gloria was going back to the Philippines. She knew it because her mother had told her so.

'Gloria has to go back to her real little girl,' her mother had said.

'No! *I* am her real little girl! I am! Me!' Bridie had struck out at her mother and Amanda had caught her hand, holding it so tight it hurt.

'You are *my* real little girl, darling,' her mother had said, in the voice she used when she was trying not to sound cross. 'Gloria's little girl is sick and she has to go home to take care of her.'

'No! She has to stay here and take care of me.' Bridie bent over and sank her teeth into her mother's hand. It felt very satisfying.

'*Ow!* You little cat!' Amanda slapped her daughter. 'Only animals bite!' Amanda looked at her hand. 'You've left teeth marks!' she said, horrified.

Bridie was delighted, even though the slap hurt.

'Hey, hey, hey, what's going on?'

Bridie's dad had come into the family room. Bridie loved her dad. He wasn't mean to her and she could get him to play Lego with her on the floor for hours and hours. He was nice to Gloria too.

'She bit me!' Amanda said, showing him her hand.

'Oh, Bridie!'

Her dad was annoyed. She didn't like that.

'She said I wasn't Gloria's real little girl. She said Gloria had a realer one in the Philippines!'

'Gloria is your nanny, darling. Mummy is your mummy.'

'I don't like Mummy. I like Gloria.'

'She's impossible,' Amanda interjected. 'Just as well Gloria has to go home. She obviously spoils her.'

'Where is Gloria?' Bridie's dad asked.

He reached up and rang a bell. Gloria appeared within seconds.

Bridie ran to her yaya. *'Soy tu verdadera nina.'*

'Mi pequeñita.'

But Bridie was not stupid. She knew being Gloria's little darling was not the same as being her real little girl, so she'd roared with rage and kicked her yaya in the shins. Then she'd run and hid in the cupboard behind the stairs.

Later, days later, she'd felt sorry. She loved Gloria, she wanted her to come back.

'Volverás cuando tu hija esté mejor?'

'Sí,' Gloria said, and Gloria always kept her promises.

Bridie had made the shoelaces as a farewell gift. She knew Gloria had made them herself when she was a little girl and sold them at the markets. Bridie had practised and practised so she would make them perfectly.

Even so, once they were finished she had seen the imperfection. Despite all her efforts, Bridie had made a mistake. She had been mortified. It was that imperfection that the grown-up Bridie could see now on her oversized TV screen.

Gloria must have given her shoes away before she flew back to the Philippines, Bridie told herself now. That was the only possible explanation. With a flood of relief, she remembered they had received a couple of letters from her nanny after she had left. She might even still have them somewhere. She remembered she'd folded them carefully and put them away safely. It couldn't be Gloria who'd been found in the forest.

But when she thought of the braid, she was not so sure. She remembered what Gloria had said when Bridie gave her the shoelaces. *'Los guardare siempre'*—I will keep them always. Gloria kept her promises. But she had never come back.

—

Bridie waited until the next day to call the number she'd seen on the screen. She felt jumpy about the whole idea. She didn't want to waste the cops' time if it wasn't Gloria—and surely it wasn't—but nor did she want to ignore the evidence in case it was. She was torn between being thought a fool and a time-waster and finding out something even worse. It wasn't until she arrived in her office the next morning that she finally screwed her courage to the sticking place.

'You think the shoelace may have been from the pair you gave your nanny when she left your family to go home to the Philippines?' Bridie had been put through to a detective in Maitland. The policewoman sounded calm and matter-of-fact.

'Yes. I made them myself, as a gift.'

'Do you think she might have left them behind or given them away to someone before she left?'

'She was on her way to the airport when I gave them to her ... and she said she'd keep them always.'

Bridie realised how lame that sounded. People said things like that to children all the time.

'Maybe she dropped them,' she continued. 'What with carrying hand luggage and all that.'

She could easily have dropped them. The last time she'd seen the laces, Gloria was holding them in her hand.

'How old was Gloria?'

'I don't know. I was five, and she had been my yaya ever since I was born. She looked younger than Mum, so she could have been in her twenties—early thirties, maybe.'

'And was she a big woman? Or small?'

'She seemed big to me, but I remember she was much smaller than Mum and Mum's no giant, so I guess she must've been small.'

'You wouldn't know what size shoe she wore?'

'No, sorry. No idea.'

'I'd like to come and see you in the next day or two, if you could suggest a convenient time. It doesn't have to be business hours.'

Bridie's stomach fell. If this policewoman wanted to drive to Sydney, the answers she had given must fit with the body they had found.

'She sent us some letters after she got home to Manila. I remember that quite clearly.' Bridie could hear the fear in her own voice.

'Do you still have them?'

'I might have.'

'Could you have a look? Or ask your mother about them? They could be very helpful.'

'I'll do my best.'

After she had hung up, Bridie got up and shut the door to her office. She turned her back to the corridor and pretended to be absorbed in a folder. Once she was sure no one could see her through the glass wall that separated her from everyone else, she began to cry. She could not bear the thought that Gloria might have been lying in a grave for twenty years, after suffering God knew what kind of death, while Bridie had got on with her life, resenting her yaya because she had left and never come back. Bridie tried to push the image of Gloria in a grave out of her mind. There was no way her yaya could have ended up in that godforsaken place. It could not possibly be her.

—

That evening, Megan paused by Constable Kumar's desk before leaving. The young woman was a hard worker.

'Arlott and I are driving to Sydney tomorrow,' Megan told her.

'To see the woman who recognised the shoelace?'

'Yeah. Can you check them out from storage tonight? We'll take them with us.'

'Did she give you a name?'

'If it *is* the woman she gave the laces to, Jane Doe may be Gloria Ramos, a citizen of the Philippines. Can you also check when she entered the country and when she left? According to Ms Turner, she flew from Sydney to Manila. I'm not sure when she arrived in Australia, but she'd been Ms Turner's nanny since she was a newborn, so try about five years before Jessica Weston heard the scream—1997 to 1998, say.'

Megan handed Kumar the notes she had taken from the phone call. She nodded. 'Gloria Ramos. Well, that'd explain the Spanish.'

'According to Ms Turner, she spoke Chavacano, a dialect of Spanish common in Zamboanga City, where she grew up.'

But Megan was not counting her chickens. The yaya of a posh Eastern Suburbs princess ending up in a shallow grave in Burraga Swamp—literally the middle of nowhere—seemed a stretch. As far as she was concerned, the body was still Jane Doe.

FIVE

Bridie was nervous. She'd been overwhelmed by a welter of emotions all day. She'd been useless at work, forgetting things and failing to concentrate. In the end, she'd pleaded a cold and left early. She was sure her colleagues had been glad to see her go. A bumbling, weepy Bridie was not someone anyone knew what to do with, least of all Bridie.

What sort of hospitality do you offer a police officer? she wondered. Not alcohol, she knew that much. Tea? She'd bought some teabags and milk on the way home. She'd forgotten sugar, but she had not forgotten biscuits. She'd bought six macaroons from La Belle Miette: two pink, two lavender and two chocolate. They looked gorgeous. She picked up a lavender macaroon and bit into it, then wished she hadn't. She'd upset the balance of the plate.

The buzzer rang. She swallowed her mouthful.

'Hello?'

'Bridie Turner?'

'Yes.'

'It's Detective Senior Sergeants Blaxland and Arlott, as arranged.'

Bridie thought she might be sick. At least she'd found the letters. They'd been neatly folded at the bottom of the little box of treasures she'd had since she was little. She'd opened them and smoothed them out. Gloria's handwriting was shaky and spidery, climbing across the page at a steep angle. This wasn't how she remembered her yaya. Gloria was always neat and careful. Bridie struggled to read the words, not just because of the handwriting but because her Chavacano Spanish dialect was almost non-existent now. She'd wanted to study Spanish at school, but her mother had stopped her. Said if she wanted to study a language it should be Cantonese. *She was always jealous of Yaya*, thought Bridie. *She knew I loved Gloria more than I loved her.*

There was a knock at the door.

Detective Senior Sergeant Blaxland was an older woman in a cheap navy pants suit, like a copper's uniform without being one. She had wiry grey hair cut short and was not wearing a skerrick of make-up. She wasn't attractive but she had a nice smile. Bridie smiled back. There was a male detective behind her, about the same age but larger.

'Megan Blaxland,' said the woman, holding out her hand. 'And this is Senior Sergeant Philip Arlott. Thanks for letting us interrupt your afternoon.'

They shook hands and Bridie ushered them in.

'You're not interrupting. I just hope I'm not wasting your time.'

'Not at all. It's our job to follow every plausible lead.'

Plausible? Bridie did not like that word.

'Tea?'

'Thank you,' the man said. The woman shook her head.

'Macaroons?' asked Bridie as she poured the tea.

'Yes, please,' said the man, taking a chocolate one.

'Don't they look lovely!' said the woman, as she took one too.

'I found the letters.' Bridie picked them up and passed them to the detectives. 'They're very short and my Spanish is very rusty, but I think she says she's arrived safely and sends her love. Just platitudes really.'

'We'll get them translated,' said the male copper.

He was putting them in a plastic bag, Bridie saw with a pang.

Her anxiety must have shown on her face, because Detective Blaxland said, 'We'll take good care of them, and we'll make sure you get them back.'

Bridie nodded, tears pricking at the back of her eyes.

'No date on them,' the woman murmured to her colleague. To Bridie she said, 'Do you have the envelopes they came in by any chance?'

'No, sorry. God knows what happened to those.'

Detective Arlott pulled two evidence bags out of his satchel and held them out. Bridie felt cold all over. She could see they contained a shoe and the shoelace from the news. Bridie turned over the bag containing the shoe. She pulled the plastic taut so she could better examine it.

'I'm sorry. I can't remember. It looks like the sort of shoe Gloria wore, but it was a long time ago.'

'And the shoelace?' Arlott was holding the smaller bag towards her.

Bridie nodded dumbly. If she tried to say anything she would cry. She did not take the bag, so the woman copper did. She did not attempt to give it to Bridie. She just put the bag on the coffee table.

'Take your time. No need to rush.' The woman's voice was kind.

Bridie steeled herself and picked it up. Tears began to flow. 'Yes,' she whispered. 'I recognise it. I made those shoelaces for Gloria.'

She twisted the evidence bag to show the two detectives where the braid was a bit wonky.

'I got the colours out of order. I was mortified about that. I wanted to take them back because they weren't perfect, but Yaya wouldn't let me. She said that was how she'd always know I made them and that it was the imperfections that were . . .' Bridie could not finish her sentence. 'I'm sorry,' she said, when she caught her breath. 'I loved her and I can't bear . . . I can't bear . . .'

The two police officers let her cry. Neither tried to intervene or offer comfort.

'I hoped it would be from a different pair, you see. I think they are common in the Philippines. Yaya—Gloria—told me how she used to make them when she was a child and sell them in the markets.'

Calmer now, Bridie found she wanted to talk. 'She was very poor. That's why she was looking after me—in Hong Kong and then here—instead of her real little girl in Manila.'

'Hong Kong?'

'Yes, that's where I was born and where Mum hired Gloria.'

'So she came with you when you moved?'

The male detective was sitting forward.

'Yes.'

'Legally?'

Bridie shrugged. She had no idea. 'I don't know. I suppose so.'

'And Gloria had a daughter back in the Philippines?' Detective Blaxland asked the question this time.

'Yes, her mother—Gloria's mother, I mean—looked after her and Gloria sent them money every month. It was because of her daughter that Gloria had to leave. She was ill. I don't know what with, but it was serious enough that she wanted to go home and look after her.'

'When was this?'

'Maybe 2002? Sometime around then.'

'And when did you all arrive in Sydney?'

'A couple of years before. Mum'd know.'

'Is the daughter still in Manila?'

'I don't know. Those two letters are the last I ever heard of Gloria.'

'But you and your family thought Gloria Ramos was in the Philippines with her daughter all this time?'

'Yes. My father even drove her to the airport.'

Detective Arlott moved in his chair.

'Do you think . . . is it possible'—Bridie leant forward, almost beseeching the two police officers—'that it's not her? That she dropped the shoelaces or gave them away and it's someone else who was buried in that forest?'

'Anything is possible at this stage,' Detective Blaxland said noncommittally. 'The first thing we need to do is trace Gloria Ramos's daughter. Do you have any contact details for her?'

'No. But my mother might.'

—

'What do you think?' Megan was looking into her rear-view mirror as she backed the car carefully out of a narrow guest parking spot under Bridie Turner's building.

'I think she's telling us everything she knows. She's clearly distressed.'

'Even after all this time.'

'I guess the people who love you when you're small always remain important.'

Megan shot a look at Phil. This wasn't the sort of remark she expected from him. He had changed a lot in the past year. Something had happened.

'Are you okay?' she asked. 'In yourself, I mean. Everything okay at home?'

Phil had turned to look out of the passenger window. All she could see was the back of his neck and the bristling grey hairs above his collar. It was as if a shutter had come down.

'Yep. Just the same. Wife can't stand me, kids hate me, dog won't sleep on my side of the bed.'

Then he turned towards her and flashed one of his cheeky grins, and she grinned back. She'd only imagined something was wrong. He was taking the piss, as always.

'Shall we pay Ms Turner a visit? Ms Turner the elder, I mean,' he said.

'No time like the present.'

—

The sandstone wall was not just high, it was impressive. There were CCTV cameras on either side of the iron gates. Phil and Megan exchanged looks. Why the need for so much protection?

'Maybe they've got a lot of art.' Megan didn't want to jump to any conclusions.

Phil pressed the intercom.

'Hello?'

'It's Detective Senior Sergeants Arlott and Blaxland, here to see Ms Amanda Turner.'

The man on the other end did not answer, but the iron gates swung open. The house was very modern, all glass, concrete and flat roofs. It was two or three storeys high; it was hard to tell exactly, because it was thrown together like cubes or children's blocks, piled one on top of the other with overhangs and sharp angles. The garden was similarly stark. Not a leaf despoiled the sweep of green lawn, every tree was architectural and trimmed, and even the flowers bloomed in formation. No real shade anywhere. *The house must cost a fortune to heat and cool*, Megan thought, looking up at the blank wash of sky.

The front door opened as soon as they put their feet on the little bridge that crossed the koi pool.

'Detective Senior Sergeants.' The woman was beaming, as if she'd been looking forward to their visit all day. 'Please come in.'

She was an older version of her daughter: a thick mane of superbly cut grey hair barely touching her shoulders and large blue eyes behind oversized black glasses. She was barefoot, in jeans and an untucked shirt, yet she managed to give the impression that she'd just left a movie set or photo shoot.

'You want to ask me questions about our yaya from twenty years ago, Bridie tells me, and of course I am happy to help.'

Bridie had obviously filled her mother in, but Megan didn't care if Ms Turner was happy to help or not. This was a homicide investigation; she was obliged to help.

'Thank you,' said Phil. 'We shouldn't take up too much of your time.'

'Take all the time you need, Senior Sergeant . . . ?'

'Arlott.'

Amanda Turner ushered them through the front door and then into a small side room, some sort of den by the look of it. She gestured towards a leather chesterfield which faced the harbour, visible through floor-to-ceiling windows. She took the chair opposite.

'Bridie has told me you think a body discovered in a forest north of Newcastle may be that of Gloria Ramos. Is that right?'

This woman liked to be in control, Megan observed. She decided to let Phil continue to take the lead.

'That's one line of inquiry.'

'Bridie told me about the shoelace. She was very upset.'

Is she blaming us for her daughter's distress? wondered Megan.

'She was clearly very fond of her.' Phil was giving nothing away.

'But it can't be Gloria,' the woman continued. 'We bought and paid for her plane ticket to Manila. And Bridie's father—my then husband—took her to the airport himself.'

'She came here with you from Hong Kong, where she had been your daughter's nanny since Bridie's birth. Is that correct?'

'That's correct.'

'Did she come here as a migrant, or on a working visa, or as a tourist?'

'I didn't know you worked for immigration, Senior Sergeant.' This was said with a smile.

Phil ignored the smile and the dig.

'We just need to establish how she arrived in this country and whether she left on that plane. Immigration will have that information and we have officers looking into it now. It would expedite matters if we had a timeframe.'

Megan was pleased that Phil was pursuing the way Gloria had arrived in Australia. If she was here illegally it would explain why no trace of her was ever found on any database.

'Would you have a receipt for the plane ticket, by any chance?' Megan interjected.

'It was twenty years ago!'

'It would be very helpful.'

'I could get my accountant to check for you.'

'Thank you.' Megan sat back and shut up.

'So how did Ms Ramos enter the country?' Phil asked again.

Amanda looked from one to the other. She was cornered. 'She came on a tourist visa.'

'And how long did she stay?'

'Two years.'

'Then she arrived in 2000?' Megan again.

'Yes.'

Megan opened her notebook and began to write.

'Why are you writing that down?' Amanda asked. 'Surely you can find all this with a few strokes of a computer key?'

'I'm old school,' Megan said with a smile.

'She was here for two years. On a tourist visa?' Phil pitched the question as if he was trying to understand.

'Bridie loved her, you see, adored her. Sometimes I thought she loved Gloria more than me.' Amanda gave a short laugh. 'And to get her in as a migrant or on a working visa was such a rigamarole, so . . . I know I shouldn't have, but mother love and all that . . . I called a few people and pulled a few strings.'

Amanda laughed for a second time, but both police officers remained expressionless.

'And at the end of the two years, Ms Ramos went back to the Philippines to care for her sick daughter. Is that correct?'

Amanda nodded.

'Would you have any contact details for Ms Ramos or her daughter? Do you know the daughter's surname? Is it also Ramos?'

'I don't remember her name—'

Of course you don't, thought Megan.

'—but I might have some contact details somewhere. Gloria used to get me to send them her pay every month via money orders.'

'All her pay?' Megan couldn't help herself.

'Yes. Gloria didn't need any money while she worked for us. We provided everything.'

Phil reached into his satchel and removed the two evidence bags. He passed them to Megan.

'Do you recognise either of these?' Megan held them out to the woman opposite.

Amanda kept her arms crossed tightly in front of her chest.

'Take your time. Look at them carefully.'

Amanda unfolded her arms slowly, took the bags and turned them both over once or twice then handed them back. 'I didn't take much notice of what Gloria wore.'

'So you didn't buy them for her?'

Amanda looked at her sharply. 'No, if she needed clothes, I gave her money for them.'

Not much money, Megan thought, as she passed the evidence back to Phil.

'And what about money for her days off?'

'Oh, she stayed here with Bridie. She didn't know anyone in Australia, didn't speak any English. She preferred to stay in the house—who wouldn't?' Amanda swung her chair around to face the view. 'She was very happy here.'

The two police officers said nothing.

'Very happy.'

Megan was not certain why she had taken such a dislike to Amanda. She was fairly sure that what the woman had told them was true—as far as it went. Perhaps it was just reverse snobbery, all this wealth and privilege contrasted starkly with the pathetic skeleton she'd seen in the grave. She remembered what Scotty had said about Jane Doe having lived a hard life. Looking at the sparkling harbour laid out in front of them in all its brilliance felt almost obscene.

SIX

Jessica hated faculty meetings. She wasn't interested in team-building or promoting the university. She was interested in birds, their habitats and some of her students, in that order. And why did they always have to begin so bloody early? To start at 8 a.m. was simply uncivilised. She found a spot at the back and passed the time scrolling on her phone. A pretty young thing was giving a presentation. According to her PowerPoint slide, her name was Nerilee Hing. She was from the university marketing department and was pitching her slides with what Jessica felt was an annoying level of gusto. Jessica had seen a million PowerPoints with complicated graphs and pictures of smiling vanilla people sourced from Getty Images. She only paid attention if they had birds in them.

'STEM is doing well at the moment,' the young woman was saying as she clicked to a graph showing student enrolments. 'STEM is cool with governments, industry and the public. You'd be surprised how rarely that happens.'

Nope, not surprised at all, thought Jessica.

'We still need to attract more female students, especially to disciplines like physics, chemistry, engineering and maths . . .'

'Our courses are dominated by female students,' said Mary Carpenter, a marine biologist.

There was a murmur of agreement around the room.

'Yes, I know, but that's actually the problem in biology.'

'Female students are a problem?' Jessica had intended to stay silent. She'd failed.

'No, no, of course not. It's just we attract more money to the other science faculties. Investments, bequests and enrolments, even by female students, are falling across the board in biology. And—don't yell at me, I'm just the messenger—we find female-dominated courses generally struggle more to attract students and funds.'

'Courses like marketing and PR?' Jessica had spoken once; she might as well do so again.

'They remain in high demand,' said the young woman as she flicked to another slide.

'Anyway, we want to do something about it, so we're spending the next few months concentrating on creating some more excitement around female-dominated subjects. And not just the ones the government wants to incentivise, like teaching, nursing and psychology.'

The picture on this slide was of a bunch of gorgeous white women—well, all but one were white—wearing lab coats and peering down microscopes or holding up test tubes filled with pastel-coloured liquid. Jessica rolled her eyes. Nerilee stuck to her pitch.

'So, we are hungry for content, for good news stories, examples of one of our less well-known faculties—like biology—contributing to the community. We're looking for things that are wild or cute, emotionally engaging or dramatic. Does anyone have a story like that?'

'Professor Weston does.'

Jessica glared at Mary Carpenter as everyone in the room turned to look at her.

'That's great!' said Nerilee. 'What's it about?'

Jessica shook her head. 'It's nothing, not relevant.'

Mary Carpenter was not discouraged. 'It's about how a lyrebird—recorded by Professor Weston—is helping police to solve a murder!'

FUCK! thought Jessica. *Fuck! Fuck! Fuck!* She could feel the excitement rise in the room. Very few of the faculty knew the story. Now she wished that none of them did.

'A murder?' said Nerilee. 'That's fantastic!'

'Not for the victim it isn't,' said Jessica dryly.

'No, no, of course not. Nevertheless, it's fantastic that your work might help solve it.'

'That's a big "might".'

Jessica looked daggers at Mary. She'd bumped into her straight after she'd returned from her interview with the police, and in a weak moment she'd told her everything. Mary was an old friend and colleague, an academic she respected and—until now—had trusted.

Ignoring Jessica's dirty look, Mary proceeded to repeat what Jessica had told her. When she'd finished, Nerilee Hing was quite beside herself.

'This is exactly what we need. Can I come and see you later this afternoon, Professor?'

Jessica shook her head, but Nerilee wasn't deterred.

'Great, I'll pop by your office around three.'

Jessica felt trapped. If Megan had wanted the world to know about the lyrebird, surely she would have mentioned it in that interview she'd done on the ABC? She'd just have to tell the marketing knobs to back off.

—

'I am not sure I am at liberty to talk about any of this.'

Jessica had spent the last few hours dreading this meeting. She had essays to mark and a lecture to prepare but she'd been too distracted to achieve much of anything. At least the marketing people had arrived on the dot of three.

Nerilee Hing had brought her boss with her—Jeff Slatter, ex-Saatchi, he told Jessica with pride. Though that meant about as much to her as if he'd said he was ex-Bunnings. Less, in fact.

Nerilee leant forward to emphasise her point. 'The last thing I want to do is hinder the investigation.'

'But it's already in the public domain,' said Jeff (he'd told Jessica to call him Jeff). 'Nerilee found a story from twenty years ago about the lyrebird mimicking a woman screaming. It didn't get much traction back then—they didn't find a body—but whatever the police may or may not want, somebody is going to break this story and it might as well be us. We can at least make sure it's accurate.'

'Let someone else break it. I don't want the responsibility.'

'I don't think you have much choice. Whoever does it is going to come looking for you. If you let us control the story, we can protect you.' Nerilee Hing was trying to sound sympathetic.

Jeff said, 'But it's more than that, Jessica . . . may I call you Jessica?'

No, you may not, thought Jessica.

Jeff took her silence for consent.

'This is highly confidential, but if we don't bring some more revenue into your faculty, we are going to have to make cuts, substantial cuts, particularly to those courses and subjects that don't wash their own faces.'

'Like ornithology,' Jessica said.

'I can't speculate on what courses they might be at this point, but if the revenue stream is not there, the academic area is at risk.'

'And how would telling this story help with that?'

'Attention, excitement and proof that what you do has practical—even important—applications in the real world.'

'Nature *is* the real world, Mr—er, Jeff.'

'You and I know that, but I am afraid the powers that be . . .' He let his voice trail away into a silence heavy with meaning.

Jessica decided she disliked Mr Slatter.

'Smug bastard,' she muttered, after she'd closed her office door behind them fifteen minutes later. But she had already agreed to do everything they'd asked—including interviews with the media. Her heart sank at the thought.

Twenty-four hours later, against her better judgement, Jessica found herself the passenger in a car driven by a journalist, stopped at the boom gate at the Paterson level crossing waiting for a train to pass. A photographer sat in the back. They were heading for Burraga Swamp.

The fully laden coal train rattled noisily as it sped past, car after dusty car. Minutes ticked by and still the railcars flashed in front of her eyes. It felt never-ending. The sight of this volume of coal made her feel even worse than she already did. *When are we going to stop doing this?* she wondered.

'Somebody murdered that woman in the forest,' Jessica said to her companions, 'and if the police catch whoever did it, they will be punished. But the people profiting from that stuff'—she pointed at the never-ending train—'they get subsidies and million-dollar pay packets and seats at all the top tables.'

The man behind the wheel, the journalist, turned to look at her. 'I guess.'

She turned her face away and stared out of the passenger window. She'd been too aggressive, too intense. It was because she felt so jumpy and because she didn't want them to think Jessica was happy about any of this, that she was some awful, attention-seeking media tart. And she felt guilty about talking to the media without telling Megan first. She'd thought about calling her last night, but she'd chickened out. Jessica felt caught between her beloved faculty and her friend. She doubled down.

'You guess? I am a scientist, and I can tell you there's no guessing about it. Burning coal is more lethal than any mass murderer who ever lived.'

There was an awkward silence. She had embarrassed them. Well, too bad. But she couldn't afford to piss them off, she reminded herself. She was doing this for her department—and for the birds.

She did not say another word until they were a long way past Paterson and bouncing up the dirt road in the forest. She had not travelled this way since that awful morning twenty years ago, but she remembered it vividly. It was just as potholed, neglected and steep now as it had been then.

She'd already given an extensive interview to the journo in her air-conditioned office. She had shown him the video and played him most of the sound recording. But that wasn't enough. He insisted on taking her up to Burraga Swamp for photographs. Jessica wanted to return like she wanted to pull her toenails out, but she had no choice. Her department had a staff of ten, including academics, sessional tutors and administrative assistants. She had three hundred and fifty students studying her subjects and five doing PhDs, and she had the birds. If the department got extra funding and attention thanks to her story, so be it.

'Have you been up here since you saw the bird doing its thing?'

The journalist's name was Brett.

'No.'

'How come?'

'There are plenty of places you can study lyrebirds—well, there were, until the 2019 fires—and I didn't have good memories of this place.'

'Must feel a bit freaky, going back.'

'Yeah.'

Jessica glanced at the photographer, who was sitting in the back. Her name was Heather. She caught Heather's eye, and the woman smiled.

'It's spectacular up here, isn't it?' Heather said.

Jessica looked out of the window. The view across the Barringtons was astonishing. The wilderness lay like a shaggy green carpet flung out haphazardly. It rose and fell at steep angles, dark crags butting up against kilometres of sunlit tree canopy.

'You know there's a plane lost out there somewhere? Crashed in '69. They send a search party out to look for it every year. They still haven't found it. There were five people on board, apparently.' Brett sounded positively chipper. 'I've been out with them once myself. Bloody impenetrable, the rainforest. No wonder they've never found the wreck.'

'Who is "they"?'

'Just a bunch of enthusiasts.'

Nutjobs more like, thought Jessica. Then she remembered what it felt like to be considered a nutjob, as she had been when she'd reported the murder all those years ago. Nutjobs were vindicated sometimes.

'Good for them,' she said.

'Which way from here?' Brett asked.

They had reached the turn-off to Mount Allyn.

'Keep going straight down the hill. The car park is at the bottom on your right.'

It was unsettling being back after all this time. It was a warm day for September, but Jessica felt cold. She pulled a cardigan out of her bag and put it on. She'd wondered if there would be a cop car around, but the car park was empty. The place looked even more isolated than she remembered. The fence around the car park had mostly toppled over, the once-solid posts and rails slowly disintegrating into the damp earth. Bright-orange fungus grew out of the rotting timbers, eating them from the inside. At first glance it looked like orange peel.

The path was heavily trampled. *Cops with their big black boots*, she thought. The hot, windy days that had replaced the rain were already drying the divots their boots had left, cracking the greying soil at the edges. Worse were the invasive species taking over from the fragile rainforest ground covers. *This is a national park*, thought Jessica. *It's meant to be protected. What hope for the rest of the natural environment?*

'You can see where the cops have been . . .' Brett was saying.

'Shhhh!' said Jessica abruptly.

'What?' he said in a stage whisper. 'What is it?'

'I want to listen to the birds.'

Brett pulled a face, then turned to the silent Heather and made a show of putting his finger over his lips.

They listened.

'There are a lot of them, aren't there?' Brett was like a five-year-old, unable to stay still and quiet for more than a few seconds.

'Not nearly as many as there used to be.'

'That's a lyrebird, isn't it?' Heather pointed into the forest, towards the bell-like sound echoing off the hills.

Jessica was impressed. 'Well spotted.'

'I grew up in the Blue Mountains. There used to be lots of them around there. You can always pick them; their voice carries—like an opera singer.'

'Is it . . . could it be . . . the one you recorded?' Brett sounded excited. He was fiddling with his phone.

'I suppose it is possible. Lyrebirds can live for up to thirty years.'

'Do you think he might do the screaming?'

Jessica shook her head. 'Wrong time of year. Lyrebirds only display in the mating season between May and August.'

Brett pulled a face. 'It's just September.'

Jessica shook her head. 'May to August,' she repeated with emphasis.

Brett looked over to the heavily forested hills. 'Take some shots, Heather.'

'You won't see anything,' Heather replied.

'Nevertheless. Bit of colour.'

They followed a bend in the path. The red cedar Jessica had clambered over two decades ago was still there, surrounded by nettles and giant stinging trees. It was in an advanced state of decay—fungi of orange, white and grey peppered its softening trunk. Someone had cut a chunk out of it to allow for the pathway. The grove of *Dicksonia antarctica* was still where it had been, their ancient, blackened trunks rising out of a frilly skirt of weeds. Jessica spotted lantana, cassia, oxalis, milk thistle, dandelions, nettles. Her heart sank. What had happened to this place?

In front of them the path was blocked by police crime scene tape, tied from tree to tree. Someone had plonked a detour sign against a sapling, and Jessica could see that walkers had trampled another path towards the swamp. *Even when we are trying to do the right thing, we fuck nature up*, Jessica thought.

Heather began taking photos.

'Where's the grave?' Brett had lifted the tape and was on the other side.

'I don't know!' Jessica's voice was shrill, almost panicky. 'You shouldn't go in there! You might contaminate the scene!' She knew they'd taken the body away and that police had swept the area, but the tape was there for a reason.

'No need to lose your shit! I'm not going any further. I just want to get a better look.' Brett stood still.

Jessica tried to speak calmly. 'I don't know where they found the body. I just know where I saw the lyrebird.'

'Where's that?'

'Over there, I think, but it's hard to tell. It's so overgrown.'

'Where?'

'There, in front of the strangler fig.'

The hide was no more, but she remembered it had been in front of the fig. The small display mound where the bird had done his compelling performance was long gone, smothered in pokeweed, hiptage and harungana.

'Can you go and stand there?'

Mercifully, the spot Heather gestured to was outside the tape, so Jessica did as she was asked. She stood in front of the fig tree feeling foolish. Heather snapped away.

'Was she killed around here?' Brett asked.

'For the lyrebird to have heard her screams, I assume she must have been. Lyrebirds have a territory.'

The three of them stood in silence for a moment. The forest was still beautiful; the birds were singing and the frogs in the swamp were calling, despite the weeds and the police tape and the carelessness of humans.

'Spooky!' Brett said after what for him was a prolonged silence. 'Awful place to be murdered.'

'I daresay anywhere is an awful place for that.'

'What's at the end of the path?' Heather had already taken a few steps.

'The swamp. It's not far. Well worth seeing.'

To emerge from the dark and dense forest into the sunlit circle was a shock. The forest stopped abruptly at the swamp's edge and a natural amphitheatre took its place. The soft, yellow-grassed, springy bog was completely round, hedged on every side by thickly wooded hills. Twenty years ago, Jessica had been able to walk out onto the bog. She remembered the wet sound of the ground sucking at her feet. Now, there was a sign warning them off, but Jessica could see by the footprints on the grassy surface that it was often ignored—like Brett and the police tape. There was rubbish everywhere too. Empty soft drink and beer cans, chip packets, biscuit and lolly wrappers, cigarette butts and, behind a rotting log, a dirty nappy.

If Jessica had thought the weeds were bad along the bush track, they were out of control at the swamp itself. The nettles were waist-high (*I hope they sting tourists regularly*, Jessica thought) and grew into the bog. But still the eerie magic of this place remained intact. The wildness of it rose above the human mess.

'Wow!' said Brett.

'Can I get you to stand by that log?' Heather asked, raising her camera.

'It was formed from a landslide,' Jessica said as she obeyed. 'This swamp was a lake at first and then became a bog. There are trees in that forest—Antarctic beeches—that are estimated to be more than two thousand years old.'

'Do you reckon there are more bodies buried out there?' Brett was pointing into the middle of the swamp.

Jessica shrugged. How the hell would she know?

'They're always digging bodies out of bogs.' Brett was excited.

'The body was not in the bog.'

Megan had said it was found in the forest.

'It was near it,' Brett said defensively.

What an idiot, Jessica thought.

'And maybe there are more bodies.' Brett wasn't giving up. 'Maybe we're standing on some right now.'

His excitement made Jessica feel queasy. She'd heard the terror in the screams the lyrebird had mimicked. This murder was not a game.

SEVEN

'Is that Ian Turner?'

'If you're selling anything, I don't want it.'

The man on the other end of the phone had a beautiful voice, deep, resonant and chocolatey. He would have made an excellent radio announcer. Against her better judgement, Megan felt herself warm to it.

'My name is Senior Sergeant Megan Blaxland. I'm from Maitland Police, and I would like to talk to you about Gloria Ramos. Your daughter Bridie gave me your phone number.'

A long silence. The way people responded to cops was often revealing. Yet Megan also knew completely innocent people were often thrown. Everyone was guilty of something.

'Gloria Ramos. That's a blast from the past. Is she okay?'

'I would really prefer to talk to you face to face. Could we arrange a time for me to drop in?'

Neither Bridie nor Amanda had known where Ian lived. Amanda had cut all ties with her ex-husband, but Bridie saw her dad a few times a year. Father and daughter always met on neutral territory—usually a pub in Annandale.

'He's ashamed of where he lives,' Bridie had explained. 'He hasn't got any money. I always buy the drinks and he always promises to pay me back, but he never does. He's a gambler. That's why Mum kicked him out. He'd been gambling away all her money, without her knowing. She had to transfer everything into her name.'

The man on the other end of the phone finally broke his silence. 'I'm, um . . . I'm between addresses at the moment.'

'Wherever you are staying is fine—hotel room, boarding house . . .'

'I'm staying with friends . . . I couldn't possibly inconvenience them.'

'This is a homicide investigation, Mr Turner. I am afraid they will need to put up with the inconvenience.'

'Is Gloria dead?' He sounded genuinely alarmed.

'We don't know, but a body has been found and we are trying to identify it.'

'I'm moving to my new place the day after tomorrow. Monday. Is that too late?'

'That will be fine.'

—

'I'm back in the saddle, love.'

'What?'

'Back on the job. I've been seconded. Do you remember that lyrebird case?'

Jason had only been a primary schooler when she first started working on it, but he'd often asked her about her cases. He liked to brag about her being a detective at school. She hadn't told him much, just that a lyrebird had mimicked a bad guy being cruel to a woman. She'd always worried about scaring him.

'Not really,' he said.

She didn't know whether to be pleased about that or not. She took another sip of her tea. She called Jason once a week, usually on a Sunday morning, just for a catch up. This Sunday was the only day off she'd had since Friday week. Tomorrow they were interviewing Ian Turner. Megan was excited. She'd been thinking about the questions they'd ask. She had a feeling he'd have some answers.

'Doesn't matter. A cold case, one of my first. It was twenty years ago but now they've found a body, right where we thought it would be—so they've asked me back.'

'You sound pleased about it.'

It didn't sound like Jason was.

'It's always nice to be wanted.'

'Don't push yourself too hard, Mum, and be careful.'

'I'm an old hand. You know that. I won't take any risks.'

She knew why Jason was concerned. He was still grieving the loss of his father. And that made him more protective of the parent he had left.

'I'll be right, love. I promise. And it's doing me good. I'm feeling more like my old self again.'

Ian Turner's 'new place' was very old. A bedsit in a converted terrace, it was dark, dingy and smelt of damp. There were three camping chairs in front of the window, but all his other possessions appeared to be in boxes.

'Sorry, the rest of my furniture hasn't arrived yet.'

'No problem.'

The contrast with his ex-wife's home was stark. Ian Turner was very tall, and Megan could see he had once been a good-looking man. Now, he was gaunt and hollow-eyed, with an unkempt beard and thinning hair pulled back in a ponytail. Perhaps he was a junkie as well as a gambler, Megan speculated. He had that look about him.

'This is my colleague, Senior Sergeant Philip Arlott.'

'I am afraid I can't offer you anything except a glass of water.' Turner looked around anxiously as he gestured for them to sit down. 'Though I'm not sure which box contains the glasses.'

His beautiful voice betrayed how far he had fallen. His educated Australian accent and his choice of words were all that remained of the life he'd once led.

'We're fine, thank you, Mr Turner.'

The man leant forward on his flimsy chair, both hands tucked under his thighs, like a schoolboy. *He is nervous*, Megan thought, *and trying to hide it*.

It was Turner who broke the silence.

'You think Gloria is dead? Murdered? That's awful!'

He took out a cigarette and lit it. There were nicotine stains on his fingers, Megan noticed. She hated smoking.

'We have not identified the body yet; that's why we're here.'

'And how can I help you? I haven't thought about Gloria for more than twenty years.'

'We have interviewed your ex-wife and your daughter, and they have both told us that, as far as they knew, Ms Ramos returned to the Philippines in 2002. They told us that you drove her to the airport. Is that correct?'

'Yes, it is.'

'Did you see her get on the plane?'

'No. I just dropped her at the terminal and drove away.'

'So, you thought she was in the Philippines too?'

'Of course. Is that where the body was found?'

'No. It was found in the Barrington Tops National Park.'

'Where?'

'It's in the Upper Hunter.'

'Well, it can't be Gloria. How on earth would she get up there? She couldn't even speak English. What makes you think it was her?'

'The remains were found wearing a shoe with handmade laces. Laces your daughter identified as having been made by her as a parting gift to Ms Ramos.'

Phil reached into his satchel and withdrew the two evidence bags, then he spoke to Ian Turner for the first time. 'Can you look at these, please, and see if you recognise them?'

Ian Turner took them gingerly. He examined them, turning them this way and that. His hands shook. Then he handed them back. 'I'm sorry. I never took much notice of what Gloria wore.'

It was almost exactly what Amanda had said.

'Are you sure she boarded that plane?'

'No, I'm not. Like I said, I just dropped her at the international terminal and left. But where else could she have gone? Though I suppose it's possible she came back to Australia at a later date.'

'If she had come back, wouldn't she have contacted your family? She was very close to Bridie.'

'I don't know. Amanda and I separated soon after Gloria left.'

'Can you remember the date and time of Ms Ramos's flight? Or the flight number?' Phil leant towards the man opposite him.

'Not the flight number, but I moved out in July, so the flight must have been sometime in May or June.' Turner was getting agitated.

'That's okay, we can find that out.' Phil's voice was soothing.

Was it Megan's imagination or did Turner flinch?

'Did Ms Ramos say anything to you during the drive to the airport? Or when you dropped her off?'

'Not that I recall. Like I said, she hardly spoke any English. Bridie did all the translating. She was fluent in Spanish in those days.'

'Ms Ramos spoke a dialect of Spanish, common in the Philippines,' Megan said.

'Did she? Sounded Spanish to me.'

'Why didn't Bridie come with you to farewell her nanny?'

'She was upset. Her mother . . . both of us . . . felt it would be too traumatic.'

'We know that Ms Ramos had long overstayed her tourist visa. Were you concerned about that when you booked her flights?'

'I didn't book them. Amanda did and she made a few phone calls. She's always been very well connected. It's not hard to get nannies and au pairs into the country if you know the right people, and Amanda has always made it her business to know them.'

'If Ms Ramos did not get on that plane, where do you think she might have gone?'

Ian Turner's voice rose. 'How should I know? I hardly knew the woman. I left all that domestic stuff to my wife. She was just Bridie's yaya, I hardly paid her any attention.'

'Why was it you who drove her to the airport then?'

'I don't know! It was decades ago!' He was almost shouting. 'Maybe I was driving that way anyway. Maybe I was trying to do the right thing. I can't remember.'

'Why didn't you just put her in a cab?'

'I wish I had now, but she didn't speak English, and she almost never left the house, except to take Bridie somewhere. Maybe I felt sorry for the poor woman. If I remember rightly, she was heading home because her daughter was ill. She was probably quite upset.'

'Probably?'

'I'm not sure I exchanged more than a few words with her, but she was a person, so I assume she was upset.'

'Do you remember which airline she was flying with?'

'No! I told you, Amanda arranged all that. I just played chauffeur.' Turner was angry.

Megan nodded and closed her notebook. She exchanged a glance with Phil and the two of them rose.

'Thank you very much for your help, Mr Turner, we appreciate it.'

Turner looked deflated. 'I didn't mean to get upset. It's just . . . it's so awful to think about Gloria and what might have happened to her. It's really shaken me. I'm just sorry I can't tell you anything helpful . . . it was such a long time ago. And, like I said, driving her to the airport was just a chore.'

'If you think of anything else, anything at all, please don't hesitate to get in touch.' Megan handed him her card.

Turner looked at it as if he had never seen such a thing before, then tucked it into the back pocket of his tracksuit pants. 'Of course, of course, but I have nothing else to tell you, I can assure you of that.'

—

It was satisfying to put Ian Turner's photo up on the board in the incident room. It was satisfying to have a suspect. Megan put him next to the slightly fuzzy shot of Gloria Ramos that Bridie had given them. She was in the photo too. A blonde four-year-old in a pretty blue dress. Bridie was smiling. Gloria was not.

The investigating team was assembled. Phil Arlott, Samira Kumar, Josh Baker and Deb, Inspector George's PA, who was there to take notes. It was a cold case. Resources were scarce. Just before they were about to start the briefing, the Inspector herself stepped into the room. It'd been a year since Megan last saw her—at Guido's funeral, she realised with a start. She hadn't changed much. Her hair was greyer, the little of it Megan could see under her police cap. She looked as if she were on her way to something more important.

'Megan! Welcome back! So glad you could come on board at such short notice.'

Megan was about to make some suitably polite response but Lisa George was clearly in a hurry. 'I've just popped in to apologise. I wanted to sit in for the briefing, but I have to go and see the Minister. Deb can bring me up to speed. And you've got this, Megan, I'm sure. It was always your case.'

With that, she was gone. Megan wasn't sure whether it was a relief or a slight. Either way, there was nothing to do but get on with it. She nodded at Phil and he rose.

'This is Ian Turner, ex-husband of Amanda Turner and father of Bridie.' Phil pointed to the two current photos they had of mother and daughter. Amanda's was clearly a professional head shot. 'Turner was the last person to see Gloria Ramos—that we have found so far, anyway. He says he dropped her at the airport but did not see her board the plane. During our interview with him, both Sarge and I had the impression he was not telling us everything he knew. He got angry and defensive.'

Megan took over the briefing. 'However, he did appear to be genuinely surprised that she had been found dead. And, of course, we have to remember we have not identified the body yet. The remains may not be of Gloria Ramos, so let's not jump to conclusions.'

'If it's not her,' said Josh Baker, 'how did a shoe with those laces end up on the body? We know they were definitely hers.'

'That's what we need to find out. The police in Manila are currently attempting to track down Gloria Ramos, her mother—if she is still alive—and her daughter. We have contact details for them from twenty years ago; Amanda Turner used to send them Gloria's pay via money orders. When we hear back from the Philippines, we'll either know Gloria Ramos is alive and well and living in the Philippines and so definitely not our Jane Doe, or we will get some familial DNA and be able to make a positive identification.'

'Do we have a cause of death, Sarge?'

'Not yet. I'm following up with Scotty this afternoon.'

—

A skeleton was less confronting than a fresh corpse. There was something anonymous, almost clinical, about bare bones. A corpse was still recognisable as a person; a skeleton was not. Everything that had made them individual had rotted away.

Scotty had been delayed and Megan was waiting in the examination room. Gloria's bones—if they were hers—were already laid out. Looking at them, Megan was reminded of a holiday she and Guido had spent in Paris, decades ago, long before she became a detective. The weather had been lousy, and they had an afternoon to kill. She'd read about the catacombs beneath the streets of Paris in a pamphlet in their hotel. The entry fee was cheap, and they were travelling on a budget. It had seemed like a good idea to head underground.

Guido had hated it—he was claustrophobic, and the tunnels were narrow and low—but Megan was fascinated. Every few feet the tunnels opened up into huge, deep alcoves. Originally fifteenth-century quarries, they were now home to millions of human skeletons stacked in their thousands. The tour guide had told them that the cemeteries of Paris had become full in the 1700s, and so city authorities had dug up the graves and put the remains in the catacombs. Each alcove bore the name of the cemetery where the bodies had originally been buried and the centuries it operated. These skulls and crossed bones were all that was left of the people who had lived in Paris in the eleventh, twelfth, thirteenth and fourteenth centuries.

The sheer volume of humanity neatly stacked in each alcove was overwhelming. As Guido hyperventilated and begged her to hurry up, Megan found she could not tear her eyes away. Every nameless skeleton had once been a living, breathing person, as vital to themselves, as caught up in the business and intensity of life, as everyone now alive on the planet. Yet here they all were: discarded, forgotten, ephemeral. *Was that why I decided to work in homicide?* she wondered now. That sense that the dead required their due?

Megan looked at the skeleton laid out in front of her. *Those buried millions were as anonymous and unknown as you*, she thought. Guido had a grave and a headstone. She visited it regularly. They'd bought the plot, but would it be there forever?

'Morning, Megan. Any luck with an ID?'

Helen Scott came into the room, drying her hands on a paper towel.

'Possibly. The laces on the shoe gave us a lead. If we're correct, her name is Gloria Ramos, a Filipina who was living here on a dodgy visa and working as a nanny for a wealthy Australian family.'

'That would explain why her DNA isn't on any of my databases.'

'We're following up on her daughter in Manila, so we may be able to get her DNA—if, of course, Gloria Ramos isn't in her home country. The family who employed her are adamant she returned home in 2002 to care for her sick daughter.'

'And that explains why no one reported her missing.'

'Any idea of cause of death yet?'

Scotty looked down at the bones. 'Well, like I said, she's had a rough life. There is evidence of old, poorly healed breaks on her left ankle, her right elbow and wrist, and a couple of ribs. See—here, here and here . . .'

Scotty handled the relevant bones efficiently yet gently. It was something Megan had always appreciated.

'How old?'

'Hard to say exactly, but the broken ankle might have happened in childhood, before the bones were fully formed. The others are more recent, but they have healed, so before death. Well, I say healed but they haven't properly—see here?'

Megan looked and nodded but she couldn't really see what Scotty meant.

'I suspect she didn't have access to medical treatment,' Scotty continued.

'The Turners might have been crappy employers, but I can't see them letting a broken elbow and wrist go untreated.'

'Worth asking them.'

'Don't worry, I will. But none of those injuries killed her, did they?'

'I'm getting to that.' Scotty stood at the head of the skeleton and gestured at its length. 'She's quite small for her age—which is about twenty-nine, by the way—almost stunted. I'd guess malnutrition as a child.'

Megan felt a wave of pity.

'Her bones tell a sad story. An unusual one in Australia too, so that backs up her being from somewhere like Manila. Unless she was Indigenous.'

Megan's thoughts returned to the skeletons stacked beneath the roads and footpaths of Paris. Many of them would have been malnourished and mistreated children, the human flotsam and jetsam that has filled the slums of big cities since there were such things.

Scotty replaced the bones she had been holding carefully, almost tenderly. 'She would have been easy to kill. Like killing a twelve-year-old really.'

Megan had to restrain an impulse to reach out and take the skeleton's hand. 'And . . . how was she killed?'

'No solid evidence on the skeleton to tell us that. Like I told you at the scene, no gunshot wound, stoved-in skull or nicks on bones from knives. It must have been a soft tissue injury that did for her. If her throat was cut, I'd expect some evidence of a knife on her neck vertebrae. My bet is she was strangled or suffocated. It wouldn't have been hard. She couldn't have put up much of a fight.'

Megan had a horrible thought. 'Buried alive?'

Helen Scott shrugged. 'Weak and small as she is, she'd still have to have been rendered unconscious first or very tightly bound.'

Megan felt sick. 'It's possible, though?'

'Yes, but not probable. No restraints were found in the grave, so only if she was drugged to unconsciousness or knocked out with a surprise blow first.'

'And if that was the case she wouldn't have screamed.'

'No.'

'So "cause of death unknown"?'

Scotty nodded. 'My guess is that she was strangled or suffocated but we won't know for sure unless you find more evidence or you catch her killer.'

EIGHT

'Have you seen this?'

'What?'

Phil Arlott threw the *Newcastle Herald* onto Megan's desk. A headline filled half the front page: LYREBIRD MIMICS MURDER. The subhead was worse: LYREBIRD'S WARNING IGNORED. POLICE TWENTY YEARS BEHIND THE KILLER.

'Jesus!'

'Your professor mate went to the media.'

Megan read the first couple of paragraphs. The story was accurate, as far as she could tell.

'You can't keep a sensational story like this under wraps for long,' she reasoned.

'Then why didn't we tell the media first and keep control of it?' Phil was angry.

Megan had never been keen on getting the media too involved in investigations. Her instincts were to do what she had always done—good, solid, unfussy police work. Take your time, be careful, check everything thoroughly, don't make assumptions and be guided by the evidence. The media had proved useful, but Megan had worried that the lyrebird angle was so sensational it could derail the investigation. Too late to do anything about that now.

'You can't control the media. Our job is to find the killer. Their job is to sell newspapers.'

'And get clicks, likes, shares and eyeballs.' Phil rolled his own.

'All that.'

'What'll we do?'

'I'll call her. I have a few minutes before my scheduled Zoom with the police in Manila. They've found Gloria's daughter—Luna Ramos. Gloria's mother, Luna's grandmother, died a few years ago.'

'Have they found Gloria?'

'No.'

'So she could still be our Jane Doe?'

Megan shrugged. 'DNA will tell us that. Until then . . .'

'But she never got on that flight.'

Samira Kumar had confirmed Gloria Ramos was not on the passenger manifest.

'She had a ticket and a seat but never showed,' Megan said.

'How much do you want to bet it's her?'

'I am not putting money on the identity of a murder victim.'

'It's just a figure of speech. Lighten up.'

Phil was right. She'd sounded priggish. Maybe she was more nervous than she'd thought about being back on the job. She was getting too intense, losing her professional distance. Talking to Scotty about possible causes of death had unsettled her. She felt protective of Jane Doe or Gloria Ramos or whoever the hell she was. The history of brutal treatment written on her skeleton, the fact she was so small and undernourished. What was it Scotty had said? It would have been like killing a twelve-year-old? But she mustn't get too emotionally involved, she reminded herself. It wasn't just her who was on edge, though. Phil was glaring at her with his arms folded across his chest.

'Sorry, that was a dickish thing to say.'

Phil raised his eyebrows. 'Apology accepted.'

'This case is getting to us all.'

But Phil wasn't having that. 'It's just another case. A bit colder than most, that's all.'

'You were suggesting it was a serial killer the other day!'

'We live in hope.'

'Phil!'

Megan was shocked, but he just grinned, making her feel like a prig all over again.

She sighed. 'I'll call Professor Weston.'

—

Jessica picked up on the first ring. 'I wondered when you'd call.'

Megan gave a wry laugh.

'Are you angry?' Jessica asked.

'More . . . curious.'

'The uni pressured me into it.'

'What do you mean? Like threatening your funding or something?'

'Oh, they'd never be that direct. They just let you know your enrolments are down, which could have an effect on how many staff you can hire and how many programs you can offer. Not-so-subtle stuff like that.'

'And publicity might help drive enrolments?'

'Yeah, now you've got it—uni speak.'

'Sounds remarkably like police department speak.'

'They also told me the lyrebird story was already on the public record from twenty years ago, and that it was just a matter of time till it broke. And . . . now it's broken. My phone's been ringing with media inquiries all morning—I'll say no to them, if you want.'

'Too late for that. The milk's spilt. Maybe getting it out there will help. Somebody knows something. Maybe media attention will jog their memory.'

'I thought you'd yell at me.'

Megan laughed again. 'What good would that do?'

'And I am sorry. I never meant to say a word, but when I came back from talking to you and . . . and seeing that video again . . . well, I ran into a colleague and blurted it all out.'

'When you talk to journalists, just stick to the facts, okay? Don't embellish.'

'Of course not!' Jessica sounded mortified. 'Just the facts. Nothing more. I wouldn't anyway.'

'No.'

'Is the story awful?'

'Apart from the headline, it doesn't look too bad.'

'I can't bear to read it.'

'Don't beat yourself up. Sometimes it's the fuck-ups that get results, and it was bound to happen eventually.'

'Drink next week?'

'I'd love that.'

Megan hung up.

Phil rubbed his chin. 'Why didn't you tell her to keep her mouth shut?'

'No point. What's done is done.'

'The media will be ringing our comms people nonstop.'

'It's their job to deal with the media.'

As if on cue, Megan's mobile vibrated on her desk.

'See?'

'But it's not my job.' Megan turned off her phone.

Phil sighed and changed the subject. 'I've finally sent Kumar and Baker to take a closer look at Boot Hill and follow up on the man with the alibi about buying eggs.'

'What took so long?'

'Paperwork seconding Baker. It got stuck in somebody's inbox, and Kumar's too green to go solo, but it's all sorted now.'

'Good.'

'It's hardly a lead.'

'I know, but what else have we got, apart from the shoelace? And we still have no idea how Gloria Ramos could have ended up buried in the boondocks. If that is who she is.' Megan looked at her phone. 'My Zoom with Manila starts in five minutes. Do you want to sit in?'

Phil pulled a chair up to sit beside her in front of her computer screen. 'If that body isn't Gloria Ramos, who is it? And where is Gloria?'

Both excellent questions, Megan thought as she clicked on the link.

The old fence sagged under the weight of all the shoes. Most of the pairs were tied to the rusting wire by their laces, but gumboots were upended on every fence post and thongs hooked onto nails. More shoes climbed the gum tree that grew beside the fence, perched on its branches like a flock of birds. Boot Hill stretched for metres each side of the tree until the shoes petered out. Samira's heart sank as she walked the fence.

'There must be hundreds of them.'

Sergeant Arlott had briefed them to collect any shoes that were not in pairs and, most importantly, to keep an eye out for any with distinctive laces.

'It's going to take us hours.' Josh wasn't thrilled either.

A noise. They both heard it and looked up. A rhythmic chutter, chutter, chutter. A helicopter, dragging an orange water bag.

'That's a water bomber,' Josh said. 'They must still be putting that fire out.'

'Fire? Didn't it rain recently, and that's why the land slipped?'

'Yeah, but that was a one-off, and the ground was so dry it didn't absorb much, which is probably why the land around the grave slipped. Since then, everything has dried out even more. A fire started up here yesterday. Remember how hot it was— way too hot for September—and windy. Mum said it's made everyone jumpy. They've got it under control now, but'—Josh looked up at the shiny blue speck above them—'obviously not completely.'

'Your mum lives around here?' Samira knew Josh was usually stationed at Gresford. 'Are you a local?'

'You could say that. Our mob's been here for sixty thousand years.'

Samira laughed.

'Ah, that local. My mob is from Mumbai via Liverpool.'

'I won't hold that against you. Welcome to Wonnarua Country.'

'Thanks.'

It was the first time Samira Kumar had felt truly welcome since she'd been posted to Maitland a month ago. She liked Josh. She was glad to be working this case with him.

'Why don't you start at one end and I'll start at the other,' said Josh, 'and hopefully we'll meet in the middle before knock-off.'

He had to raise his voice. The helicopter was lower now, positioning its trailing water carrier over a thin plume of smoke rising from the thickly wooded ridge line opposite. As they watched, shielding their eyes against the sun, the chopper dropped the water in a silvery rush. The smoke shrank for a moment or two, then returned as a wispy grey smudge.

Samira eyed it warily. The locals weren't the only ones feeling jumpy.

'Nothing to worry about unless the temperature soars or the wind turns nasty,' Josh assured her.

'And what do we do then?'

'Get the hell out.' Josh put his hands on his hips and considered their task. 'Where will we put the shoes if we find them?'

'There?' Samira pointed to a large log lying on the grass in front of them.

'Good a place as any.'

Samira looked back at the plume of smoke. The helicopter and its empty water bag had disappeared over the ridge. A car drove by. She knelt and put on her protective gloves. The sun was hot. It was going to be a long day.

'Thank you so much for joining us this morning, and thank you for all your hard work, Detective Cruz. This is my colleague Senior Sergeant Arlott.'

'Good morning.' Phil's face filled the screen.

'Nice to meet you both.' The Filipina detective was formal and polite. 'I hope you don't mind, but Ms Ramos was very keen to meet you and find out all she could. I thought she could answer any questions you might have directly and vice versa.'

Megan had noticed the younger woman sitting beside the detective. She had hoped it was Gloria's daughter.

'We are delighted to meet you, Ms Ramos.'

The younger woman nodded but did not smile. She was very pretty and very like her mother, with the same curly dark hair and wide-set eyes.

Megan wondered if Gloria's daughter could speak English.

'May I talk to Ms Ramos directly?' she asked the detective.

'Of course.' The young woman answered for herself. Her English sounded good and her accent was light.

'Thank you. If there is anything you don't understand, I am happy to clarify.'

'Thank you, but I think I am up to it.'

Neatly put in my place, thought Megan.

'You were expecting your mother home on Qantas flight nineteen, landing at six fifty p.m. on the seventh of July 2002, is that correct?'

The woman nodded.

'Did you go to the airport to meet her?'

'No. I had pneumonia and my grandmother couldn't leave me. My mother was catching the bus.'

'But she never arrived.'

'No. We waited and waited, but she did not come that night, or any night.'

A shadow passed across the young woman's face. It must have been awful waiting and wondering, never getting an answer.

'Did you call anyone to try to find out where she was?'

'My grandmother could not speak English and she had no phone and no money. Eventually she persuaded my doctor to call on our behalf.'

'Who did your doctor call?'

'Mrs Turner, the woman who had been sending us the money. But she didn't speak to Mrs Turner; she spoke to her husband.'

Phil caught Megan's eye.

'And what did he say?'

'He said he had dropped my mother at the airport.'

'Did you or your grandmother ever hear anything from her?'

The young woman, who had been so composed, looked upset. 'Maybe,' she said.

'Maybe?' asked Megan.

'We got a letter, but neither of us believed it was really from her.'

'Why not?'

'It was in English. Why would she write a letter to her Chavacano-speaking mother and five-year-old daughter in a language we didn't understand?'

Megan was puzzled. The letters to Bridie were in Chavacano dialect, according to the translator. Why would Gloria write to these two in different languages? Was she trying to tell them something? Or perhaps she didn't write to them at all. Megan made a quick entry in her police notebook.

Luna Ramos looked as if she was trying not to cry. 'We knew then that something horrible had happened to her.'

'You said you spoke Chavacano with her?'

'Yes, it's a Spanish dialect from Zamboanga City, where she grew up. My mother and grandmother could also speak a bit of Tagalog, but nothing else.'

'When did they move to Manila?'

'My mother was in her twenties. I was a baby. My dad had died, and they'd lost his income. They came seeking better paying work. My grandmother wanted her daughter and her granddaughter to have a better life than she'd had. When Mum got the job as a yaya in Hong Kong, she thought she had succeeded.'

A better life? Megan was saddened. As Scotty had pointed out, the bones they believed to be Gloria's told a very different story.

Samira and Josh had gathered about twenty shoes without a mate. Some of them were children's shoes, some—judging by their size—were probably men's, but there were around eight that could have been worn by women: a floral sandal, a red gumboot, a selection of petite running shoes and one rather large hot-pink high heel. Samira placed a small mauve running shoe on the log, then she stood and stretched her back. It was aching from bending over and painstakingly sorting through the never-ending shoes. It was dirty, smelly work and the footwear was infested with insects and spiders. She was glad she was wearing protective gloves.

She turned and saw the helicopter heading back with another load of water. It had made at least three trips while they had been working, chugging methodically backwards and forwards, yet still the thin haze of grey smoke plumed upwards.

'The fireys call it a candle. They can be hard to put out.'

Josh had come up behind her, holding a running shoe. 'What do you think about this? Is it a match for the one in the grave?'

Samira took the filthy shoe. It was so blackened with dirt, mould and damp that its original colour was hard to tell, but the laces were woven. Samira removed one of her gloves and scratched at the dirt on the shoelace with her thumbnail. It looked promising. 'Maybe,' she said.

'I'll bag it.'

'If it is, does that means someone around here did it?' Samira glanced around, half-expecting the culprit to jump out from behind a tree. She wasn't used to the bush. It made her nervous.

'Nah, more likely someone driving past. Locals don't hang boots at Boot Hill, only tourists do.'

'It's a good find, though,' Samira said.

Josh put the shoe in an evidence bag while she went back to her tedious task. Above her head, so did the helicopter.

By the time the two cops met at the tree growing at the top of Boot Hill, the sun was low in the sky and the helicopter appeared to have stopped for the day, even though the thin plume of smoke was still visible. There were probably fifty shoes around the log now. They still had to bag and label every one and put them in the back of Josh's police four-wheel drive. And then they had to follow up on the twenty-year-old alibi. Samira was hot and grubby and her back was killing her. All she really wanted was a cold beer.

The driveway was steep and rutted and the vehicle juddered and bounced all the way to the small weatherboard at the top. The shoes made a hell of a racket as they banged around in the back. The house came into view around a curve. It had seen better days. Once bright blue, it was peppered with raw, greying boards which must have replaced those that had rotted decades ago. Nobody had bothered to paint them. Maybe someone had cared about the place once, Samira thought, but not anymore. The window frames had lost all semblance of paint, and the corrugated-iron roof was red with rust. A large dog began barking furiously and straining at its chain as they approached.

Behind the house a pair of derelict chook sheds were visible, but that was the only sign this used to be a chicken farm. It was hard to believe anyone lived here now. The grass was high in what once must have been a garden, and rotting car bodies and appliances littered the home paddock. Apart from the angry dog, a large, unkempt quince bush was the only sign of life. There was something almost frightening about the place, like it was the setting for a scary movie.

'Do you think there's anyone home?' Samira asked.

'There's always someone home. Trev Farrow and his sister Nan live here. Nan never goes anywhere. She's in a wheelchair. Always has been.'

Poor Nan, thought Samira, scanning their surroundings.

Josh kept talking as he negotiated the rutted path. 'Some sort of brain damage at birth, Mum said. I don't know the details.'

'Is she the one we need to speak to?'

Josh looked at her. 'Nan can't speak. Her mind's okay, as far as anyone can tell, but her disability makes her impossible to understand. Trev usually speaks for her. He's done that since they were kids.'

Looking at the broken, weed-infested pavers, Samira wondered how on earth you'd get a wheelchair out. The house was at the end of a winding dirt side road. Then there was the driveway, all but impassable, and the property was on the very edge of the forest. She thought of the helicopter and the thin plume of smoke. How the fuck would Nan get out if there was a fire?

Before they reached the front door, a woman in a wheelchair had opened it and rolled herself out onto the small porch. Unlike her surroundings, the woman was clean. Her hair was neatly brushed and coiled into a bun at the back of her head. Her clothes were old and faded but laundered and ironed. The woman's face lit up when she saw Josh. He smiled back.

'Ibid!' she said.

'Hello, Nan. Is Trev in?'

Nan shook her head, and babbled affectionately at Josh: 'Ibid, ibid, ibid.' She took his hand, nodding both a welcome and her pleasure at seeing him. She smiled warmly at Samira, who found herself smiling back. Suddenly the tumble-down house didn't seem so sinister.

'No worries. You heard about the body in Burraga Swamp?' Nan nodded her head. Her smile disappeared.

'Do you remember, way back, the cops coming to ask you about a bloke who bought eggs from you? They were investigating a possible murder. It would have been about twenty years ago. Do you remember?'

Nan was staring at him. Josh tried to jog her memory. 'It was a woman detective, Megan Blaxland. Do you remember her?'

Nan nodded, but her smile had not returned. Samira supposed a copper asking her questions would be one of the most exciting things that ever happened to this housebound woman. A visit from the police was like that for most people, even those who had a life.

'We're just rechecking old evidence, Ms Farrow, that's all. We've reopened the case, now that we've found a body.' Samira followed Josh's lead and spoke gently. 'According to the case notes at the time, you confirmed to Detective Blaxland that a local— Leo Blake—had bought a dozen eggs from you that morning. It's a long time ago, I know, but he drove a red four-wheel drive, if that helps jog your memory.'

A kettle began to whistle inside the house. Nan looked over her shoulder but did not move. Samira followed her gaze but saw nothing. The kettle clicked off.

'Do you want to get that?'

Nan shook her head.

'Anyway, do you remember the man buying the eggs? Do you remember telling the police officer about him?'

Nan nodded her head. Then she babbled again. 'Ibid. Ibid.' It seemed to be all she could say.

'Was Trev here when Mr Blake called?' Josh asked.

Nan shook her head.

'Do you know where he was?'

She raised both her hands and shrugged.

'You don't know?'

Another shake of the head.

'Or you don't remember?' Samira this time. Nan was looking tired.

The woman nodded.

That made sense. While she might remember the copper's visit, after twenty years why should she remember where her brother was?

'Are you sure Trev isn't here?' Josh was looking over her shoulder into the dark hallway.

Nan nodded her head.

Josh handed her his card. 'Thanks, Nan. Get Trev to give us a call.'

'Why do you want to speak to her brother?' Samira asked, when Nan had closed the front door and they were out of earshot.

'Like I said, he speaks for her. They've always lived together—they're twins, in fact—and she doesn't get out much.'

'She looks well cared for.'

Josh nodded. 'They used to have carers, but since Trev retired he seems to do it all himself.'

'They should get her one of those electronic speaker things.'

Josh and Samira—as they were now calling each other—climbed back into the four-wheel drive.

'I don't think Trev's got two cents to rub together since he gave up farming the chickens.'

'Why'd he stop?'

'Got too old? I dunno.'

'Couldn't he have sold the farm?'

'They grew up on the place. Inherited it from their parents. Well, Trev did. He's a bit of a recluse too. They've always been on their own, apart from the occasional carer.'

'But what about the NDIS? Surely that could help them.'

'Who knows? They keep themselves to themselves. People around here respect that.'

Samira looked back towards the decrepit house. She couldn't help wondering if Nan was happy to keep herself to herself.

NINE

'The DNA results are in. Scotty's on her way over.' Kumar had popped her head around the door.

Megan looked up and smiled. 'Good.'

The more Megan saw of the young woman, the more she liked her. Kumar reminded her of herself as a young cop. Naive in some ways, a bit too eager to please, but quick on the uptake. She'd seemed shy at first and Megan had worried that she might not be tough enough for the job, but the younger woman had begun to warm up. Kumar might be rather too well versed in the police handbook—like many young coppers—but she had a sense of humour. Megan still didn't know much about her personal life. Didn't know if she had a partner or what she did when she finished her shift. She was vaguely aware that Kumar had come from Sydney. She probably didn't know many people in Maitland and, like many regional towns, it could be a bit cliquey. She remembered her own loneliness when she'd first moved up here forty years ago, and she'd had a husband.

Megan made a mental note to get to know the young woman better, but a friendly chat would have to wait—a lot was riding on this DNA.

She'd put a rush on the results comparing Luna Ramos's DNA with that of their Jane Doe, but even so they'd taken a couple of days. In that time, Baker and Kumar had been up to Leo Blake's place only to find it all locked up. Megan had been pushing for another interview with Ian Turner, but he'd also proved hard to pin down. He'd checked himself into a short-term mental health clinic, strictly no visitors allowed. She could have pushed the issue, but she decided it was better to wait. Let him stew. He could not avoid them for long. Nonetheless, she was growing increasingly impatient. Until they knew who their victim was, they'd gone about as far as they could. If the DNA gave them a positive ID, they were away—hopefully. Bridie had confirmed that the lace on the running shoe Kumar and Baker had found at Boot Hill was part of the pair she had given her nanny, so Scotty's results were even more vital.

Megan got up and grabbed her notebook. 'Get the team together. Whatever the result, we can review.'

Kumar nodded.

The other shoes the two constables had brought back were laid out on a large table in the incident room. Megan was not sure what to make of them. They were a motley assortment without any obvious connection. Some were left shoes, some right. They were all different sizes, makes and colours. The only thing they had in common was they had no mate—not hanging on the fence at Boot Hill, anyway.

Megan studied them as she waited for the others to arrive. One shoe stood out: a hot-pink high heel. Megan pointed to it as Josh Baker entered the room. 'It's got to have been put there as a joke, surely?'

'People hang bras on the fence sometimes. The farmer whose land Boot Hill is on doesn't like that, so he takes them down. I'm kind of surprised he left this one there.'

'It's just a shoe.'

'Yeah, but it's a sexy shoe.'

'A fuck-me shoe.'

Kumar had joined them. They both turned to look at her.

She's full of surprises, Megan thought. *Good*.

'Don't look at me like that,' the young woman said. 'It's what they're called.'

'You wouldn't wear them up there, though,' said Megan. 'You'd break your neck.'

'I dunno,' Baker said. 'There are weirdos everywhere.'

'It's a *Priscilla, Queen of the Desert* shoe.' Phil was standing behind them.

'You're right,' Megan said. 'It's big for a woman's shoe.'

'Do you think it has any relevance? Or is it just some day-tripper having a laugh?' Phil had his arms crossed.

'Who can say? But it's hard to ignore.'

'If Gloria's shoe is a trophy, could the person who wore this be another victim?' Kumar asked.

Megan swept her hands wide. 'We don't know enough yet, but it's possible any of them could be.'

'Or all of them,' Phil said. 'Serial killers like trophies.'

'There are fifty-two shoes!' Baker was incredulous.

'Surely no one could get away with killing that many people?' Kumar was shocked.

'People lose shoes in the river all the time, especially when it's running fast, and Boot Hill's a convenient place to leave the one that's left, and some of them could have been souvenired,' Baker pointed out. 'Tourists stop at Boot Hill constantly. They add old shoes—and, no doubt, take them away. Animals and weather might have taken others. It floods up there sometimes, particularly in the last few years.'

Josh Baker's local knowledge was proving helpful. Megan was pleased she'd added him to the team.

'We're lucky we found Gloria's other shoe then.'

They heard the door behind them open. Helen Scott had arrived. She looked at the bagged running shoe Megan was now holding in her hands and shook her head.

Megan's heart sank. 'The remains aren't those of Gloria Ramos?'

Scotty shook her head a second time. 'There is no familial match between the DNA provided by Luna Ramos and the body found in Burraga Swamp fourteen days ago. If we accept the authenticity of the DNA sample sent by the Philippines police, the remains are not those of Gloria Ramos.'

'Fuck! Back to square one.' Phil spoke for all of them.

'Here, let me show you.'

Scotty put her laptop onto a nearby desk. The police crowded around.

'See, that's Luna Ramos's DNA profile, and that's from our Jane Doe.'

Two parallel columns of horizontal lines filled the screen. Scotty hit a key and the two slowly merged. The differences were stark.

'Shit,' Phil said. No one else spoke.

'But we know the laces on the shoe worn by the corpse were given to Gloria Ramos,' Megan said. 'So how did they end up with some other woman's body?'

'And if she's not Gloria, who is she?' Baker leant in to examine the image on the screen, as if it could offer up answers.

'And if she's not the woman in the grave, where is Gloria Ramos?' asked Kumar.

All good questions.

'We've got a murder *and* a missing person on our hands now,' Megan said.

Baker stepped back from the computer. 'Could Gloria be buried up near Burraga Swamp and we just haven't found her body yet?'

'I think we'll have to do another thorough search of the area,' Megan agreed. 'That bird mimicked a Spanish speaker. We know Gloria spoke Spanish. Maybe it heard Jane Doe being killed, maybe it heard Gloria . . .'

'Or someone else.' Phil sounded disheartened.

Scotty closed her laptop. 'I wish I could have brought you more answers, but DNA doesn't lie.'

'Could the sample have been contaminated?' Phil was clutching at straws.

'Unlikely but I can ask for another one.'

'I'll do that, Scotty,' Megan said. 'We'll also have to tell Luna Ramos that the body is not that of her mother.'

Scotty put a hand on her shoulder. 'Rather you than me.'

Megan smiled at her friend. She was dreading that conversation. Awful though it was to know your mother had been brutally killed, it was better than knowing nothing. And she'd already seen the toll a missing mother had taken on the daughter Gloria had left behind. What was it Bridie Turner had called her? Gloria's 'real little girl'.

'What next, Sarge?' asked Kumar.

'All we can do is follow the leads we have,' Megan said. 'It looks to me like Jane Doe and Gloria Ramos must have known each other or come into contact in some way. How else did Jane get those shoelaces? So if we find Gloria—dead or alive—we might also find the identity of our current victim. Let's do what we would have done if we'd had a positive ID.'

'Get Ian Turner in for another interview,' Phil said. 'I've been doing a bit of digging. Just a hunch I had after Bridie said he was a gambling addict—and bingo! He was up to his ears in debt to some very dodgy characters. Worth having a chat about, I reckon. I'm talking organised crime, human traffickers, evil fucking bastards.'

'Great! That gives me enough to bypass the rules of that crisis centre where he's been hiding. Bring him in.'

Megan patted Phil Arlott affectionately on the back. He could be irritating sometimes, and old fashioned, but he was an outstanding copper. Human trafficking had occurred to her too; the way Gloria had arrived in the country, her lack of legal status—all made her vulnerable. But Megan had not known about Turner's dodgy past. Phil's digging gave them a new lead.

'Good work.'

Phil grinned.

'Constable Kumar, can you follow up on the letter Luna Ramos received from her mother—or someone pretending to be her mother? I'd like to get a copy.'

'What about searching Burraga Swamp?'

'I'll ask Inspector George about that. It's a national park, a protected area. We'll have to get permission from the relevant authorities . . . not to mention more manpower.'

'And what in hell are we going to tell the media?' Phil wasn't about to let that grievance go.

What indeed? Megan wondered, but it was what she was going to tell Luna Ramos that concerned her the most. She'd wait until she had Scotty's written report. That'd buy her a couple of days, and maybe by then she'd also have some better news to report—by better news, she meant any substantial lead at all.

—

Jessica carried two chardonnays back to the table, holding them high above her head as she pushed through the crowd at the bar. It was her shout—the least she could do after setting the media onto Megan. The older woman looked tired.

Jessica didn't like that. She wanted Megan to be in charge. Jessica's worry about her wayward daughter had become even worse since they'd found the body. She knew it was irrational. Whatever had happened had happened twenty years ago. There was nothing for her to fear now. But the feeling she'd had as she ran through the forest clutching her camera was still with her.

A feeling that someone sinister was watching her every move. She was relying on Megan to solve the mystery, catch the bad guy and put everything back to rights.

'You look beat,' she said, putting the drinks on the table.

'Good deduction. I am beat.'

'How's the case going?'

'Slowly. We thought we'd found the identity of the victim, but the DNA doesn't match.'

'What'll you do now?'

'Keep going with the leads we've got.'

'I'm still really sorry about the media.'

'No worries. I'm letting police comms deal with them.'

'JESSICA!'

Jessica almost jumped out of her skin. Both she and Megan turned towards the sound and were dazzled by a staccato burst of camera flashes.

'Thanks, ladies!'

As she blinked into the dark, Jessica felt sick. Just as she had feared, someone was watching her.

―

TOP COP AND LYREBIRD LADY DROWN THEIR SORROWS

Megan threw the newspaper across the room. For fuck's sake! As if she didn't have enough to deal with. The photo was terrible. She and Jessica both had their mouths wide open and looked half-pissed, although neither of them had had as much as a sip.

Phil came into the room just as the paper hit the bin.

'You've seen it, then.'

'Bloody rubbish! But how the hell do they know we still have no ID on the victim? Is someone leaking?'

'Your bird lady?'

Megan shook her head. 'Honestly, I don't think so. She's mortified. But I won't tell her anything, just in case.'

She wished she'd never told Jessica about their dead end. Had her friend set her up? She'd lost her ability to judge character if that was the case. She decided to change the subject.

'How are you doing, Phil? I've hardly had a moment to chat to you. How's Clare?'

'Away.'

'On holidays?' Megan was trying but Phil was giving her nothing.

'At her mother's.'

Phil sounded positively hostile. They'd always got on well; was he really that shitty about the publicity? Perhaps he'd wanted to run this investigation? No, Phil wasn't like that. He was always happy to be part of a team.

'Is everything all right? I mean with you, not the case.'

'Yeah. Why wouldn't it be?'

It was like talking to a brick wall.

'Look, I am sorry about the paper, but we were both taken completely by surprise.'

'Shit photo.'

Megan laughed. 'Yeah, but I can live with "Top Cop".'

'Not sure the rest of us can.'

Phil was grinning again. She grinned back, but she was still uneasy. Something wasn't right.

'Ian Turner's in the interview room. He looks awful. He's brought a lawyer with him.'

It was the next morning. Phil seemed like his old self. Perhaps Megan was just finding it hard to get back to their usual rhythm.

'Courtesy of Amanda, I imagine; there's no way he could afford a lawyer on his own.'

'Why would she help him out? She didn't want a bar of him.'

'Fear of scandal?' Megan guessed. 'Bridie twisting her arm?'

'Why would Bridie want to help him?'

'He's her dad. She stays in touch. They must have some sort of connection.'

'Lucky him.'

Megan looked up at her colleague. 'Where'd that come from?'

'Nowhere. Too long on the job. Seen too many fucked-up families.'

That grin again, shutting her out.

'Maybe someone else paid,' Phil suggested. 'Worried about what Turner might say.'

'Possibly.'

'Do you want me to do the interview?' he asked.

'Worried I might be rusty?'

'Well . . . it's been a while.'

'It's like riding a bike,' Megan scoffed. 'This bastard is mine.'

Megan intended to get the truth out of Turner no matter what it took. She was getting sick of slow and steady. It was time to turn up the heat.

Ian Turner and his lawyer had been sitting in the interview room for about fifteen minutes by the time Megan and Constable Kumar took their seats across the desk. Always a good idea to let suspects sweat. Kumar turned on the tape. Phil was watching the interview remotely from another room.

'You were the last person to see Gloria Ramos before she disappeared,' Megan began.

'If you say so.'

'It's not up to me to say so, with respect. It's up to you.'

'I just mean that the people at the airport and on the plane must have seen her . . .'

'We've checked that, and it appears she did not get on that flight and might never have been at the airport. You have not told us all you know.'

'What I know? I just dropped her off . . .'

'If you dropped her off, where did she go? She seems to have vanished without a trace.'

'How should I know where she went? I've already told you all this.' Turner's voice was shrill.

His lawyer leant towards him and whispered something in his ear. Turner's eyes were wide. He was terrified.

'But we now know you were up to your eyeballs in debt at that time,' said Megan. 'Your ex-wife told us that's one reason she divorced you. She was about to lose the house. You owed money to some seriously scary people. Do you deny that?'

'No comment.'

'Let me paint a picture. Your daughter's pretty twenty-nine-year-old yaya has to fly back to the Philippines to care for her sick child. She speaks almost no English, officially she's not even in the country, she's got her passport and you offer to drop her at the airport. Am I right so far?'

Turner's left leg was jiggling.

'You owed some very bad people tens of thousands of dollars. They are not the type to let such a debt go unpaid. Either you cough up the money or they hurt you. Am I getting warmer?'

'Amanda and I had plenty of money. If I had such a debt, I could have just paid it.'

'Mrs Turner has already told us that she had isolated all her funds from you and taken possession of your credit cards. She was aware of your gambling problem and had taken steps to protect her assets. You couldn't "just pay it", not anymore, could you, Mr Turner?'

Turner looked at his lawyer. The man leant towards him as if to whisper in his ear again, but Turner pulled away, forcing his lawyer to give his instructions aloud.

'You are not obliged to answer that question.'

Turner's leg was jiggling so hard it was banging the underside of the table. He looked at Kumar, then at Megan, then back at his lawyer.

'I'm not obliged to answer that question,' he parroted.

'We are obliged to continue to investigate, Mr Turner. And we will interview every one of the people you owed money to, and one of them will tell us what we want to know. It will be better for you if you cooperate and tell us yourself what happened. We know you didn't drop Gloria at the airport.'

Megan didn't know this, not for sure, but she was becoming more convinced by the minute.

The lawyer whispered in Turner's ear again. Whatever he said had been a mistake. When Turner looked at Megan there was something defiant about him.

'Can you repeat the question?'

'You couldn't just pay your gambling debts anymore, could you, Mr Turner? Not in cash, anyway. But you could pay it in kind. You could give Gloria to the bad men and let her work off your debt.'

Ian Turner slammed the table with his fist. His lawyer looked agitated.

'My client is distressed. I think we should stop the interview and give him time to compose himself.'

'NO!' Turner shouted.

The lawyer started. Megan and Kumar were still.

'No,' he said again, quietly this time. 'I want to go on.' Then he turned to his lawyer. 'Fuck you. I know who you're here to defend and it's not me.'

The man looked down at his notes and said nothing.

Turner drew a breath then looked Megan in the eye. 'What do you want to know?'

'Did you traffic another human being?' Megan kept her voice expressionless.

Turner's eyes filled with tears. He nodded. His face was working as he battled to remain in control.

'They were threatening Bridie! They said they'd kidnap her, do horrible things to her. I knew they could, and I knew they would. She was five! I had to do something!'

Megan felt a twinge of pity.

'You could have spoken to your wife. Told her the truth. Surely she would have done anything to protect her daughter?'

'I was ashamed.'

Not as ashamed as you are now, Megan thought.

'You could have gone to the police,' she said. 'You had options.'

'They'd have killed me! You don't know these people. They have no souls.'

'So, you delivered a vulnerable, friendless young woman into the clutches of people with no souls?'

'I didn't think they'd kill her. I thought she'd work off her debt and go home.'

'*Her* debt?'

'My debt. I misspoke.'

'Tell us where you took Ms Ramos.'

'I took her to a brothel in Pitt Street.'

'On the spur of the moment? Or had you planned it in advance?'

'In advance.' Turner was quieter now, looking down at his hands.

'With whom?'

'Sammy. Sammy Lee.'

That name was familiar, but Megan couldn't place it.

'Who is Sammy Lee?'

'He . . . I thought he was just a croupier. He used to lend me money. Let me put bets on tick. I thought he was my friend . . .'

Turner began to cry. Tears of self-pity.

'He'd give me free drinks, listen to me complain about Amanda. I thought he liked me.'

'But he only liked your money.'

'Amanda's money. Everything changed when I told him she'd cut me off.'

'What did you arrange?'

'I already told you.'

'Tell me again.'

'Sammy asked me how I intended to pay back the fifty grand he said I owed him. When I said I didn't know, he suggested he kidnap Bridie and demand a ransom from Amanda. He even said he'd demand a hundred thou and cut me in for a percentage!' Turner sounded outraged. 'I refused, of course.'

What does he want? Megan wondered. *A medal?*

'That's when he mentioned Gloria. I remember he said something about how pretty she was and that maybe she could work off the debt. That really freaked me out. If he knew about Gloria, knew she was pretty, then he'd been watching us! Watching Bridie! I nearly threw up.'

'I'll ask you again. Why didn't you go straight to the police?'

Turner met Megan's eyes. His own were dead in his face. 'They'd have killed me. And now I wish they had.'

'How did you persuade Gloria to go into the brothel?'

'I told her—I got Bridie to tell her—that I had to pick up some papers on the way to the airport. That's the thing about that brothel; it looks just like an office block. I drove into the underground car park and Sammy Lee's blokes took care of the rest.'

'Took care of the rest?' Megan wasn't going to let him off that easy.

'They wrenched open the door and grabbed her. She screamed at me—reached out to me, begging me to help her. I just sat there and stared straight ahead.' He shuddered. 'I'll never forget the sound of her voice ... She kept saying: *"Ayúdame".*'

TEN

Megan stood beside the grave they'd thought was Gloria's. Baker was removing the police tape. By the look of the footprints and trampled undergrowth, it hadn't kept many people away from the crime scene, but out here, what could you do? And once it was in the media . . .

She turned back to survey the twenty or so cops gathered in a ragged half-circle. She'd briefed them carefully, but it was going to be a tough search through thick, overgrown forest on steep crags. A ranger was telling them about the plants and trees they should not touch. He was putting the fear of God into everyone about the giant stinging trees.

'Do not touch any part of these trees, particularly the leaves.' The ranger was pointing to a tall, large-leafed tree behind them. Every head turned. 'The pain is horrendous and even a mild sting can last for hours. A major one can have you in agony for months. Gloves won't protect you from the stinging hairs, nor will your clothing. Just give them a wide berth.'

'There are a bloody lot of them.' Phil Arlott was looking around. He was right; now they knew what to look for, the searchers could see the vicious trees everywhere.

Great, thought Megan. *As if this job wasn't hard enough already.*

'They grow more quickly and widely in areas of rainforest that have been logged, damaged by storms or otherwise disturbed,' the ranger explained. 'That's why there are so many.'

'Otherwise disturbed? Like if someone dug a grave?' Baker was standing beside Phil.

'Possibly.'

They had travelled to Burraga Swamp in a convoy of vehicles, including a small bus and four police four-wheel drives. The novelty of this police presence in such a sleepy valley made it impossible to keep their mission under wraps. By the time they'd reached the car park, they were accompanied by a phalanx of curious bystanders and a handful of representatives of the local media, including Brett Collins and Heather Maxim from the *Newcastle Herald*; it seemed they regarded the lyrebird case as 'their' story. There was also someone from local ABC radio and another from the *Dungog Chronicle*. None of the major media had bothered. In these straitened times, they only turned up at a place as remote as Burraga Swamp if a major announcement or discovery was on the cards. Especially if there was also the chance of some juicy visuals.

Megan had managed to contain the sightseers to the car park. Some of the locals had offered to help in the search. At least they'd claimed to be locals. Megan was too experienced a homicide detective not to know that the perpetrator often returned to the scene of the crime to enjoy the mayhem they had created. She asked Constable Kumar to take down all their details. None of those gathered looked a likely prospect . . . but you never knew. Likely or not, she wouldn't be using any of them in the search. Lack of manpower notwithstanding, enthusiastic amateurs caused more trouble than they were worth.

The coppers fanned out into a wobbly and idiosyncratic line. Megan had divided the search area into grids and each group of five was assigned specific ground to cover, but she knew the search areas were dictated by the terrain and not by any logic. Given what she had to work with, it was the best she could do. Megan had managed to scrounge a couple of cadaver dogs and their handlers. She was pinning a lot of hope on them.

It had been a gruelling week, starting with informing Luna Ramos that the bones were not those of her mother. She'd had to deliver the news over Zoom, of course.

'Firstly, I want to thank you for providing the DNA sample. It has been very helpful, although not in the way we expected.'

Even over the internet, Megan could see the young woman tense.

Luna leant forward, her head looming large on the computer screen. 'What do you mean, not in the way you expected?'

'The body we found in Burraga Swamp, wearing the running shoe with the shoelaces Bridie Turner gave to your mother, is not that of Gloria Ramos. There was no familial relationship between the DNA of the dead woman and your sample. I have forwarded the forensic report to Detective Cruz. I am sure she will provide you with a copy.'

The young woman's face crumpled. The agony of not knowing would continue.

'Rest assured we have not given up searching for your mother, or for the killer.'

'I assume from her footwear that the woman in the grave either knew my mother or must have come across someone who had.'

Luna Ramos had regained her composure. She had grit.

'I think that's a fair assumption.'

'I will come to Sydney. Bridie Turner has very kindly offered to let me stay with her.'

Fuck, thought Megan. That could get complicated given what Bridie's dad had done to Luna's mother.

They'd charged Ian Turner with deceptive recruiting and trafficking in persons. He was on remand and faced a maximum sentence of twelve years. Megan was pretty sure he'd be convicted. His guilt and shame were so overwhelming, she doubted he'd even try to fight the charges. Bridie must know by now what he had done. His arrest had been all over the media. WEALTHY PHILANTHROPIST'S EX CHARGED WITH HUMAN TRAFFICKING, screamed one headline, illustrated with a recent photo of Amanda, champagne flute in hand. Amanda had also featured prominently in the TV news stories, head down, flanked by lawyers, running the gamut of the media pack.

'Will you post bail for your ex-husband, Amanda?' one of the journalists had yelled.

The question had stopped the woman in her tracks. 'I will not.'

Her reply was so vehement Megan had barked an admiring laugh as she'd watched Amanda disappear inside her high iron gates. Nor should she. Turner deserved what he would get. But talking to Luna, Megan had stayed neutral.

'Are you aware of Ian Turner's involvement in your mother's situation?'

'I know what he did, Detective.' The young woman's face was expressionless.

'All right. Just so long as you are aware.'

'What chance is there that she is still alive?'

'I can't speculate about that.'

Luna Ramos nodded. 'She would have contacted us if she was.'

Megan admired the young woman's clear-eyed ability to face reality, however bad it might be.

'Your grandmother did a good job.'

'The money orders made all the difference. My grandmother spent them on me. I am grateful to my mother and the Turner family. Without them, I might have been forced into the kind of life my mother had.'

Megan had not thought of that, but it made a horrible kind of sense.

'Maybe I could have ended up in a grave in a forest, with only the native birds as witness.'

'We are doing everything we can.'

Despite the young woman's composure, it had been a tough conversation.

The next blow was discovering that Sammy Lee was dead. He'd been killed in a gangland hit a few years ago. No one had been convicted of his murder. Megan had discovered quite a lot about the brothel Gloria had been taken to, even though the same floors in Pitt Street were now occupied by a very respectable accountancy firm whose staff were both shocked and titillated when they found out who the previous tenants had been. The Sydney cop who had headed the investigation into Lee's murder was still alive. He'd retired about the same time as Megan and now lived in Tea Gardens, only a couple of hours drive from Burraga Swamp.

In the forest, the ragged police line had begun to make its way forward. There wasn't much more Megan could do here, unless they found something. She looked at the time on her phone. If she left the search in the capable hands of Phil Arlott, she'd still have time to go and talk to the retired detective.

'Anything else you need from me, Phil?'

'Nope. Unless you've got an antidote for giant stinging trees.' The big man looked around him warily.

'Think of the compo,' Megan said cheerily. Poor Phil. He could handle the meanest of streets, but the bush? His worst nightmare.

—

'Detective Senior Sergeant Blaxland! Detective Blaxland!'

The minute she emerged from the bush track Brett Collins was in her face, Heather Maxim was snapping photographs, and the ABC journo was thrusting a mic at her. There weren't a lot of press, but they still managed to be as annoying as a swarm of mosquitoes. She wanted to swat them away. *It is so bizarre*, she thought, *this fuss in the middle of nowhere.* She wondered if there were any lyrebirds around taking mental notes for their mating repertoire.

'Have you found any more bodies?'

'Have you any idea who the killer is?'

'Do you know who the victim is yet?'

'How is human trafficking linked to this case?'

All excellent questions. She wished she knew the answers. Megan stopped and spoke to the throng, using the line the police media people had given her.

'Once we have some news, rest assured we will make a statement,' she said.

'But it's been almost a month since you found the body and nothing. I understand they called you out of retirement to head up the investigation. Do you think you might be past it?' Brett thrust his phone in her face.

Jesus Christ! thought Megan. *They don't pull their punches.*

'As I said, we will make a statement as soon as there are any developments.'

The comms woman had called this technique 'broken record'. 'Just keep saying the same thing over and over,' she'd advised. 'They can't do anything with that.'

'But Ian Turner has been charged with human trafficking. What has that got to do with the body in the forest?' Brett kept pushing.

'When we have an announcement, you will all be kept fully informed. Now, if you will excuse me, I have an appointment.'

The four media people plus some of the local gawkers stood between her and her car, and she was forced to push past them. She kept her head down and forced herself to show no sign of irritation. Just for a moment she had a flash of fellow feeling for Amanda Turner. It was horrible to be besieged.

Even once she had closed her door and buckled her seatbelt, the journalists continued to press against the vehicle. She had to drive slowly out of the car park to ensure she did not bowl over any of the fourth estate—however momentarily satisfying that might have been.

—

Andrew Weymouth had a beautiful garden, filled with climbing roses and pink and white bauhinia trees. His small lawn was freshly mown and his garden walls, protecting his plants from the salty estuarine breeze, looked as if they had been erected yesterday. He was waiting for her on his front verandah, tea and biscuits on the table. She had called ahead to make sure her visit was convenient, and he had greeted her suggestion of a chat with enthusiasm. However frustrating this case was becoming, his delight at her visit reminded her how glad she was to be working again. Even though she had friends, including Scotty, retirement had been lonely and, she finally acknowledged to herself, boring. She'd felt useless. She'd thought about volunteering or joining a local committee dedicated to something or other, but it had all felt a bit desperate and pointless. Tracking down a murderer had brought her back to life. She recognised the irony of that but it didn't make her pause. She was determined to crack the case. She owed it to Luna, Bridie, Gloria and that woman in the grave—whoever she was.

Weymouth stood up to greet her. They'd not met before, and she was surprised to see that he was a small man with a pronounced pot belly. She expected cops from the organised crime squad to be big, hard men; Weymouth looked like your grandad.

'Tea?' he offered.

It was in a proper pot with a flowered tea cosy. Lovely.

'Please. White, no sugar.'

Once they had settled back on his sunny verandah, Megan got straight to business. 'I assume you know why I am here.'

Weymouth nodded and smiled. 'Phil Arlott briefed me. We go way back. Went to the Academy together. You think the body you've found has some connection with the Pitt Street brothel run by Sammy Lee?'

'In a nutshell.'

'That wouldn't surprise me; it was a bloody awful place. When we shut it down, I pulled a drunk fifty-something off a little Thai girl who turned out to be thirteen. You know what he was pissed off about? That I wouldn't let him "finish". Disgusting old pervert.'

'Did you notice this woman?'

Megan showed him the slightly fuzzy photo of Gloria that Bridie had given them.

He looked at it carefully, his bifocals on the end of his nose. 'Filipina?'

Megan nodded.

'Most of them were from the Philippines or Thailand,' he said. 'During the Balkan wars we got a lot of Eastern European girls as well. Now it's probably Sudanese, Syrians and South Americans. Wherever life becomes insupportable, women will be vulnerable. Men cause the problems; women pay the price. Watched that my whole career.' He handed the photo back. 'I don't remember her, sorry.'

'Who else could I talk to? Are any of the girls still around?'

'Nah. Sadly, when we raid the places and rescue the women who have been trafficked they eventually get deported. They're here illegally, you see. That's one of the reasons they don't go to the police even if they get the chance. They're between a rock and a hard place. I reckon we should let them stay, but too many of those bloody politicians can't shake the idea that they're whores and won't pass the character test.'

'Even the thirteen-year-olds?'

Weymouth nodded. 'Even the thirteen-year-olds.'

'Could Gloria have been deported?'

'Very likely, if she'd been caught up in a raid.'

'But she'd have been deported to the Philippines, and there's no record of her ever going back. And she's never contacted her family.'

'Sometimes they're so ashamed of what they've had to do, they go to ground. Awful. It's not like they had any sort of choice.'

'Anyone else I could contact?'

'You could talk to Coco. As far as I know she's still around.'

'Who's Coco?'

'She was the madam.'

'Wasn't she arrested?'

'Yeah, went to jail, but she's served her time and last I heard she was managing a legit place in Surry Hills.'

'Not a human trafficker any longer, then?'

'I don't think she ever was, really. She just managed the place—front of house, accounts, kept the books, that kind of thing. Sammy had something over her. She was just as terrified of him as the other girls were. I never found out what it was; gambling probably. She was a ladyboy—or that's what Sammy called her. Maybe that was an issue. Maybe she owed him for the op.'

'Any idea where I might find her?'

'Try the brothel she runs now. It's even called Coco's. She's become a bit of an icon.'

'Are there any doubts about Lee's murder?'

'Only that we never found a body. But that's very typical. The people he worked for are very professional. If they decide to get rid of someone, they never leave any evidence. They just disappear.'

'Got something!'

They all stopped in their tracks. The dog handler was holding up his hand and his dog was whining and pawing at the ground. *Holy shit*, thought Samira. *I hope it's human remains.* Then she felt ashamed. What a horrible thing to wish for.

Scotty had sent a couple of her assistants to help with the search. They scurried forward, suited up, each one carrying a trowel. Samira's heart sank. Digging up a body buried in a peat bog with a couple of trowels could take all day. She knew they didn't want to destroy any evidence or damage the body, but she hadn't realised that'd mean they'd have to go slow.

'Keep searching.' Phil Arlott had joined them. 'Where there's one, there may be more.'

Samira thought of all the shoes on the evidence table. She suddenly had a feeling that the ground beneath their feet was crunchy with bones. She and the rest of the uniforms did as they were told, continuing to creep forward in formation, poking at the ground, alert for anything unusual or out of place. The work was quite mesmerising, so Samira wasn't sure how much time had passed before she heard her name being called.

'Constable Kumar.' It was Arlott. 'Can you radio Senior Sergeant Blaxland from the car park and tell her it might be worth her while to return? Then call Professor Scott and get her up here as well.'

It was a body all right, and because it had been buried in the peat bog it was better preserved than the first one. As the forensic guys carefully brushed the dirt from the skull, Samira leant over to Josh, who was standing beside her.

'Do you think it could be Gloria?'

He shrugged. Samira hoped it was and also hoped it wasn't.

'Kumar!' Arlott yelled. He gestured towards the car park. Samira turned and ran.

She was out of breath when she got to the four-wheel drive. The journos and bystanders were taken by surprise. They'd been chatting and leaning against their cars, waiting for something to happen. A few must have given up because their numbers had thinned. It was the lady photographer who first spotted Samira at her car. She jumped up and began snapping photos. A bloke waving a recording device wasn't far behind.

'What's happened?' he asked.

Ignoring him, Samira climbed into the car and proceeded to deliver the messages as Senior Sergeant Arlott had instructed.

When she returned to the search she sensed an increase in excitement among the other cops. Arlott was busy giving orders, waving his arms about, and Scotty's assistants were busy digging in another spot. She looked at Josh and raised her eyebrows.

'The dogs have found another one,' Josh whispered.

'Strangulation. He buried this one with a cord still around her neck. It's nylon, so it's relatively intact.'

Scotty gestured towards the neck of the corpse lying in its boggy grave. Megan leant in to get a closer look and saw a fragment of something blue and white embedded in the remaining flesh. Though filthy, it was recognisable as the kind of rope used on washing lines.

'Safe to guess the other women were strangled as well, then?'

Scotty nodded. 'This certainly increases the possibility.'

Megan had driven back to the swamp after her afternoon tea with Sergeant Weymouth. She must claim her mileage, she reminded herself. They'd unearthed two bodies by the time she'd arrived and Scotty had been deep in the process of preparing them for transport to the morgue. The sun was low in the sky and none of them wanted to leave the remains in the open any longer than necessary.

There wasn't much more to be said about the discoveries. Both were buried much as the first Jane Doe had been, and there was no real evidence at the scene after two decades in the wilderness. At least the cord around the neck gave them a cause of death. *And*, Megan thought as she looked down at the mud-stained bones, *every fact we unearth leads us closer to the killer.*

'Maybe one of them will be Gloria,' said Phil's voice behind her as he entered the Scene of Crime tent.

'Let's hope so. Either way, this will mean Lisa will have to release some manpower. Obviously we're going to have search every inch of this area.'

'It's a killing field. The media will go nuts!'

Knowing the journalists would have taken note of her return and Scotty's arrival, Megan grimaced, steeling herself for the inevitable confrontation when they returned to the car park.

ELEVEN

'Can you put a hurry-up on the DNA?'

It was the next morning, and Megan had joined Scotty at the morgue. She was keen to know if one of these two new bodies was Gloria; she wanted to be able to give Luna and Bridie some news as soon as humanly possible.

'I marked it as urgent,' Scotty said, 'but you know how it is—the results take as long as they take.'

'And murders that happened twenty years ago never take priority over the ones that are happening right now.'

'Got it in one.'

'And I asked before.'

Scotty nodded.

'Is there anything you can tell from the bodies themselves? Anything for us to be getting on with?'

The skeletons were lying side by side on two examination tables. They looked like children in twin beds.

'They're both women, young women. Particularly this one.' Scotty pointed at the remains closest to her. 'She's not out of her teens.'

'Were they mistreated like the previous Jane Doe?'

'Not to the same extent, but they are both small. Undernourished in childhood, I'd say.'

'And you think strangulation was the cause of death for all three?'

'Given the cord and the lack of evidence of anything else, that's my best guess.'

'But apart from the cord and until we get the DNA, that's all we've got?'

'You know you're dealing with a serial killer. You've got that.'

Scotty was right. This was the case of Megan's career. Nevertheless, as she looked down on the two small skeletons laid out on their stainless-steel slabs, looking so vulnerable and exposed, Megan felt nothing but profound sadness.

Coco Potts sat on the very edge of her chair.

'It was my drag name. My last name really is Potts, so . . . it seemed funny at the time. And when I transitioned, I kept it. I'd changed so much about myself I just couldn't change anything else. Sometimes I wish I had. I seem to go through life explaining it. Every time I say my name, I get the look. But it's too late now.'

Megan laughed sympathetically. 'From a copper's point of view, it makes you easy to find.'

'Yeah, that hasn't worked out so well for me either.'

Kumar and Megan were sitting in the lounge area of Coco's brothel. A large neon sign with the establishment's—and owner's—name was shining in electric pink and purple above their heads. It exactly mirrored the one on the high wall outside. Megan appreciated the possessive apostrophe.

They were still waiting for the DNA results, but they continued to work the case. Knowing they were dealing with a multiple murderer had given everyone a new sense of urgency. There was even some excitement about what the increased manpower Lisa had allocated to the search might unearth in the forest. Of course the death of one woman mattered, Megan reminded herself, but three? Shit was getting serious. Following their next lead was what had brought the two cops to this plush sofa in Surry Hills.

'You own the place?' Megan asked.

'I got a little something from Sammy Lee's will. Enough to start my own business. Only good thing that bastard ever did was get himself killed.'

'How come you were a beneficiary?'

Coco gave Megan a long look, as if considering how much to tell her. 'I'm his half-sister. Or, as he liked to say, brother from a different mother. He was always misgendering me. He didn't approve, which, considering what he did for a crust, was fucking hilarious.'

'If you had the same father, why is his name Lee and yours Potts?'

'Sammy had his mother's name. She was Chinese, that's why we didn't appear to be related. Unlike my poor mother, his mum never married Dad. He treated her just as shit, though.'

Coco was tall and broad-shouldered with long red hair, startling blue eyes and the kind of white skin that looked like its possessor must drink a pint of cream every day. The hair might be a wig, the blue eyes coloured contact lenses, but there was no faking that Irish skin.

'I didn't know Sammy Lee,' Megan said. 'He was notorious in Sydney, I believe, but I'm stationed in Maitland. I'd never come across him.' *His name keeps coming up now, though*, she thought.

'Eurasian. Hated gweilos. Except me—maybe.'

'What about his dad? Your dad, I mean?'

'Hated him worst of all. Not a nice man, Leonard Potts.'

'Tell me about the Pitt Street brothel.'

'Do I have to? I hate thinking about that place. It was literally the pit of hell. I learnt what not to do by working there. The girls working for me now choose to be here. I pay them properly, look after their health and safety, and if they want to leave, we have a farewell party with a cake and a card, like regular workplaces. Sammy's girls were drugged, terrified and desperate. That's how I felt too, most of the time I worked there. But my misery was self-inflicted.'

'Did you know the girls were trafficked?'

Coco looked at her hands, clasped in her lap. 'Of course I did.'

'Why didn't you go to the police?'

'He'd have killed me. He might not have wanted to, but the higher-ups would have insisted.'

'Higher-ups?'

'Yeah. Hong Kong bastards. Triad bosses. Scariest fucks in the world.'

'Why did you get involved in the first place?'

'I was a junkie. Sammy gave me all the dope I wanted.'

Coco was wearing an elegant silk shirt with long, flowing sleeves. Megan glanced at her arms. It was only a brief flick of the gaze, but Coco noticed.

'I kicked it in jail. They offered rehab. I was terrified of going inside, and it was tough, but I reckon I'd be dead by now if I hadn't.'

Megan looked at the beautiful, stylish woman in front of her; she did not like to think about what might have happened to her in jail.

She handed Coco the photo of Gloria. 'Do you recognise this woman?'

Coco nodded. 'That's Gloria. I liked her. Is she okay? She's one of the girls I managed to get out of the place. I hoped she'd make a better life for herself. I could only help a handful, but when I saw an opportunity, I took it.'

'You helped her leave the brothel?'

'Our regulars often had favourites and some of them fancied themselves in love. They were sad bastards, most of them. Sometimes they wanted to talk more than fuck. I'd encourage them to take the girl to live with them. It only worked if the men were single and prepared to buy out the girl's so-called debt, but if I could persuade them, I did. I figured one bloke was better than an endless stream. And the ones that fell in love were often big softies. A bit naive. I figured they'd be the safest bet.'

'You may have figured wrong—at least as far as Gloria was concerned.'

'What do you mean?'

'We've found three women's bodies buried in a remote part of the Barrington Tops National Park. We think one of them may be Gloria Ramos.'

'Oh my God!' Coco's shock seemed genuine. 'And who were the other two?'

'We don't know. We're concerned there may be more.'

'Jesus! You mean I delivered them from hell into a worse hell?'

'Perhaps.'

Coco jumped up from the couch and walked to the door. For a moment Megan thought she was about to leave, then she turned and walked back again, but she did not sit down.

'I can't believe that! I can't bear to believe that! It was the one comforting thought I had about that place. That I'd got some of them out. But if I just delivered them into the hands of a psychopath . . .' She sat down abruptly and Megan could see the woman was fighting to stay in control.

'You weren't to know.'

'How does that help? Who gives a fuck about my good intentions? They led nowhere but the grave. I should have left them where they were. They would have been found in the raid and sent home. Gloria would still be alive if not for me.' Coco stood up again for a moment, quivering. Then she burst into tears.

'We haven't confirmed the identity of any of the women as yet,' Megan told her.

Kumar, who was taking notes, kept her head low and her eyes on the page. She was calm and quick to pick up on emotional cues, Megan had noted.

'I'm sorry.' Coco dabbed at her eyes. 'I've tried to leave the dark behind me, but it follows me wherever I go. Sammy and me, Leonard Potts's kids, we were children of the dark. It was our inheritance.'

'Andrew Weymouth—Sergeant Andrew Weymouth—spoke highly of you. He made it clear that you were not one of the bad guys.'

Coco gave a rueful laugh as she sat back down. 'That was decent of him. I was a junkie, though, and junkies might not be bad, but they are useless.'

'Well, it's possible you have information that could be useful now.'

Coco nodded, but she did not look up.

'Who did you sell Gloria to? And who were the other women you sold?'

Coco's head jerked up. '*Sell?* I didn't sell her! I didn't make a cent out of her or any of the other girls. I was as captive to Sammy and his thugs as any of them. My addiction meant I was chained just as much as they were.'

'The girls were chained?'

'Sometimes, at night. Sammy was scared they'd try and run off.' Coco's face was whiter than white.

'I apologise for my poorly worded question,' Megan said. 'Who bought Gloria? Who was the man you persuaded to help her?'

'I don't know.'

'What do you mean, you don't know? I thought you just told us that you picked the men carefully, the ones who fell in love with the girls—who had a favourite. How did you not know who they were?'

'We didn't use names for our clients. Everyone had a pseudonym.'

'What was his?'

'Zorro.'

Megan frowned. 'Zorro?'

Coco shrugged. 'The men chose them. They often picked superhero names. Pathetic, really.'

'How did he pay?'

'Cash. One hundred percent cash up front. That was the rule.'

'What about when he bought off her debt?' Ian Turner's debt, Megan silently corrected herself.

'Above my pay grade. Sammy handled that directly.'

'Did Zorro buy any other girls?'

'Yeah, he said they were for a friend.'

'A friend?'

'That's what he said. I didn't ask. I was just pleased to offer more girls an escape route.'

Coco looked up at Megan and her eyes were brimming with tears. 'I wish I had asked now. But it was beaten into us—literally—that questions could get you killed.'

Megan flashed a look at Kumar. So they were looking for two men? Or was Zorro's talk of a 'friend' just a cover story?

'And you don't know this friend's name either? Weren't you curious about him buying more girls?'

Coco shrugged. 'Curiosity killed the cat. More than my life was worth to do any wondering.'

'But you thought you'd helped them, done them a favour?'

'Zorro was gruff, but he seemed harmless. It was the best I could do.'

'And the friend's name?' Megan repeated.

Coco shook her head, her eyes on the floor once more.

Megan had seen this before, when she was a uniform. Sex workers often kept their eyes down, especially when their pimps were nearby. She'd hated it then and she hated it now. It made the women look beaten.

'Do you know who the other girls were?'

'Siriporn, Concepcion and Yulia.'

'Did they all go together?'

'One at a time.'

'Didn't you wonder what had happened to the previous one?'

'Yes, but I didn't dare ask.' Coco looked up. 'I suppose I hoped they'd been let go, or got away, or something. Stupid of me. I see that now.' Then she paused and looked Megan straight in the eye. 'I knew it was stupid at the time, if I'm being honest, but then Siriporn came back, and so I let myself believe the others were okay too.'

'Siriporn came back?' Megan's heart leapt. This was a real break.

Kumar spoke up for the first time. 'Do you know her last name?'

Coco looked at her. 'No, strictly first names only.'

'Do you know where she is now?'

'No idea. I saw her once, years ago. That's how I know she came back. She waited for me outside Coles. She was smart and spoke a bit of English, unlike most of the others, though she kept that to herself for ages, until she'd decided she could trust me. Sammy and the others had no idea she understood what they were saying. Like I said, she was smart.'

'You said she was waiting for you at Coles?' Megan prompted.

'Yeah, she knew the day and the time I did the shopping, so she waited for me there. Again, smart: none of the blokes would have been seen dead at Coles.'

'What did she want?'

'Money. She told me she'd run away with nothing but the clothes she was standing in.'

'What did you do?'

'I gave her a hundred dollars. I'd been creaming a little bit off the grocery money—buying stuff on special when I could. Sammy thought he counted every cent, boasted that he could have been a forensic accountant and that he knew exactly where every dollar went, but he didn't.'

'So you gave her some of the money you'd squirrelled away?'

Coco nodded.

'What happened then?'

'She skedaddled. Last I saw of her.'

'Did she say anything about Zorro or his friend? Or any of the other girls?'

'Not a word and I didn't ask. Like I told you, nobody asked questions at Pitt Street. That's what cops do.'

'Maybe you didn't want to know,' said Megan.

Coco gave her another long look. 'Maybe I didn't.'

'Did the fact that she'd run away worry you?'

'No way. Why wouldn't she? I might have hoped the girls I helped would have a better life than the horror they endured at the brothel, but I wasn't completely deluded. No one wants to be a captive. And I knew Siriporn could do what the other girls couldn't because she spoke some English. I was thrilled for her. I guess I still am.'

'We need to find her,' Megan said.

'No doubt, but I have no idea where she went.'

'Do you have a photo? Anything we can use to identify her?'

Coco shook her head.

'Would you sit down with a police sketch artist and help us get a photofit?'

'If you think it'd be useful.'

Megan reached down into her bag and pulled out two more photographs. 'Do you recognise this shoe?'

'That was Gloria's. I'd know those whacko shoelaces anywhere.'

'It wasn't found on Gloria's body but on the unidentified remains.'

'Probably Concepcion then. They were tight. Always rattling away in Spanish. Unless Sammy was around. Then they shut up pronto. He'd punch any girl who spoke to another girl in their shared language. But he couldn't be around all the time. I was supposed to stop them chatting, but I didn't.'

'You don't know anything about Concepcion except her first name, correct?'

'That's right. I don't think she was Filipina, though; she was from somewhere in South America, I think. Colombia? Maybe I heard that mentioned. I can't remember.'

'Do you recognise this one?'

Megan showed her the picture of the hot-pink high heel.

Coco looked at it for a long time. Then she handed it back. 'It's mine.' Her voice was expressionless.

'Can you explain how it came to be hanging on a fence in the Upper Hunter Valley?'

'I have no idea.'

Megan wasn't sure if she believed her or not.

TWELVE

The angry faces of protestors filled the screen. They were midway through a twenty-four-hour anti-coal blockade of the port of Newcastle. *Good on them*, thought Jessica. *It's time we got serious about saving the planet.*

She and Sheridan were eating dinner in front of the TV. It was just too exhausting to try to have a sit-down-at-the-dinner-table meal when it was just the two of them, whatever the parenting experts might argue. *What is it about parenting experts that always manages to make actual parents feel like shit?* Jessica wondered. She took another forkful of the pasta she had pulled together from the leftovers in the fridge. She had to get to the supermarket—another thing to add to her list.

A journo was thrusting a mic at a young woman at the front of the crowd. She had her back to the camera but, with a sinking feeling, Jessica felt a strong sense of recognition. She looked at her daughter. Her daughter looked back. Her face said it all. Then the girl on the screen turned around.

'The fossil fuel industry, this government and everyone who stands by and does nothing as we approach a global climate tipping point is playing Russian roulette with my future and that of all young people. We are fighting for our lives!'

The Sheridan on the TV screen was full of confidence and zeal. The Sheridan sitting beside her mother eating dinner—not so much.

There was a huge roar of approval from the people around her. A super had popped up on the screen. It read: *Sheridan Weston, Convenor, School Students 4 Climate Action.*

Jessica took such a deep breath she almost choked on her pasta carbonara. As she reached for her glass of water she glared at her daughter, who was concentrating so hard on sprinkling parmesan you'd think it was gold dust. She did not speak until she had caught her breath. She kept her voice low, but there was no hiding her fury.

'What the fuck?'

'I told you I was going.'

'And I told you that you weren't!'

'Yeah, well, this issue is too important.'

'That's not the point.'

'You think it's important! You're the one who taught me to care about the environment. You've been banging on about climate change since I can remember!'

Sheridan was right; Jessica knew she was. Nevertheless, she was mortified by her daughter's disobedience and by the public way she had been defied. She felt like a fool.

'You told me you were at the library.'

She'd been so delighted when Sheridan had said she'd be late because she was going to study after school. She'd even thought that maybe they'd turned the corner and that her truculent and rebellious fifteen-year-old was turning back into to the conscientious, high-achieving primary schooler she remembered so fondly. What a gullible idiot she was.

She also felt guilty. When Sheridan had asked her if she could join an anti–fossil fuel blockade, Jessica had forbidden it. Not because she disagreed with the cause, but because demonstrations could be dangerous and the idea of Sheridan in the middle of one made her feel sick. When she'd told Sheridan no, the sick feeling went away. Stupidly, however, she had not bothered to check when the blockade was to be held, nor consider what she might do if Sheridan disobeyed her.

'You lied to my face!'

'If I'd told you where I was really going, you would have stopped me.'

How was it that Sheridan now made her feel as if it was Jessica's own fault her daughter had lied to her?

'You could have not gone!'

'Ending fossil fuel exports is more important than not lying to your fucking mother. You do realise we pay them billions in subsidies . . .'

'Of course I realise!' Jessica was not about to be lectured about fossil fuels by her daughter. 'The worthiness of the cause is not the point. I have to be able to trust you.'

'You treat me like a child!'

This came out as a wail. Sheridan jumped up from the table—upending her pasta—and fled to her room. She slammed the door so hard that, yet again, Jessica cast an uncertain look at the old ceiling. It shook but remained intact.

Then Sheridan flung the door open.

'And they voted me convenor and you don't even care!'

SLAM!

This time, a little smattering of falling dust. Jessica winced. She didn't know where she'd find the money to repair the ceiling if it collapsed.

She went back to her pasta. It was lukewarm and tasted like sticky cardboard. Maybe she should have let Sheridan go to the protest, she thought as she chewed another mouthful. She was just as worried by the lack of action on carbon emissions as her daughter. But demonstrations could be violent. People would be watching, taking photos. Lots of academics she worked with, especially those a little older than her, boasted about their ASIO files, courtesy of their work in the moratorium movement in the sixties and seventies, but she didn't think having an ASIO file nowadays was the same as back then. Not with the internet, facial recognition technology and the vested interests that were willing to do anything to protect their profits. She hated being at loggerheads with her daughter. She recognised something of her teenage self in Sheridan's fiery determination to do what she thought was right. Then she remembered how bad she had felt about that behaviour when her own mother had been killed so abruptly. So much of their short time together wasted in fights and bad feelings.

She got up from the table and went to her daughter's emphatically closed door.

'I know you are doing what you believe is right and I respect that,' she said to the keyhole. 'And I think it's great they elected you convenor, I really do. But if you lie to me . . . well, I can't trust you. And if I can't trust you, I have to keep a tighter rein on you. You do see that, don't you? But I hate fighting with you. I fought with my mum and I really regretted it when—'

Sheridan's door flew open. For a moment Jessica thought she'd got through to her, then she saw the expression on her daughter's face.

'Don't emotionally blackmail me with your dead mother again. I'm sorry she was killed, I really am, but this is my life and my future; it's got nothing to do with you and your mum.' Then she slammed the door shut again.

Selfish little bitch! Jessica thought. What was the point in reaching out, if it was just going to be thrown back in her face? Sheridan was fifteen. Convenor or not, she could leave saving the world until she went to university.

THIRTEEN

First thing Friday morning and Megan was sitting with Scotty in Scotty's office at the morgue. Maybe to dispel any reminder of its sinister setting, the forensic scientist had made an effort to create a room as friendly and welcoming as any office in a government-owned institution could be. It had flowering plants along the windowsill, photos of Scotty's family and friends on a bookshelf and a knotted wool rug that Megan knew Scotty had made herself. There was even a shot of Megan receiving a commendation among the cluster of framed photos and pictures that hung on the wall.

'I don't know why you give that photo such pride of place.'

Scotty knew exactly which one she meant. 'You're my mate, that's why. Plus, women don't win enough accolades in this business and I like to remind everyone who comes in here of the ones that do.'

Megan pulled a face.

'Don't be so bloody humble,' Scotty said, pouring some tea from her very beautiful blue-and-white teapot. 'Women are far too good at humility. They brought you out of retirement, my friend. They don't do that for just anybody.'

Megan smiled but changed the subject. 'The first dead woman—the one wearing the shoe with Gloria's laces—may have been Colombian, but all we know about her so far, if we're right about her identity, is her first name: Concepcion.'

'Pretty.'

Not anymore, thought Megan.

She had been summoned by the forensic examiner via a text message as she left for work that morning, so she knew that Scotty had something important to tell her. She'd hoped it was DNA results—positive or negative. The more they knew, the more they knew. *That's what detective work is*, Megan thought. *It's like a jigsaw puzzle, and you keep putting the pieces together until you can see the whole.*

'Were the other two women killed at around the same time as the one we think is Concepcion?'

'More or less. Might have been a few months or a year apart; it's hard to tell exactly. And'—Scotty paused for effect—'I can confirm that the body with the cord around her neck is Gloria.'

Megan felt a wave of relief—and not just for the sake of the case. At least Luna would know something with certainty, however terrible. Then she thought of Bridie, the child who had loved and been loved by Gloria. To know that it was your father who had delivered the woman who was like a mother to you to such a fate must be unbearable.

Luna will be on her way to Sydney by now, Megan thought, *and about to arrive at Bridie's.* She wondered what this bombshell might do to them both. She hoped the two young women could be support for one another but given the circumstances, that was a big ask.

'DNA match?'

'Yep. Luna is Gloria's close relative.'

'And the first body? Concepcion? Or the third one? We think her name might have been Yulia.'

'Still no idea. No result for either from our Australian database. Women who are trafficked often have no identity, no protection. They fly under every possible radar.'

'Which is why they are preyed upon.'

'You did bloody well finding Gloria's identity. And to have names for the others, even if nothing else, that's impressive.'

'It's my job . . .' Megan paused. 'We believe there may be a woman out there who knew all three of them in the brothel on Pitt Street and may well have escaped the same killer. We're looking for her now.'

'Good luck.'

'I'll need it. She's all we have to go on. She was sold to the same bloke as the others.'

'Do you know who he is?'

'Nope. He called himself Zorro.'

Scotty snorted.

'The clients often called themselves by superhero names, apparently.'

'Pathetic!'

'He may have had an accomplice, but I don't know if that's bullshit or not.'

'Lyrebirds, three bodies and counting, a missing witness, sex trafficking, an unsolved gangland hit . . . Did you realise what you were taking on when they talked you into coming back?'

'I've never come across a serial killer before—if that's what he is. If I catch the bastard, it'll be a nice way to end a forty-year career.'

Megan put a brave face on it, but this case was a lot. No sooner did she pull on one thread than a whole lot of others unravelled.

'Were those bodies wearing one shoe, like the first?' she asked.

'Only the remains of a rubber thong on Gloria, but it's too big for her.'

Megan felt a wave of pity. The thought of Gloria scuffling along in oversized thongs was unbearable.

—

It was almost midday by the time she returned to the station. She headed straight to the incident room. Finally, she had hard information.

'The second body we found is Gloria Ramos,' she announced.

Apart from a sharp intake of breath from Kumar, no one made a sound.

'At last!' Phil Arlott exclaimed, expressing the relief in the room. It was horrible to feel pleased to know who had been violently murdered, but such was police work, Megan thought. *Our job is to find the killer and we can't do that unless we know who has been killed.*

'And as we know, the cause of death—likely for all three women—is strangulation.'

The mood in the room became sombre again.

'Let's get on with catching the bastard then.' Phil again. He didn't like too much emotion. He was right not to. Coppers didn't want to lose their capacity to feel for victims, but nor could they let it cloud their ability to do their job. Phil was still puzzling her though. They were old colleagues and had been in some tight spots together. He'd been nothing but helpful, but he'd kept her at arm's length. Was it her imagination, or was he gruffer than usual? Making a mental note to try to talk to him again later, she moved on to the next thing.

'Constable Kumar?'

Kumar scooted her chair out from behind her cubicle.

'Yes, Sarge?'

'Have you followed up on the guy Jessica Weston saw when she drove to Burraga Swamp—the one the woman at the egg farm ID'd?' Zorro and his mysterious friend were niggling at Megan.

Kumar checked her notes.

'Leo Blake? We've called around a few times but he's never there. Neighbour says he's on holiday in Tasmania.'

'Any idea when he's back?'

Kumar shook her head. 'We'll keep trying.'

'Good. Maybe check his social media.'

'We have. He doesn't post much. More of a lurker.'

'What's a lurker?'

'Someone who doesn't post much.'

Megan laughed. It was good to see Kumar relaxing a bit. She turned back to Phil.

'I'm going to see Professor Weston this evening. I'll update her on these developments.'

'Great. We can read about it in the *Newcastle Herald* tomorrow.'

Megan ignored the sarcasm. 'The comms people are making an announcement this arvo, so I won't be telling her anything that won't already be on the public record. We might have been able to keep one body fairly quiet, but three?'

If Phil thought they could keep a lid on that, he was kidding himself.

'Will you inform Luna Ramos that her mother's body has been found?' Phil had changed the subject.

Megan looked at her watch. 'I think she's in transit, on her way to Sydney. I'll ring her to make an appointment when she arrives.'

—

Megan sat on the couch while Jessica fetched some cheese and biscuits.

'Where's Sheridan?'

Megan had always had a soft spot for Jessica's little girl.

'She says she's at rehearsals for the school musical.'

'Says?'

'I can't trust her as far as I can throw her these days. Just a week ago, her face was all over the TV as one of the leaders of an anti-coal blockade.'

'Apple doesn't fall far from the tree and all that. You've always been pretty gung-ho about climate change. Even twenty years ago, when it was on hardly anyone's radar.'

'I'm a biologist. We understand the science. Anyway, tonight's the first time she's been allowed out for a week—and only to a school thing, where I can drop her off and pick her up and check with her teacher.'

Jessica looked at her half-empty glass. 'Would you like another? I'll be stopping at the one, obviously.'

Megan shook her head. 'I'm driving too.'

Jessica, having half risen to get the bottle from the fridge, sat back down. 'I saw on the news that two more bodies were found. It really upset me. Knowing more people had died made me want to throw up.'

Megan nodded. 'I blame myself for letting the case go cold,' she said. 'Maybe those women wouldn't have died if I'd refused to let go.'

Jessica reached across the table and put her warm hand over Megan's. 'You were the only person who tried to do anything. If anyone should be blaming themselves it's that Sergeant Arlott.'

Phil? thought Megan, taken aback by Jessica's vehemence. But the other woman had a point. Phil been scathing about the whole case twenty years ago, and his scorn had stung. Maybe that explained why he was acting a bit weird at the moment: because he felt bad. That'd be like Phil. He made up his mind too quickly, but he was soft-hearted underneath and he cared about justice.

'No one has a crystal ball,' Megan said aloud. 'We had nothing to go on, and police resources are always limited.'

'Like university resources. Anyway, how are *you* coping?'

Megan shrugged. 'It's my job. I failed to prevent them being killed; the least I can do is bring their killer—or killers—to account.'

'Killers?'

'Just a theory. Nothing much to go on yet.'

Jessica winced. 'I really am sorry—about the media and all that.'

'I know.'

Megan suddenly felt weary. Maybe it was because, sitting here with Jessica, sipping wine, she had allowed herself to relax. Searching for Siriporn felt like an overwhelming task. It was sheer luck they had found Gloria. She doubted they'd be that fortunate again. It was dumb-arse luck they'd ever discovered anything about the murders at all. Without that lyrebird, without Jessica, no one would ever have known. If the killer was still alive, if he was still out there, he'd realise that too—the story had been all over the media. From the point of view of the investigation that was a good thing. Fear of being caught often made people do stupid things and make mistakes, and this guy—or guys—must have really thought they'd got away with it after twenty years. Then, another thought. Why had the murders suddenly stopped? Had the murderer died, moved away? Surely the brothel being raided and shut down wasn't enough on its own?

'There was a woman who got away,' Megan said. 'Her name was Siriporn.'

'Thai?'

Megan nodded. 'If we can find her, we'll find him. Or them.'

'If anyone can find her, you can.'

Megan wished she felt half as positive as her friend. Siriporn had very good reason to make sure she was swallowed up and never seen again. She'd had twenty years to practise not being found. But what was it Jason said whenever she felt sorry for herself? *Too bad, so sad.* When she'd agreed to come out of retirement, she'd agreed to follow this case through to the bitter end.

'I gave it up once before and look where that got me.'

'I gave up too.'

'It was my job to find the killer. It still is.'

The front door opened with a loud bang and both women jumped.

'Mrs Roberts gave me a lift home and I am *early*!'

They heard Sheridan before they saw her. Megan was pleased; she'd hoped to see the girl again. She and Guido hadn't been able to have any more children after Jason and she'd always wanted a daughter. Maybe that's how she'd felt about Jessica, too, when she was that young, wide-eyed student, terrified about what she had heard in the forest. Maybe that was why she felt so protective towards her.

'Oh!' Sheridan stopped in her tracks when she saw Megan. 'I didn't know you had visitors.'

'This is Megan Blaxland. She's the lead detective on the lyrebird case. Do you remember her? You knew her when you were little.'

'The lyrebird case? Cool!'

Sheridan seemed genuinely impressed.

'Lovely to see you again, Sheridan. I'm sure you don't remember me, though. It was a long time ago.' Megan and Jessica had mostly met for drinks after work or coffee in restaurants and cafes. They'd talked about their kids but never brought them.

'Yeah, sorry. I don't.'

'You were about five when I saw you last. Just starting school, and now you're what . . . fifteen?'

Megan could see no resemblance between the teenager with the dreadlocks and piercings and the cute little blue-eyed blonde of her memory. She looked a lot older than fifteen, but girls often did. Megan remembered how Jason had still looked like a kid when he was in year nine, while all the girls in his class had looked like grown-ups. *It must be hard for them*, she thought. The world reacted to them as if they were adults, but they weren't. It made them vulnerable. She began to understand Jessica's anxiety about her child. *Girls and young women are especially vulnerable*, she thought, looking at this apparently confident teenager. If there was one thing she had learnt in her forty years on the police force, it was that.

'Yeah. I gotta go learn some lines.'

Sheridan disappeared up the hall.

Jessica had fetched the chardonnay and was holding it over Megan's still half-full glass. 'I can't tempt you?'

Megan shook her head.

'She's driven me to drink,' Jessica said.

'Not sure you can blame her—I seem to recall you were hideously hungover the first time we met.' Megan grinned at her friend.

'Bloody coppers. Never forget a single transgression.'

Megan took a large swig from her glass. 'Like I said, it's my job.'

FOURTEEN

Megan had called Bridie Turner first thing Monday morning. Luna Ramos had arrived crack of dawn Sunday.

'She's still asleep,' Bridie told her.

'I'll call her this afternoon.'

'Any message?'

'Just tell her I'll call.'

Megan was not looking forward to that phone call. Being the bearer of terrible news never got any easier.

Now, she was standing behind a desk at the station, looking over the shoulder of the photofit expert. She was relieved the photofits were finally happening. It had taken a couple days to get anyone with the right skills up to Maitland. In the meantime, they'd had a frustrating time searching fruitlessly for Siriporn. She and Kumar had contacted Thai community organisations, they'd even trawled through Thai restaurants in Sydney and in some of the larger regional centres. All to no avail. Megan had figured it would be hopeless, but they couldn't just sit around on their hands.

The photofit guy and Coco Potts were huddled over a computer. They'd been at it for more than an hour, going through every permutation of Thai features. They had already created a photofit of Zorro. That had taken much less time. Megan examined the printout of the man. He looked like a throwback to the seventies, all long straggly hair and ZZ Top beard. Megan kept her feelings to herself, but her heart sank when she saw it. Twenty years on, he'd likely look very different and, if he knew they were looking for him (given the media coverage, he would), a beard was the easiest thing to get rid of.

'It's tough,' Coco said. 'Siriporn would be in her forties now, late thirties at best.'

'I can age her up,' said the expert, manipulating the mouse. Megan had forgotten his name.

'Bob's a genius with this stuff,' Coco said, smiling at him.

Shit, thought Megan, *she's flirting. Oh well, I guess that's how she's survived all these years.*

Bob blushed.

Megan looked at what they had compiled so far: a pretty Thai woman with long dark hair and large dark eyes. She looked sullen but Megan realised that was just because most images of Thai women showed them smiling demurely. No one in a photofit ever smiled. No one in a photofit had any reason to.

'Did she have any identifying features?' Bob asked. 'Birthmark? Mole? Scar? Tattoo? Piercing?'

'She wore a lot of earrings right down her left ear, and she had a small scar on her forehead, above her right eye.'

Bob got busy. 'Like this?'

He put up a series of ears with many earrings. Coco began to look at them carefully, one by one.

'I'll let you get back to it,' Megan said. 'But before you leave, Ms Potts, would you mind giving me a couple of minutes of your time? I'd just like to follow up on a few details.'

Megan watched Coco carefully. If she was concerned, she showed no sign. She was holding something back, Megan was certain of that, and there was still the mystery of how her shoe had found its way to Boot Hill.

'No problem.' Coco did not raise her eyes from the screen.

'Thank you, I appreciate that. Interview room five. Bob can show you the way.'

'Do I need a lawyer?'

'Of course not. It's simply a good spot for a private chat.'

An hour later, Megan and Coco were sitting opposite one another.

'Thanks for giving us a bit of extra time. I've just got a few more questions.'

Megan passed Coco a plastic sleeve containing an emailed copy of the letter Gloria had written to her mother and daughter. Luna Ramos, as requested, had brought the original with her to Sydney. Another reason Megan needed to visit her in person.

'What can you tell me about this?'

Coco sighed deeply. 'I'd forgotten.'

'The daughter of Gloria Ramos told us that it was when she and her grandmother received this letter they knew something awful had happened.'

'Why?'

'It's written in English, a language Gloria didn't speak and they didn't either. Gloria's daughter has informed me that her grandmother had to pay to get it translated. Money they didn't have, especially as the payments from Gloria's nannying work had stopped.'

Coco held up her beautiful hands. 'No need to rub it in.'

'Did you write them?'

Coco nodded. 'I wrote letters in pencil and got the girls to trace over them. Sammy's stupid idea. He thought they'd look more convincing if they were handwritten. I wasn't so sure, but I hoped they might help stop the families from worrying. He hoped it would stop them from making inquiries. Not that any of them knew how to do that. That's why the traffickers pick the poorest ones. I warned Sammy that writing them in English was foolish, but he was worried about what they might write if we let them use their own language.'

'And these?' Megan passed her another plastic sleeve. It contained the letters Gloria had sent to Bridie.

Coco glanced at them and nodded. 'Needless to say, I am ashamed.'

'The family who received them were more easily fooled. Bridie was five and her mother wasn't interested. Her father knew it was bullshit. But they were in a Spanish dialect, not English. Why is that?'

'Sammy insisted. He said the guy who sold Gloria told him his family would know something was wrong because she didn't speak and couldn't write English. And unlike Gloria's family, Mrs Turner could have made inquiries.'

'Do you speak Spanish?'

'No. Sammy held a gun to Gloria's head and made her write them. Just the one sentence in each. That's why her writing was all over the place. She was terrified.' Coco looked back at Megan. She was stricken. 'I'm not proud of that.' She shifted her gaze to the pale-green wall above Megan's head.

'Did you know Ian Turner?'

Still staring at the wall, Coco nodded.

Megan continued, 'He trafficked Gloria Ramos, whose body we found in the Barrington Tops, to pay off his gambling debt.'

Coco nodded again.

'Did he frequent the Pitt Street brothel?'

This time she shook her head. Was she trying not to cry?

'No. I only saw him once or twice, when he came for meetings with Sammy and some thugs. I assumed he owed them money.'

'You assumed right.'

'He always emerged looking terrified. I'd seen that a few times. Gamblers—in way over their heads.'

The two women sat in silence. What a dark world, thought Megan. And Coco had been trapped in it by birth. Another thought. Sammy Lee had been similarly trapped from the moment he drew his first breath. Coco had hung on to some humanity, Sammy not so much.

Megan picked up the evidence bag by her chair. She took the hot-pink high heel out of it and put it in the middle of the table. It was filthy, but still impressive.

'I feel like Cinderella.'

Megan smiled. 'Actually, that's a good idea. Can you try it on?'

The shoe fit perfectly.

'And you shall go to the ball . . .' Coco kicked her leg high. 'I told you it was mine.'

'But you have no idea how it found its way to Boot Hill in the Upper Allyn?'

Coco's gaze was frank and steady. 'None at all.'

'Do you remember the last time you saw it?'

'We're talking about a pair of shoes I owned two decades ago! And I never really liked them. Sammy gave them to me and insisted I wear them. He thought they added to the vibe. All I remember is how relieved I felt when it was time to take them off.'

'But surely you must have noticed when one shoe went missing? Shoes are not earrings or socks.'

'I don't recall that at all. It's possible they both went missing.'

'Can you think of anyone who might have taken them? Gloria? Concepcion? Siriporn? Yulia?'

Coco pulled a face. 'Why would they? They all had teensy little feet, not like my great clodhoppers.'

'Could Zorro have taken them?'

'It's possible, I guess. As I said, I kicked them off any chance I got—mostly when I knew Sammy was out—but I can't remember missing them.'

'If Sammy insisted you wear them, wouldn't he have noticed they were gone?'

Coco sat back in her chair. 'He would have done, he was such a control freak, but I have no memory of that.'

'Could he have taken them—or one of them?'

'Why would he?'

'Can you think of any reason?'

'He wasn't a secret cross-dresser, if that's what you are implying.' Coco laughed. 'Though given what a hypocrite he was . . .' She stopped and gave Megan a half-smile. 'You'd know better than most, given your job, that we are all most mysterious to ourselves.'

Megan liked Coco. There was something gallant and undaunted about her. That was also what she admired in Luna Ramos. They'd both taken shithouse situations and refused to be beaten by them.

'It's my job to solve mysteries,' Megan said, smiling. Then she stood up and walked to the door. 'Thank you, Ms Potts. That's all the questions I have for now. If you do remember anything about the circumstances around the disappearance of this shoe—or its mate—please let me know.'

Coco got up and went to the door, then she turned and looked at Megan. 'Maybe Sammy was an even darker horse than I imagined. He was a sweet little boy. I often wondered what had happened to him—apart from Dad, of course—to make him what he became.'

Megan walked into her office, closed the door and sat down at her desk. She looked at the time on her computer screen. It was 5 p.m. She could not put off calling Luna any longer. She was beat. It had been another huge day. But she was probably not as tired as poor Luna. It was hard flying halfway across the world at the best of times, but coming to a country where your mother has been brutally murdered? Megan hoped she and Bridie were getting along all right.

'Hello? Can I speak to Ms Ramos?'

'I'll get her.' Bridie had answered the phone.

It took a minute or two for Luna to come to the phone. 'Sergeant Blaxland?'

'Yes. I hope I didn't wake you.'

'You have news for me?' Luna ignored the pleasantry.

'I do, but I'd prefer to tell you in person if that is okay?'

Megan heard a sharp intake of breath. Her heart went out to the young woman.

'Please don't keep me in suspense any longer. The not knowing is excruciating.'

Megan hesitated. It was better to do death calls face to face, but Luna Ramos already knew what she was going to tell her, and Megan could see no purpose in making her wait another miserable night just to tick a box. 'All right, but I will need to come and see you in person as soon as possible.'

'Of course.'

'We have discovered two more bodies in Burraga Swamp. One of them is a familial match with your DNA.'

For a long moment, the girl on the end of the phone said nothing. Megan suddenly realised why death calls were done in person. Unable to see Luna's reaction, she was gripped by worry for her, bereaved and alone, among strangers in a strange country. Had she made a dreadful mistake?

'There is no doubt it is my mother?'

Megan felt better. Luna sounded like herself.

'DNA is very accurate.'

'Thank you for telling me.'

'Are you all right? I can come now, if you like?'

'No. I am okay, and Bridie is here, and we can look after one another.'

Megan could hear Bridie sobbing in the background. Luna did not sound as if she had shed a tear.

'Tomorrow then?'

'I don't know. I can't think about that yet. I will call you in the morning, when I have had more sleep and can think more clearly. But'—a pause, and Megan's anxiety rose—'do not worry about me or Bridie. We have both been expecting this news for some time.'

—

Coco's apartment was high above the city. It was small but had a panoramic view of the harbour. It was dark by the time she got back from Maitland, and she was tired. The interview had forced her to think about things she'd spent a lifetime trying to forget. All the way home, her mind had been filled with images from the past, from back when she and Sammy had been children living with their respective mothers. A few times a year, during school holidays or when her mother was dragged off to rehab to dry out, Coco had gone to stay with her father, stepmother and half-brother. She'd been Graeme then, and miserable in her own skin. The only happy memories she had were of spending time with Sammy. He was eight years younger than she was and she had loved having a little brother to fuss over and care for.

'He's like a second mother to him,' she remembered Cindy Lee saying.

She'd meant it kindly, but it had earnt Graeme a beating from her dad for being a 'sissy'. Leonard was always punishing her for being too soft and too girly. She was terrified of her father, and he knew it. It enraged him.

'Toughen up, you big girl.' She could hear her father's voice now, dripping with disdain—no, worse, disgust. 'No son of mine will be a poofta.'

'Way more than that, Dad.' Coco had said this out loud as she accelerated past a slower car that had finally pulled out of the right-hand lane. 'Your son was actually your daughter.'

Did she wish Leonard had lived long enough to see her as she really was? No, she did not. Not because she still feared his scorn, but because she sincerely wished he had never lived at all. He'd done nothing useful while alive. All he had ever caused was pain. Her mother had become a hopeless alcoholic and died in her fifties of cirrhosis of the liver, and Cindy Lee had died by suicide. Leonard Potts was poison; anyone who came close to him was doomed. Coco had hated him. But she had loved Sammy—until he grew up and began to copy his father. He had mocked and belittled her too, especially when she became Coco. He never called her anything but Graeme, no matter where they were or how much she begged him not to.

Coco put down her bag and kicked off her shoes. She stood for a moment in the dark, admiring the kaleidoscope of lights through the window. None of it mattered now. She was alive and they were all dead. She was wealthy and they had nothing but the coffins they were buried in—and Sammy didn't even have that. She was legit and they were all crooks.

Then, another thought: wasn't she poison too? Look at what happened to Gloria, Concepcion and Yulia. She'd believed she was helping but . . . maybe everyone who came into her orbit was doomed too. Maybe she was more like her dad than she realised. The thought made her feel sick.

She went into her bedroom and pulled off the elegant dress she was wearing. She took a gauzy dressing-gown off the hook on the back of the door and put it on over her bra and knickers. She tied the three pink silk ribbons down the front into droopy bows. The edges of the top ribbon were fraying slightly. She'd have to get it mended. How old would the dressing-gown be? Thirty years? Forty? It had been Cindy's. But kind though her stepmother had always been, that wasn't why Coco had kept it, nor why she was putting it on now. She was wearing it for Sammy, for the bewildered little boy he had been when this gown was brand-new.

Coco slid one of the ribbons between her fingers. A vivid memory rose in her mind. Sammy at four years old, maybe, walking around in the bedroom they shared when Graeme came to stay, wrapped in his mother's dressing-gown. It had fluttered out behind him as he twirled and danced, stroking the silk ribbons over and over, while the two children tried not to listen to their father beating the living daylights out of Cindy downstairs.

It was the next morning when Samira and Josh went into the Gresford post office. They'd already been to the IGA across the road. They were hoping to find someone who recognised either of the photofits. The bored teenager behind the till at the IGA had given them short shrift, but the manager had agreed to stick both images on his front window. It was a small place; maybe one of them would jog someone's memory. Samira had been taken by surprise to see Christmas decorations already up around the store, and also at the post office. The ads for Christmas cards, wrapping paper and gifts were jarring. It was only October!

There was a queue of people waiting for service in the post office and every head turned as the two cops entered.

'Hello, Sadie.'

The woman behind the counter looked up.

Of course Josh knows the postmistress (if that's what you call them these days), Samira thought.

'Hello, Josh. What can I do for you?'

'No rush, happy to wait our turn.'

Community liaison was constantly drummed into them. No big swinging-dick coppers anymore, whether they had actual dicks or not.

'Don't be silly,' said the postmistress. 'No one here is in a hurry except you.'

Everyone in the queue is dying to know what the police wanted, Samira thought. No one was leaving before they found out. No one, that was, except a mother with a bored and fractious toddler. She looked like she wanted to throw something or burst into tears. Samira felt sorry for her.

'Maybe serve this lady first. Looks like she's got her hands full.'

The boy's mother flashed Samira a quick smile. She had various bills to pay, so Samira and Josh showed the two photofits to the other customers. No one recognised either of them.

'Sorry, love, I'm new to the area.'

'We only come up every couple of weeks.'

'My mother might know. She's lived here all her life.'

Samira gave this woman a copy of each of the photofits. 'Show her these.'

'I will, but don't get your hopes up—she barely recognises me these days!'

An older man with no hair examined both portraits carefully.

'Jog any memories?' Samira asked.

He shook his head. 'I thought there was something familiar about the bloke, but a lot of men looked like that back in the day.'

'Some of them still do!'

It was Sadie the postmistress. She'd finished serving the mother and was looking expectantly at the two cops, her meaty forearms folded on the counter.

Josh stepped forward with the flyers. 'Two things,' he said. 'First, do you recognise either of these faces? And, second, would you mind putting them up in your window?'

'Happy to.' She held out her hand for the flyers he was holding. 'Here, let me have a squiz.' Sadie looked at the picture of the man first but shook her head. 'It could be anyone.'

'What about the other one?'

She studied the second flyer for a few seconds. 'You know, I think it's a woman I picked up on Masseys Creek Road decades ago. Looks just like her.'

FIFTEEN

Bridie had never been inside a jail before. It was a strange and disorientating experience, and this was just the waiting room. Everyone looked tired, grumpy and poor. Bridie had carefully dressed down, worn distressed jeans and an old t-shirt, yet still her runners were too white, her blonde ponytail too bouncy and her jeans too just-the-right-length. She felt ashamed of her privilege, as if there were something vulgar about it. She looked at her hands, then curled her fingers into her palm to hide her perfectly manicured nails. There was too much misery in this place. She was miserable too, grieving for Gloria, shocked and horrified about her father, guilty about her family's casual cruelty. But something about the weary hopelessness of those around her revealed a level of suffering that she knew nothing about.

The only good thing to come out of this whole awful situation was meeting Luna. She'd arrived in Sydney a few days ago. They'd been awkward with one another at first, but then they received the call from Detective Blaxland. Having some certainty had broken the ice. They'd wept together, then drunk far too much wine. And they'd agreed to keep the policewoman at arm's length for a few days. They knew they'd have to meet up with her eventually, but Luna had been adamant that she couldn't deal with sympathy or fuss or questions yet and Bridie had turned into a lioness, protecting her friend, making excuse after excuse every time Detective Blaxland called. She'd taken leave from work and was letting Amanda's calls go straight to voicemail.

In the days after they had received the news, holed up in Bridie's apartment, they had discovered a shared passion for *The Crown*. Something about all those unhappy royals wandering about in luxurious locations was comforting. Maybe this was because it was safely in the past, maybe it was the sense of otherworldliness, or maybe it was just the thrill of plain old gossip. Whatever it was, both of them enjoyed curling up on either end of Bridie's sofa and immersing themselves in the palace intrigues of the last seventy years. Discussing the ins and outs of the show had given them something safe and painless to talk about. For the first time in a long while, Bridie had felt secure. Then she had decided to visit her father.

The woman in the next seat had two small kids. She seemed disconnected from them, as if she was just too exhausted to try to make them behave. She was letting them squabble and bicker in front of Bridie's chair and Bridie pulled her feet back, trying to take up as little room as possible. The children were fighting over a toy, yanking it this way and that. The little girl suddenly let go and the toy flew up in the air and landed in Bridie's lap.

She was about to hand it to the children's mother, when the girl stood up and put both hands on her hips.

'It's mine.' She stuck out her bottom lip. Bridie gave her a smile and went to hand it back, but the little boy let out a howl.

'No, it's not. It's mine!'

Bridie froze. She had no experience of children. No brothers or sisters, no nieces or nephews. She'd seen other people clucking over kids, she'd even made similar noises herself when a colleague brought a new baby into the office, but she'd always known she was acting. Kids didn't look cute or remotely appealing to her, just strange. And these two, with their jutting chins, naked aggression and stinky little toy, were positively repellent.

She was wondering what to do when the weary woman next to her rose up and gave each child a resounding smack. The suddenness of it shocked Bridie. No one had ever raised a hand to her. She'd never even seen someone give or receive a blow, except on television.

Both children were howling. The woman sat down. 'Shut up or I'll really give you something to cry about.'

Bridie was still holding the noxious little toy. She handed it to the woman. 'Sorry . . . I . . .'

The woman looked her up and down. 'I haven't seen you here before.' It was a statement, not a question.

'This is my first visit. My father's on remand.'

The woman nodded and took the toy. 'No bail? You look like you could afford bail.'

Bridie blushed. 'No bail. My dad has no money, and my mum won't help him.'

'Smart woman. We should all stop helping them.'

Bridie didn't know what to say, so she just smiled. The woman looked her up and down a second time, then turned to the person sitting on her other side.

The waiting room was bad enough, and having to leave everything—bag, phone, wallet, the lot—in a locker was sobering. She'd been frisked by a female corrections officer and walked through a metal detector, all made worse because no one smiled, not even when Bridie grinned at them. Her charms just fell uselessly to the floor. She could almost hear the pathetic little tinkle they made when they hit the concrete.

Why did I come? she wondered, as she waited for her name to be called. She had been shocked to the core when she found out the part her father had played in Gloria's fate. Her feelings about him had always been complex. She loved him, he was her dad. She despised him, he was such a loser. She felt sorry for him, her mum was so mean about him; she felt protective of him, he annoyed and bored her. She felt obligated to him, she resented feeling obligated. She identified with him. Neither of them was a match for Amanda. And now she was ashamed of him, while also consumed with pity. How in hell's name was anyone meant to unpick all that?

—

'Hi, Dad.'

The visiting room was filled with desks set out in rows, like an old-fashioned classroom. Around the walls were some shabby couches and a box of battered toys. The kids from the waiting room were fighting over them. Ian was waiting for her at one of the desks, but he had his head in his hands so she couldn't see his face.

'Hi, Dad,' she said again.

'Hi,' he mumbled through his hair.

'How are you?'

A shrug.

Bridie felt a wave of irritation. Did he expect her to feel sorry for him?

'Can you at least look at me? I've come a long way.'

He looked up at her. 'I didn't ask you to.'

'You're still my dad. Did you think I'd just abandon you?'

'I wouldn't blame you if you did.'

'Mum thinks I should.'

'She's right.'

'Maybe, but nothing was more likely to make me come and see you than mum telling me I shouldn't.'

Ian smiled.

Bridie was surprised at how good that made her feel. She leant forward, her courage boosted. 'How could you do it, Dad? How could you sell Gloria?'

Ian slumped again, hiding his face. 'I was desperate. I thought I had no option. They were threatening to kidnap you, Bridie—or worse. I'd sell anyone to prevent that from happening.'

Bridie frowned. Was he trying to shift the guilt onto her? Five-year-old her?

'Why didn't you tell Mum? She'd have paid off your debts to keep me safe. You know she would.'

'The police asked me the same question.'

'And?'

Her father looked up at her for a second time. Tears were streaming down his cheeks. 'I was ashamed. I couldn't bear to admit to the mess I'd got myself into.'

'So you sacrificed another person to get out of it?'

Ian groaned, then nodded. 'I was a fool.'

'No, Dad. You were a slaver.'

Ian nodded again and wiped his face with the back of his hand. 'I know.'

They sat in silence for a few moments.

'How's jail?'

'It's okay. I feel better in here than I have in decades.'

'What do you mean?'

'I'm where I belong. I'm being punished at last.'

'You're paying your debt to society?' Bridie's voice dripped with sarcasm.

'If you like.'

'Too late for Gloria.'

'I know, but I did try to help her once, not long after I'd sold her into hell. Until the police knocked on my door, I thought maybe I had.'

'What do you mean?'

'About six months after I'd left her in that underground car park, I made an anonymous phone call to the police and tipped them off about the human trafficking at the Pitt Street brothel. Not long afterwards, I heard there had been a raid.'

'Too late for Gloria,' Bridie repeated. She wasn't sure whether she believed her father or not. She wanted to and he seemed sincere. What was the point in lying now?

'I know that now. And I understand if you don't believe me. Why should you? But it's true. I was terrified that Sammy Lee and the rest of those bastards would find out it was me, but they never did. They'd have killed me if they had.'

Bridie felt something tight inside her abdomen uncoil a little. At least he had tried. At least she had that to hold on to.

—

'Did you see him?'

The pizza they'd ordered for dinner that evening had arrived. It turned out neither Bridie nor Luna could cook. They ate takeaway almost every night, or cheese on toast, but the wine was always excellent. Amanda's regular deliveries made sure of that. *Her way of making restitution*, thought Bridie. It was more useful than her dad's.

Bridie took a big bite and nodded. She waited until she had swallowed her mouthful before she answered. 'Yes. He was sort of a mess.'

'Sort of?'

'He said jail was okay, that he felt better being inside than he had for ages. That it was where he belonged.'

Luna looked at her. *She really is very pretty*, thought Bridie. She'd noticed how much Luna resembled Gloria. Bridie was a bit jealous of that.

'He has a conscience,' Luna said.

'A conscience? After what he's done?'

'He feels remorse. You have to have a conscience to feel that.'

'He says he tipped off the police about the human trafficking at the brothel and that's why they raided the place.'

'Do you believe him?'

'Yes, I think so.'

'So he did a terrible thing, but he is not a terrible person.'

'I think he's pretty terrible.'

'God tells us to hate the sin but not the sinner.'

Luna was a Catholic, like her mother. Bridie had a sudden flash of the golden cross Gloria had worn around her neck. She'd like to play with it when she was very little, when Gloria had held her close, trying to catch it as it swayed back and forth, sparkling in the light. She wondered where that cross was now.

'I don't hate him,' she said. 'I wish I could. It'd be easier.'

'Sometimes I used to hate my mother.'

Bridie was shocked. Hate Gloria?

'Why?'

'Because she wasn't there and because she never came back.'

Luna ate her pizza daintily, taking small bites which she chewed and swallowed carefully. She was neat and tidy, like Gloria, and always put a napkin across her lap when they ate—as they always did—on the couch. She was very like the Gloria Bridie could remember. Was that why she'd taken such an instant liking to her? It wasn't just that, however; even though they didn't talk about it much, they were both grieving for the same woman. Luna, Bridie realised as she took another bite of pizza, was the closest thing to a sister she was ever going to have.

'I felt like that too,' she said. 'Gloria was the only person who ever showed me any affection—well, except for Dad. He used to rumble with me, and I loved that.'

'Your mother wasn't affectionate?'

'Not really. I knew she loved me, but she mostly expressed it by trying to improve me and that just made me feel like I wasn't good enough. I still feel like that.'

'That's how my missing mother made me feel too—like I wasn't worth coming home for.'

'But you were her real little girl.'

'Was I? It didn't feel like that. It felt like you were. Her letters home—the ones she actually wrote—were full of you: what you were doing, how you were growing, cute things you'd said. I hated you.'

'Do you still have those letters?' Bridie was eager to see what her yaya had written.

'No. I burnt them in a fit of spite. I wish I hadn't now.'

Bridie was surprised by how bereft she felt.

'It was mean of me,' Luna said, leaning forward.

'But understandable.'

'My mother did the best she could. It wasn't her fault that she was so vulnerable.'

'It was ours. My father had options. He chose the wrong ones. Your mother had none and even so she did her best. I envy you her.'

'That's funny—I feel the same about you. You knew her. I did not.'

Luna's phone vibrated on the table. 'It's Detective Blaxland again,' she said.

They had stopped answering her calls but they both knew they couldn't avoid the policewoman much longer.

'Shall I answer it?' Luna asked.

'Only if you want to.'

Luna sighed but picked up the mobile.

Bridie got up, meaning to make herself scarce and give Luna some privacy, but her friend motioned for her to stay.

'Hello, Detective.' She listened without expression then said, 'I will be at Bridie's flat all day . . . Yes, nine o'clock would be fine.'

'Well?' said Bridie, when Luna had ended the call.

'Friday morning, nine o'clock.'

'Why not tomorrow?'

Luna shrugged. 'She said she was not available until Friday morning.'

'Something to do with the case? I wonder if they've caught someone?'

Luna shrugged a second time. 'I don't know, and I didn't ask. She wouldn't tell me anyway.'

Bridie picked up another piece of the now lukewarm pizza and took a large bite. 'Shall we watch another episode of *The Crown*?'

Luna picked up the remote.

SIXTEEN

'Your name is Sadie Margaret Lewis, and you operate the East Gresford post office. Is that correct?'

Megan had asked Kumar to start the interview with the postmistress. *Kumar has started well*, she thought. *She sounds confident and professional.*

Sadie nodded.

'Could you answer aloud, please?' Kumar gestured towards the recording device. 'For the tape.'

'Yes, I am the postmistress,' Sadie said loudly. 'Australia Post calls me the post office agent these days, but I prefer postmistress.' She folded her arms across her chest.

'You identified the woman in the photofit that Constable Baker and I showed you as someone you gave a lift to. Could you tell me how that came about?'

'I picked her up and gave her a lift.'

'Maybe start at the beginning, Ms Lewis.'

The postmistress shot a look at the senior officer. '*Mrs* Lewis,' she said, with emphasis.

'Apologies, Mrs Lewis. In your own time, just as you remember it.' Megan was pleased with Kumar, but she would take the interview from here.

'It was a while ago, but I remember it all right. I'd been making some deliveries in the van up the top end of Masseys Creek Road. I had to take it slow. The road was bad then—it's even worse now. The floods last year washed away all the gravel and gouged out all those potholes. Whole families could live in some of them. Postal vans aren't built for dirt roads, even well-maintained ones. They take a hammering, but you try explaining to the bigwigs in head office why delivering the post up there isn't like doing it in the suburbs of Sydney.'

Having lurched and bounced down Masseys Creek Road herself, Megan could sympathise, but she wanted Mrs Lewis to stick to the point.

'When did you see the woman?'

'I'm getting to that. You never pass many people on that road, especially on weekdays. Maybe the odd farmer, or someone else making a delivery, but pedestrians? Not unless their car's broken down or blown a tyre in a pothole. Anyway, that's why she stood out like dog's balls, limping along in shoes that were too big for her. And she was foreign! Honestly, it was like a Martian had landed.'

'You hadn't seen any other Asian women out that way?'

'I think Nan may have had a couple of carers who were from overseas, but I never saw them. They never stayed long. Who could blame them? Stuck in the middle of nowhere.'

A little alarm bell went off in Megan's head. Baker and Kumar had told her about Nan, and she vaguely remembered interviewing the woman in the wheelchair herself as part of the original investigation. Her carers had been from overseas? She needed to look into this later.

'What did you do when you saw her?'

'I pulled over and wound the window down. "You right?" I asked her. We do that in the country, especially in out-of-the-way places. "I need a lift," she said. "Hop in," I said, and she did. Like a fool, I didn't ask where she was headed until after she was in the passenger seat and we were on our way. "To the nearest train station," she said. That set me back a bit.'

'Why?'

'The nearest station is Paterson. That's nearly fifty k away!'

'Where did you take her?'

'To Maitland station in the end. Maitland's even further, but when I got to Paterson she looked like such a fish out of water—and I had no idea when the next train was coming, and they don't come often—I felt sorry for her. Once I'd picked her up, I couldn't just leave her. I was stuck with her.'

'That's a long drive.'

'You're telling me.'

'What did you talk about?'

'Not much. Just that she needed to get to Sydney.'

'You didn't ask her name?'

'I don't remember, but I can't have done, can I? Otherwise I'd know what it was.'

'Did she tell you how she came to be on—what was the name of the road . . . ?'

'Masseys Creek? I asked her if her car had broken down or something. She said she'd been travelling with her boyfriend and they had a fight, and he kicked her out of the car and drove off.'

'Did you believe her?'

'Why wouldn't I? How else would she have got out there?'

'You didn't think she might have been one of Nan's carers?'

'Never crossed my mind.'

'Did she say anything else?'

'Hardly a word until we got to the station. If I asked her a question, she claimed she didn't understand English very well. Understood it well enough when she asked me for money.'

'Did you give her some?'

'I did. Twenty dollars. She said she'd left her wallet in her boyfriend's car. I felt sorry for her, and in those days twenty dollars would get her back to Sydney.'

'Did she say anything else?'

'Just "thank you" and "goodbye".'

'Did you ever see her again?'

'Not until she'—Sadie jerked her head towards the younger woman—'brought that picture into the post office. Hadn't thought about her either.'

'Not even when you heard about the bodies in the forest?'

'Why would I? She was alive last time I saw her. Is she all right? Has she done something wrong?'

'Not as far as we know. She may be able to help us with our inquiries, that's all.'

'About the bodies?'

'Do you have any idea where she might be now?' Kumar asked.

'Could be in Timbuktu for all I know.'

'Did she tell you her boyfriend's name?'

'Nope.'

'Did you pass his car on the road at any point?'

'No. Come to think of it, I didn't, and I should have, shouldn't I? When I was driving in to Masseys Creek Road to do my deliveries.'

'Could you have seen him drive past but forgotten?'

Mrs Lewis shrugged. 'Possibly. Who remembers every car they've passed? Unless they practically force you off the road or something.'

'You've been very helpful, Mrs Lewis.'

'I hope you catch the bastard. We're not used to having murderers up this way. A few wife-beaters and a heap of whoopee weed-growers, but murderers? No, thanks.'

—

Megan sat in her office and looked at the picture of Siriporn. There was no doubt that this young woman was smart and resourceful. If she did not want to be found, and Megan was pretty sure she didn't, then the search was going to be difficult. Yet Megan was also sure she held the key to breaking the case wide open. Siriporn knew who Zorro was. She may also have known what he was doing, given she decided to run. The problem was how to find her. Siriporn was a common Thai name, and she could have ended up anywhere. The fact that she had asked for money from both Mrs Lewis and Coco indicated that this was a woman who knew how to look after herself. She must've trusted Coco to seek her out once she'd returned to Sydney. She sounded too smart to take any unnecessary risks, even for a hundred dollars.

Megan opened her police notebook and wrote *Suspects* at the top of a blank page. Zorro, obviously, but who was he? Was it Trevor Farrow, brother of Nan? The mentions of carers made him a candidate. But was Nan an accomplice? Seemed implausible. And how about Leo Blake, still somewhere in the wilds of Tasmania? He was a long shot. The only reason he was on the list at all was because he had been on the road at the same time as Jessica Weston twenty years ago. They'd only bothered to check him out back then because they literally had nothing else to go on. And then there was Coco Potts; Megan still had a sense that there was something Coco wasn't telling them.

Megan started a second list: *Interviews*. Trevor and Nan Farrow, Leo Blake, Coco Potts and Siriporn—if they could find her. They were posting the photofit far and wide; maybe someone else would recognise her, like Sadie Lewis had. The fact Sadie identified her straight away was heartening. It must be a pretty good resemblance—or resemble how she looked twenty years ago, at least. Also on the plus side, the postmistress's encounter with Siriporn on Masseys Creek Road had narrowed the search area. It seemed more likely that they were looking for a local. They hadn't had a single hit on the photofit of Zorro, though. Had Coco deliberately led them astray?

Fuck. More than a month into the investigation and all she had was questions. And the more leads she followed, the more questions she had. *But it's always like this*, she reminded herself. *You always feel like you'll never solve the mystery until suddenly you do.* Then another voice, nagging at her: *Yeah, but you don't always solve it. Sometimes the bastards get away with it.* Megan closed her notebook. This was not one of those times. They would solve this case. Even after two decades, they'd find out who killed these three women. *Were there more victims?* she wondered. A small team was still searching. Coco claimed to have only sent four girls to Zorro and they were all now accounted for. Still, she'd keep the search going for a few more days. Coco had secrets. Maybe another body was one of them.

She glanced at her watch. It was late. She had to be up early tomorrow to drive to Sydney to see Bridie Turner and Luna Ramos. She logged off her computer, grabbed her bag and made her way through the station.

'Sarge?'

Samira Kumar was still in her cubicle.

'Why haven't you gone home?' Megan asked.

'Just going over the shots of the shoes we collected. It was interesting that Siriporn was also in shoes that didn't fit.'

'Good observation. Did you find anything else?'

'Not really. But do you think the killer lived in Masseys Creek? Or is local?'

'It's starting to look more likely.'

Kumar was showing signs of being a good cop. Maybe she should give the young woman something even more challenging to do.

'Want to come with me to Sydney tomorrow?' Megan asked.

It would be a death call. Every cop worth their salt had to get used to doing those. But this one should be easier than most, given Luna and Bridie already knew the worst.

'Morning, Sarge. I got you a coffee and a pastry.'

Samira felt more relaxed with the senior detective now. While not the chattiest of bosses, Megan was both reasonable and fair. And she could take a joke. No doubt she'd had to develop that ability when she started out in policing forty years ago. It was blokey enough now; Samira could not imagine what it must have been like then.

They travelled in companionable silence most of the way to Sydney. Samira was pleased to have been asked to partner with Megan (that's how she liked to think of it), but she was nervous about the conversation with the two young women. They were both around Samira's age, and the thought of losing her own mother in such circumstances made her shudder. Not, of course, that her very respectable maths teacher mother would ever have ended up trafficked to a brothel. Yet maybe the women in her family were just lucky. Notwithstanding women from war-torn parts of Europe, sex trafficking disproportionately involved brown women. They were still the most susceptible to the offer of a better life—and not just for themselves but, as with Gloria, for their families.

Samira looked over at her boss, who was concentrating on the fast-moving traffic on the M1. The only reason she was sitting here, as a serving member of the NSW Police Force, a graduate from the Police Academy, the holder of an undergraduate degree in criminology, was because her parents had made the huge decision to migrate to Australia soon after their marriage. Her father, a dentist in Mumbai, had struggled for years to get accredited in this country and had driven a cab while he waited. He had a thriving practice now. Samira often thought of how much she owed him . . . probably because it had been hammered into all his kids as far back as she could remember. It was why she and her siblings had studied so hard. But she also knew she had been a disappointment. Her father had been strict when they were growing up, pushing his children to do well. He'd been furious when Samira had decided to go into policing rather than study law. But Samira did not like studying; she liked doing.

Samira's mother could hardly speak English when she first arrived in Australia. She had worked as a school cleaner while her children were little. It was the school's deputy—a woman who was always in her office after hours—who had persuaded her to apply to do a master's degree in teaching, when she'd discovered that Mrs Kumar had an honours degree in mathematics from the University of Mumbai. Mrs Kumar's English had improved by then, and she and the DP had become good friends, sharing many cups of tea in an otherwise empty school.

'If I'd had different parents, I could have ended up in that brothel,' she said aloud.

Megan glanced over. 'So could any of us, I guess,' she said.

Samira shook her head. 'No. Australian women have choices. A lot of brown women don't. Gloria didn't.'

'There are plenty of white Aussie sex workers.'

'I know, but they're often drug addicts or state wards, homeless ex-foster kids, that kind of thing.'

'Same diff.'

'No. It isn't the same. They are vulnerable because of their circumstances, sure, but not because of the colour of their skin or the country they were born in.'

'What brought this on?'

Samira shrugged. 'I was just thinking about how lucky I was and how hard my parents worked to make that luck.'

'Gloria tried to do the same thing for her daughter.'

'That's what I mean. That's why it's as much luck as it is hard work.'

'Gloria succeeded. She couldn't save herself, but she did save her daughter.'

Samira looked at Megan. She had not thought of that.

'Why did you decide to be a police officer?' she asked her boss.

'Me? My dad was one and I thought he was amazing. It was also the most interesting job of the ones I had the marks to apply for. I didn't fancy being a secretary, a receptionist or a filing clerk. Mind you, when I first entered the force, those were the jobs I spent most of my time doing. What about you?'

'I studied criminology, mostly inspired by watching decades of cop shows. My mum was an addict—to the shows, I mean, not substances.' The idea of her mother so much as sipping a shandy made Samira want to laugh. 'I didn't get the marks for forensic science. My dad wanted me to go on and do law, but I didn't, so . . . here I am.'

'You're good at it.'

Samira was unused to praise. She didn't quite know how to react.

'Thank you,' she said.

'Ms Ramos, as I explained on the phone, we have positively identified the second set of remains found in the Burraga Swamp as those of your mother, Gloria Maria Ramos. I am very sorry for your loss.'

Megan had known she had to do this death call, but she'd thought this one might be easier. Now it was upon her, this one felt harder than most. Maybe it was because they had waited so long before they could confirm what they all already knew. It made the interview feel performative, like it was just a formality. Fake.

Then, Luna's eyes filled with tears and Bridie, who was sitting next to her friend on the couch, put an awkward arm around her shoulders. The sweetness of the gesture was moving and Megan's feelings quickly changed. She had to make an effort to keep her expression professional and impassive.

'I'm sorry,' Luna said, dabbing at her eyes. 'I've known it was her for days and yet, hearing it from you in person . . . I don't know why that should be so upsetting.'

'Don't apologise. Most people get emotional, even if they have known the worst. Our presence makes it official. Removes the last vestige of hope.'

'Can we see her?' Bridie passed Luna another tissue.

'Yes, of course. She is in the Maitland morgue.'

'I can drive us both,' Bridie said.

Megan felt better. She was glad she had come. She was reassured by the relationship that appeared to have developed between the two women who used to be the two little girls that Gloria had worked so hard to care for. Their concern for one another was a tribute to the character of the woman whose murderer they sought.

'Do you know . . . ?' Luna could not finish the sentence, so Bridie finished it for her: '. . . who did it?'

'We have photofits of the man who—I am sorry, I can't think of a better way to put this—who bought your mother, and another of one of the trafficked girls who managed to escape. If we can find her, we hope she'll be able to identify the perpetrator. We believe her name is Siriporn.'

'May I see the images?' asked Luna.

Kumar, who had so far remained silent, passed them over.

Luna and Bridie studied both carefully.

'I don't recognise either of them,' Bridie said.

Luna just shook her head.

'Can we keep them?' Bridie asked.

'Of course,' Megan said. 'Show them around if you like. Every pair of eyes helps.'

—

Megan and Samira had only stayed at Bridie's flat long enough to finish their tea. The whole visit had not lasted more than half an hour, but their car had been sitting outside in the sun while they delivered the bad news. Even with the air-conditioning pumped up to full blast, it was sweltering.

'What's the temperature outside?' Samira asked.

Megan looked at the display on her dashboard. 'Thirty-four degrees.'

'At ten thirty! Phew.'

'And it's still only October.'

They didn't speak again until they were a fair way along the M1, heading home. When they did, they returned to the weather.

'It's getting very dry,' Megan commented. It seemed easier to make inconsequential small talk after a death call.

Samira looked up at the featureless blue sky. 'We're in for another bad fire season, they reckon.'

'So they're saying.'

Samira looked out the window at the passing countryside. Everything drooped in the heat, and the grass looked parched. It was as if the rain that had fallen a month ago had never happened. A clump of trees on the median strip stood out among the tangled green. They were dead, all of them blackened and brown, burnt to a crisp.

'Cigarette,' Megan said.

'What? Thrown out of a car?'

'Happens a lot in summer, especially when it's dry.'

'It's not summer yet.'

Samira turned to look as the brown-and-black scrub disappeared behind them. She hated fire. It frightened her. It was what she had dreaded when she'd been posted to the country.

The thought of floods or gales or cyclones didn't worry her, but fire was so all-consuming. It just devoured everything.

'Do Maitland police have to attend bushfires?' she asked.

'Sometimes, especially uniforms. It's usually just to get people out of harm's way and then make sure they don't get back into the fire zone. We leave the actual firefighting to the experts. Of course, if the fireys see signs of arson, they hand it over to us.'

As a 'uniform' herself, Samira was only mildly comforted. She would be glad to get home to her nice little flat, right in the middle of Maitland. The only greenery she could see from her small balcony was the well-mown grass bank running down to the Hunter River, and that was just the way she liked it. Then, unable to distract herself any longer, her thoughts turned to the two young women they had just left. Their distress had been upsetting. She'd admired the calm but compassionate way Megan had handled the situation. She'd thought this would not be as hard as other death calls, given what all of them already knew. Yet it had been hard. Really hard. Awful to see the last shred of hope ripped away.

Samira made a mental note. She would ring her parents when she got home.

SEVENTEEN

Amanda sat on the couch in Bridie's flat. She could hear her daughter and Gloria's in the kitchen. They were fetching wine and the food Bridie had ordered. The young woman from the Philippines didn't cook. This surprised Amanda. Bridie had told Amanda the woman's name, but she had instantly forgotten it. All she knew was that this young woman was Gloria's daughter. Her presence in Bridie's flat felt like an accusation.

A shout of laughter from the kitchen, followed by a clattering of cutlery, gave Amanda a pang of jealousy. She remembered feeling the same when she'd hear Gloria and Bridie having fun together all those years ago. Why had she never been able to have a relationship like that with her daughter? She still could not understand how Bridie could be so like her in some ways and yet so different in others.

Another shout of laughter. Gloria had been a good cook, Amanda recalled. She'd sometimes prepared an Asian feast for them all. Amanda's sense of being on the defensive increased.

She hated remembering Gloria. Not only had she envied her relationship with Bridie, but Amanda felt guilty about her fate. Not that she *was* guilty, of course. It was her fuckwit of an ex-husband who had delivered the poor woman into the hands of human traffickers, not her. What she had ever seen in Ian Turner she did not know. No doubt it was the bits of Bridie that reminded her of him that were the most irritating.

To distract herself, Amanda looked down at the coffee table. It was untidy, with keys, chargers, receipts and what looked like the entire contents of Bridie's letterbox strewn about. Amanda reached down to straighten the papers and clear a space. As she did, something caught her attention.

'Why do you have a picture of Sara Stanhope on your coffee table?' Amanda asked Bridie, who was entering the room carrying food and drink. Gloria's daughter was right behind her, holding plates and cutlery.

'Who?' Bridie asked.

'Sara Stanhope,' Amanda repeated, picking up the flyer.

'The police told us her name is Siriporn.'

'Well, she's the living spit of Sara.'

'Who is Sara?' It was the other young woman speaking. Gloria's daughter.

'She's Sydney's most exclusive caterer, booked months—if not years—in advance. Married to Brian Stanhope, ex–Reserve Bank.'

'Is she Thai?'

'I don't know. Could be. She's from somewhere in Asia, anyway.'

The young woman whose name Amanda couldn't remember—Laura? Lisa? Laverne?—sat down suddenly.

'The police think she knew my mother and maybe knew my mother's killer too.'

Amanda stared at her. 'Sara Stanhope? I hardly think that's likely.'

She felt irritated with the girl. As if someone like Sara would mix in the same circles as Gloria Ramos.

'We better tell the police,' the girl said, turning to Bridie.

Feeling dismissed, Amanda's irritation intensified.

'I'll call Detective Blaxland.' Bridie was already looking for her phone.

'Don't be silly!' Amanda snapped. 'It's just a chance resemblance. Lots of Asian women look . . .' She stopped herself just in time, but her unspoken remark hung in the air.

'Asian women look the same? Is that what you were going to say, Mother?'

'Well, they do. To our eyes, anyway. We probably look the same to them.' Amanda smiled at the other young woman, trying to charm her into agreeing.

'Whether it is Siriporn or not, we must tell the police,' Gloria's daughter said.

Amanda felt awful. Not only had she been unfairly accused of racism, now she'd probably be subjected to another humiliating interview about life with a husband she'd really rather not remember. She picked up the glass of wine Bridie had put in front of her and took a slug. Then she squared her shoulders and utilised her greatest asset, her superlative social skills.

'Anything I can do to help get justice for Gloria I will do happily,' she said, smiling at the two young women. And to Gloria's daughter: 'I am very sorry for your loss, dear.'

'Her name is Luna,' Bridie said.

'I know. You introduced us earlier.'

Bridie rolled her eyes.

—

'We're here to see Ms Sara Stanhope.'

Megan and Phil stood in the foyer of Raw and Cooked. It was a converted warehouse in Surry Hills, all white walls, rusting industrial pipes and huge wooden pylons and beams. The place was buzzing with people, yet strangely hushed. The staff sat at long trestle tables in front of screens. They were all wearing headphones. Adding to the quiet, everyone padded about barefoot on the timber floor, shoes neatly lined up just inside the front door. A sign asked everyone who entered to remove theirs. Phil and Megan ignored it. Their shoes echoed noisily as they walked from the door to the reception desk.

'Do you have an appointment?'

The young man behind the desk had his blond hair in a bun. He wore flowing, neutral-coloured clothing, a cross between what hippies had worn when Megan was young and what people from Asia and the Middle East had worn for centuries, but he was as Caucasian as Caucasian could be.

'No.'

'I am afraid Ms Stanhope never sees anyone without an appointment.'

Megan and Phil took out their IDs. It was the part of police work they both thoroughly enjoyed, watching how the person who had brushed them off responded when the tables were turned.

'Detective Senior Sergeants Megan Blaxland and Phil Arlott,' Megan said. 'I'm afraid Ms Stanhope will have to make an exception. We are investigating a multiple homicide.'

The young man went pale. 'Oh. Oh, I see.'

He jumped up and scarpered, presumably to fetch Ms Stanhope. A few moments later he reappeared. 'Follow me.'

They climbed a spiral staircase. The young man skipped up noiselessly. Phil and Megan clomped behind him, every footfall clanging noisily on the metal steps. At the top stood Siriporn. If the photofit was accurate, there wasn't a shadow of a doubt that this elegant woman was the person they had been searching for. She looked exactly the same, minus the multiple earrings lining her left ear. The twenty years that had passed sat lightly on her; only a stylish streak of grey hair across her forehead gave any hint. She was dressed similarly to the young man, all linen and layers, all oatmeal and clotted cream.

'To what do I owe the pleasure?' she asked.

'We are investigating a murder and we have reason to believe you may be able to help us with our inquiries.' Phil's voice echoed off the walls.

'Do tell me more.'

If the woman was startled by their sudden appearance, she gave no sign of it. Rather, she inclined her head towards a seating nook beneath a huge industrial apparatus. *Once a working part of this warehouse*, Megan thought. *Now just a style statement.*

They sat, but before Megan could ask her first question, the young man appeared again with some kind of herbal tea in a glass teapot.

'Tea?' Ms Stanhope asked.

Phil shook his head. *Bugger*, thought Megan. *That means I'll have to try it.* She was a purist about tea. She felt about herbal tea the way she felt about oat, almond and all the other milks that weren't milk. Why couldn't people just leave well enough alone?

'Lovely,' she said. Phil gave her a grin. She ignored him.

Siriporn poured Megan a cup, or rather a glass, then one for herself. As the two women sipped their vaguely minty hot water, Phil spoke up.

'The bodies of three women have been found in the Barrington Tops National Park,' he said. 'They were buried there around twenty years ago. In the course of our investigations, we have been told that you may have information that could prove helpful.'

Phil sounds like a police officer speaking to a media scrum, Megan thought. *Deliberately neutral and unemotional.*

'Me? Are you sure you have the right person?'

'We are looking for a woman who went by the name Siriporn twenty years ago. She was a human trafficking victim and, we believe, narrowly missed being murdered herself.'

Megan watched the woman opposite her, searching for any sign of nervousness or discomfort. She saw none.

'My name is Sara Stanhope.'

Megan handed the photofit to her.

Ms Stanhope looked at it carefully. 'She does look like me, I'll give you that.'

'Even down to the scar.'

A flicker of something, perhaps, in Ms Stanhope's dark gaze. She had a small scar over her right eye, just like the Siriporn in the photofit.

'Coco Potts, who ran the establishment which trafficked and exploited these women and others, has worked with our photofit expert to create this likeness of the woman she knew as Siriporn. Do you know Ms Potts?' Phil still sounded like he was reading from an autocue.

'A great many people know Ms Potts.'

Megan got straight to the point. 'Are you Siriporn?'

'I think I should call my lawyer before I answer any more questions.'

—

Once they were outside the weathered brick of Raw and Cooked, Megan turned to Phil. 'She's Siriporn, all right. Why else would she need a lawyer?'

'How long do we wait before getting her in?'

'Twenty-four hours, no longer. In the meantime, seeing as we're in the neighbourhood, let's drop in on Coco Potts. She must have known who Siriporn was all along.'

—

Coco was calm and in control as she sat opposite the two cops on her expensive couch. Coco's was her territory. She felt safer here than in any police interview room. She smiled at Megan and then at Phil.

Megan refused to be charmed. 'Did you realise the photofit of Siriporn resembled Sara Stanhope? Apparently you two are acquainted.'

Had Coco deliberately sent them on a wild-goose chase? Megan didn't believe so, especially given the East Gresford postmistress's emphatic ID, but they needed to check all the same. Good police work, as she had told Samira, left no stone unturned.

'Acquainted? I think we may have attended some of the same events—fashion week, fundraisers, that sort of thing. We may have been introduced, but that's all.'

'But you must have recognised her. She looks just as you described.'

'I see that now you say it. But it never occurred to me before now. It was the context, I suppose. I never would have expected Siriporn, funny little Siriporn, to turn up in such places. I honestly thought she was just Sara.'

Was this credible? Megan wasn't sure. Coco was either sincere or a consummate liar. Megan could not make up her mind.

'So you didn't do it to embarrass her, or throw us off the scent?' Phil sounded aggressive.

Coco gave him a long look. 'Of course not. I want you to catch this cunt.'

Megan could almost feel Phil's shock. No matter. She would be the good cop.

'You created the photofit in good faith?'

'Of course I did.'

'So when you saw Ms Stanhope at various events, her resemblance to Siriporn never struck you?'

'Not really. Maybe I thought she looked familiar, but I dismissed it. Who would believe that the Siriporn I knew could have ended up married to an ex-governor of the Reserve Bank? And anyway, what would I have done with the realisation? March up to her at some swanky do and ask her if she was the hooker I worked with twenty years ago?'

'Why didn't you think to tell us about the resemblance while you were putting together the photofit?'

'I told you: I didn't even think about it. I don't think I've seen Ms Stanhope for years. The resemblance had faded from my memory.'

Megan had been prepared to accept most of Coco's answers, but not this one. She was holding something back, Megan sensed; something important.

'What is it you are not telling us, Ms Potts? I believe you when you say you want to see Zorro brought to justice, but I don't believe you about Siriporn. Does she know something you don't want us to know?'

'Of course not. I have been completely open with you.'

'Whatever it is, we'll find it out eventually,' Megan warned. 'Better you tell us everything now.'

'I have.'

But Megan was not convinced.

'We will be interviewing Ms Stanhope shortly. We may need to interview you again after that.'

Coco nodded and smiled. 'Anything I can do to help.'

EIGHTEEN

Leo Blake's house was as neat as a pin. It was large and sat on a concessional block on a tongue of land on the Allyn River. As they pulled up beside the post-and-rail fence, Josh and Samira could see the man himself on the other side of his immaculate lawn, moving methodically forwards and backwards on his ride-on mower. The two cops stood and watched him until he got to the river. He was wearing earmuffs, so there was no point calling out to him. They would have to wait until he turned around.

He did eventually, and when he saw them he killed the machine and waved. Then he got off it and walked towards them.

'Sorry,' he said with a smile once they drew near. 'I go into my own world.' He gestured towards the mower. 'Very meditative. The lawn was practically up to my knees. It must've rained while I was away, though you wouldn't know it now.'

They followed his gaze. The Allyn had been reduced to a sluggish trickle through sun-baked rocks.

'Yeah, she's dry, all right,' Josh said. 'Have you got a moment, Mr Blake?' Mandatory weather talk was done.

'Call me Leo, Josh.'

'I'm here on official business.'

The man looked them both up and down. It was another sweltering day, and there were large sweat rings under the arms of their regulation police shirts.

'You'd better come inside then. I've got the air-con on.'

He ushered them up the steps and through the front door.

Once they were seated in his pristine lounge room—on matching pale green sofas so clean they made Samira perch nervously on the edge—Blake cut to the chase. 'Is this about the bodies in Burraga Swamp?'

'We want to check something you told the police twenty years ago,' Josh said.

Blake tipped his hat onto the back of his head. He was completely bald. 'Twenty years! That's going back a bit.'

'Yours was the only other vehicle on the road when a witness went into the forest early one morning. You may recall being asked about it back then. You told the detective you were buying eggs from a neighbour. This was later confirmed by that neighbour.'

'You have a witness to the murders?'

'I'm afraid I can't go into details.'

'We are simply rechecking your whereabouts at the time,' Samira interjected. 'You were questioned about it then by Detective Constable Megan Blaxland. Do you recall that?'

Blake turned and smiled at her. He looked like a wrinkled walnut, but friendly enough. 'Vaguely. They suspected there may have been a murder in the forest but never found any evidence?'

'That's right.'

'And now you have. The whole district is alive with gossip about the bodies you've discovered. Nothing this exciting has ever happened up here. Not even the willy-willy that uprooted trees and stripped roofs from houses outside Paterson, or the lightning strike that killed six pregnant cows in one go!'

Leo Blake was almost making fun of the murders.

'Three women have been killed.' Samira could not help herself.

Blake's smile evaporated immediately. 'Of course, sorry. It's how I cope. This is serious, I understand.'

'Do you recall what you told Constable Blaxland at the time?' Josh asked.

'I do. I told her I'd been to buy eggs from Farrow's farm on Masseys Creek Road.'

'And do you stand by that statement?' asked Samira.

Leo Blake looked at her again. 'I do, young lady.'

Young lady? She immediately felt diminished, like a schoolgirl rather than a police officer. But he was of a different generation. He probably meant it kindly.

She held out the two photofits. 'Do you recognise either of the people pictured?'

Blake took the flyers out of her hands and looked at them carefully. 'We all looked a bit like that, back in the day.'

Samira was taken aback; the man in front of her was as bald as an egg.

'Alopecia,' he said. 'I don't have a hair anywhere on my body anymore.'

Too much information, Samira thought. *Way too much information.*

Blake studied the photofit of Siriporn. 'And I think I'd remember if I'd ever seen her.'

'What do you think?' Samira asked Josh as they walked back to their car.

'If we're going on the evidence, I think he was just on the wrong road at the wrong time.'

'He's a bit sexist.'

Josh shook his head. 'He's just an old-fashioned country bloke, not up on political correctness.'

'It's not political correctness to treat me as a professional. It's just basic good manners!'

Samira turned and looked back at the shiny house on the beautifully landscaped tongue of land. 'And he's got a pretty fancy spread for an old-fashioned country bloke. Where did he get his money from?'

'No idea,' said Josh. 'We never ask questions like that in the country.'

'You do when you're a copper. I reckon we should have a bit of a dig around.'

'Sure, but is this just because he called you "young lady"?'

'No. It's what Sarge said—leave no stone unturned.'

They were driving north from Gresford, on their way to Masseys Creek Road to show Nan and hopefully the elusive Trevor the photofits, when Samira started to feel hungry.

'Shall we stop for lunch soon?' she asked, as her stomach rumbled.

Josh looked at the time displayed on the car's dashboard. 'Sure. We can sit by the river. It'll be cooler near the water.'

'What little water there is.'

'There'll be more further up; always is. Less farmers using it for irrigation the closer you get to the forest and more trees along its banks, slowing the evaporation.'

Samira was always impressed by how much Josh knew about his local area. 'You love it here, don't you?'

'Of course. It's my country. It's in my blood.'

Maybe that's why I feel like such a stranger, Samira thought. It was the crowded streets of Mumbai that were in hers.

They found a quiet bend in the river, parked the car, scooted under the wire fence—Josh swore he knew the landowner and that they wouldn't mind—and clambered down a grassy bank to sit themselves on a log that had been washed up in the last flood or the one before that. Josh was right: it was cooler than up on the road, and the river here still chortled and babbled over the rocks. Just listening to it made Samira feel fresher and cleaner.

Josh got up and went over the river's edge. He squatted, cupped his hands and scooped up some river water, drinking it thirstily. 'You won't find sweeter water than this, anywhere.'

He gestured to Samira to try it. She stood and joined him, dipping her fingers in. The water was cool and refreshing. She sucked a few drops from her fingertips. If Josh said it was safe to drink, she believed him.

Returning to the log, she took a bite from her chicken and salad roll. 'You don't think Leo Blake could be a suspect?' Samira asked after she swallowed her food.

Josh, who had just sat down and taken a large bite of his own roll, shrugged. 'They're all suspects, I reckon, until they prove otherwise.'

Samira nodded. That made sense.

'Shush!'

Samira hadn't said anything. She looked at Josh, startled.

'Wha—'

'SHUSH!' he hissed, more insistently. He pointed downriver.

She turned. A lyrebird had come out of the forest onto a gravelly little beach on the opposite bank. Samira froze. She'd never seen one in the wild. Correction, she'd never seen one at all, except in Jessica Weston's video. The bird was only a few feet from them, but it seemed unaware of their presence. It walked to the water's edge and lowered its head to drink. The two police officers sat as still as statues until the wild creature had slaked its thirst and headed back into the tangled undergrowth.

'Wow!' said Josh. 'You don't see that every day.'

'Is it an omen, do you think?'

Josh looked at her. 'Nah. It's because of the drought. The wildlife have to get closer to humans when the water sources in the forest start to dry up. It's either that or die of thirst.'

'I can see why Professor Weston has made them her life's work.' Samira was gazing at the spot where the bird had disappeared. She wanted to see it again.

'Must be weird, though,' Josh mused. 'Studying a bird that has such an association for her. That video she took is really chilling.'

Samira thought of the footage they had all watched at least once. Chilling was exactly the right word, but seeing a lyrebird now felt different. It felt exciting. It felt like a privilege. A window into a world that usually remained hidden.

—

Nan looked at the photofits and shook her head emphatically.

'She doesn't know them,' her brother said unnecessarily.

As far as Samira could tell, Trevor Farrow looked just like all the other old blokes living in the backblocks. He was grey-haired and clean-shaven and built on a large scale, muscle running to fat. His hands were huge and ingrained with what looked like a lifetime of dirt. Yet when he had given Nan her cup of tea, he had been gentle and solicitous.

'Do you?' Josh asked.

'Nope.'

'Leo Blake said you all looked like that back in the day.' Samira couldn't resist.

Farrow turned towards her. His eyes were very blue under their hooded lids.

Farrow shook his head. 'Can't see it myself.'

'What happened to Nan's carers?' Josh asked. 'A few people we've talked to mentioned them.'

'Why? 'Cos they were Asian and all Asians look alike to them?'

'Were they Asian?' Samira took over the questioning.

'Not all of them.'

'What happened to them?'

'They didn't like it here. Too out of the way. Stayed a few months, then left.'

'Where did they go?'

'How should I know? I paid them what they were owed and that was that.'

'How did they get out of here? It's not on a bus route, is it?'

Trevor gave Josh a look over Samira's head. 'Same way they got here. I picked them up from the station and I drove them back there.'

'Why don't you have a carer for Nan now?'

'No need since I've retired. I can save the money and do it myself.'

Trevor Farrow gave little away. His face was mostly expressionless, yet he somehow managed to convey his contempt for Samira. She wasn't sure if he despised her because she was a woman, Asian, a cop, or all three.

'Can you check the photofit again? Her name is Siriporn. Are you sure she wasn't one of Nan's carers?'

He did not even glance down at the flyer in Samira's hand. 'Of course I'm sure, and so is Nan . . . aren't you, love?'

'Mrs Lewis from the post office recognised her as a woman she picked up on this road a couple of decades ago,' Josh said.

Farrow shrugged. 'Nothing to do with us.'

Nan nodded. The brother and sister seemed very tight. They looked alike, although Nan was as small as he was large. Their gestures were similar. Their obvious bond was both touching and slightly weird.

—

'Did Nan seem nervous to you?' Samira asked. 'More nervous than the last time we talked to her?'

She and Josh were walking down the rutted driveway to their car.

Josh shrugged. 'I didn't notice.'

'Maybe it's because Trevor was there. Do you think he mistreats her? People with disabilities are disproportionately victims of abuse.' Samira was aware her recent graduation from the Police Academy sometimes showed. She'd written an essay about the groups in society who were most at risk.

'Never been any reports of anything like that,' Josh said.

Samira said nothing. She looked back at the isolated, run-down house. *How would Nan ever make a report?* she wondered, but she kept her doubts to herself.

'No injuries, no bruises, no hospitalisations.' Maybe Josh had been thinking the same thing.

'Still, they're weird together.'

'They're twins.'

The dog was straining on the leash again. Growling and slavering as if it would tear them from limb from limb if only it could get at them. Samira was glad the chain looked sturdy.

'Yeah, you told me.'

They got in the car and Josh started the engine.

'Nan nearly died when they were born, Mum said. Trev was the big twin and took all the blood and the nutrition. He's why Nan is the way she is.'

NINETEEN

Jessica dropped her bag on the table, kicked off her shoes and grabbed some cold water from the fridge. It was so fucking hot. Leaving the air-conditioned biology building had been like stepping into an oven. The air was so close it was hard to breathe. *Since when did Newcastle become Singapore?* she wondered. There was a nasty hot wind blowing too, coming straight off the Western Plains. Was it her imagination or could she catch the whiff of bushfire? She looked at the *Hazards Near Me* app on her phone. Nothing yet, except the general warning: *Extreme Fire Danger. Total Fire Ban.* They'd sent that to everyone on the east coast, she imagined.

The cold water was refreshing. She sat down on the nearest kitchen chair. It was a relief that Sheridan was not home from school yet. They had been at each other's throats for weeks now. Sheridan took offence at everything she said, reading meanings into her words, even into her facial expressions, that Jessica felt were both bizarre and unfair. *It's so peaceful when she's not here,* she thought guiltily. *I love Sheridan. I do. I just don't like her very much at the moment.*

There was a folded piece of paper on the table, with *Mum* underlined twice. Even the flourish looked angry. When had Sheridan left that? Had she wagged school and come home early? Rage rose in Jessica's throat. For fuck's sake, what did she have to do to get her daughter to behave? It wasn't like she was strict. She wasn't one of those parents who had rules about much—but going to school? That was her daughter's fucking job. Her contribution, like slogging away teaching indifferent university students in an increasingly hostile and underfunded institution was hers.

I've gone to Dad's. I need a break. S

She needed a break. Was she fucking kidding? Well, her father was welcome to her. He could deal with the condescension, downright rudeness and teensplaining. He could run around after her like a blue-arsed fly, washing her clothes, cooking her food, cleaning up after her as she whinged and complained and picked fights over every little thing. He could drive her about like a chauffeur and fund her excursions. It was his bloody turn.

'Where are you?'

She had dialled her daughter during her furious internal monologue.

'At the bus stop.'

'And you're going to Dad's?'

'That's what I said.'

Jessica could hear the irritation in her daughter's voice.

'You don't always do what you say.'

'Oh, fuck off, Mum. Just fuck off!'

'Don't speak to me like that!'

'I'd rather not speak to you at all!' Sheridan hung up.

Jessica stared at her phone. If that was the way her daughter wanted to play it, she was only too happy to oblige.

Then she thought about ringing Megan. She needed some advice, someone who knew a lot about conflict, human nature and wayward teens, but she hesitated. She knew Megan was up to her neck in the lyrebird case and probably had no space to listen to her complain about her rebellious daughter, but Megan was the closest thing to a mother figure Jessica had... *Bugger it*, she thought, bringing Megan's number up in her contacts. *Maybe she'd like to talk about something else for five minutes.*

You've called Megan Blaxland. I can't come to the phone right now—

Jessica hung up. She'd just have to deal with her fury on her own.

—

Megan was staring at Sara Stanhope's nails. They were long and pointed, polished to perfection in ice blue. Megan wondered how she ever managed to cook anything with nails like that. The amount of shortcrust pastry dough that would get caught up under them didn't bear thinking about. Though shortcrust pastry wasn't very fashionable anymore, Megan reminded herself, so it probably didn't matter. It was hard to tear her attention away from the nails as Ms Stanhope was drumming them rhythmically on the interview table. Was she nervous?

Beside Ms Stanhope sat her lawyer, a Sydney solicitor of considerable renown, or so his client had assured them. Megan had never heard of him, but she doubted bigwig lawyers often visited places like Maitland. They were not compelled to allow him to sit in on the interview, but Sara Stanhope was not a suspect, and maybe having her lawyer beside her would help her feel safe enough to tell them the whole story.

Phil turned on the tape and did the usual ident. Then he turned to the lady with the ice-blue nails.

'State your name, please.'

The nails stopped thrumming.

'Sara Siriporn Stanhope.'

A very good sign, Megan thought. *She's here to tell us the truth.*

'Before we begin'—the lawyer paused and cleared some phlegm from his throat—'Ms Stanhope wants it made clear that she intends to tell the truth, and the whole truth, but she wants her evidence to remain confidential if possible.'

'We keep all witness statements confidential,' Megan said.

'Nevertheless, the evidence Ms Stanhope is about to give you is startling.'

'As I am sure you have already informed your client, Ms Stanhope may be subpoenaed to give evidence in court, should the case ever come to trial,' Phil said.

The lawyer nodded. Ms Stanhope worried at a piece of skin by her thumbnail.

Megan leant across the table. 'What made you decide to talk to us?'

Ms Stanhope had her head lowered. She raised it. 'What choice did I have?'

'You had choices, but I am glad you made the one that you did.'

'You can compel me. There's a fine.'

'Not of a magnitude that would worry you.'

'I like to obey the law, be a good citizen.'

'I see . . .'

'And I thought about the murdered women and that maybe I was the only person who could get justice for them. That kept me up at night.'

'And multiple murderers can do it again,' Phil added. 'Putting Zorro behind bars could save lives.'

'That's not what we called him. That's the stupid name he gave himself.'

'What did you call him?'

'I don't like to say. It's not very polite.'

'We've heard everything,' Megan assured her. 'Be as graphic as you like.'

'He had very big balls. Like eggs. Or maybe they just looked big beside his small dick. And he was from the country. He sometimes talked about his chickens.'

Megan and Phil looked at one another.

'We liked to come up with nasty nicknames for the men we had to'—Ms Stanhope stopped and took a sip of water—'service. He was the Egg Man. Gloria was brilliant. She came up with the best ones—Long Dick, Big Belly, Hairy Monster, Cunt Face, the Egg Man, No Balls—all in her version of Spanish, of course. Concepcion sounded different when she spoke, but they could understand each other. She'd do drawings to explain. Her cartoons were hilarious. It helped us to be able to laugh at those men, put them down behind their backs—and to their faces. We'd call them by their nickname in our own language, say it to their face as if it was an endearment. They liked it, but we'd laugh. "*Mnusy khi*," I'd say to the Egg Man, as if I was calling him my darling. Taking them for fools made us less afraid. At first, anyway.'

Phil leant forward and put the photofit of Zorro in front of Siriporn. 'Do you recognise this person?'

Siriporn stared at the image, frowning.

'Is it Zorro?' Phil pressed.

'It looks like him.'

'So, it's him?'

Siriporn didn't sound certain. 'Yeah, but a lot of Australian men I met looked like that back then, especially if they lived in the bush.'

Many still do, Megan thought, remembering some of the bikies, drug addicts and domestic violence perps she had arrested over the years.

'But you think it's him?' Phil was persistent.

'I'm pretty sure, but it could be the other bloke too. He was a lot darker, but otherwise . . .'

Megan and Phil exchanged a glance. Had Coco deliberately led them astray?

'Would you sit down with our photofit expert and put together an image of the third man?'

Siriporn nodded. 'If you think it will help.'

It was a good question. Would it help? Megan wondered. They were drawing a blank with the picture of Zorro.

'Are you still afraid of Zorro?' she asked gently.

'Are you kidding? I'm terrified. I didn't know what he was capable of back then.'

'Are you afraid he'll kill again?'

Siriporn shook her head. 'No, he stopped killing after I escaped. Coco saw to that.'

Phil and Megan looked at one another a second time. Coco? Had she been involved all along? Megan had known Coco was holding something from them. She reminded herself to proceed slowly.

'We will get to Coco Potts in good time, but I'd really like you to tell us what happened to you, right from the beginning.'

She looked at Megan. Her dark eyes were solemn. 'I was seventeen and the eldest girl. We lived in Chiang Mai and we were very poor. My mother had died, and my dad had remarried—a girl about my age. She did not like me, treated me like I was her servant, and she was mean to my younger brother and sisters too. I could hear her complaining about me to Dad at night when she thought I was asleep. Making up stories about things I had done. Most of them were things she had done to me! But if I ever tried to tell Dad, he just got upset.'

She wiped her eyes with the back of her hand.

'One day they told me they had found me a great job as an au pair in Sydney and that I would be leaving the next morning. I didn't know what an au pair was, of course, but they told me it was looking after children, and I knew I was good at that. I was pleased at first, because I was glad to get away, but then I began to worry about what would happen to my sisters. I wasn't so worried about my brother; he was a boy, and maybe that made him less of a threat to her. And it certainly gave him more choices. I still worry about what has happened to my sisters. I have not heard anything about them from that day to this and I am forty now.'

She stopped and said nothing for a moment or two. Megan and Phil let the silence be.

'Of course there was no such job. They had sold me to human traffickers. I want to believe it was all my stepmother's doing and that my dad knew nothing about it, but . . . I don't think that would have been possible. He sold me. I am terrified he may also have sold my sisters.'

'We may be able to help you look for them. I can talk to the human trafficking squad. They're highly skilled.' Megan spoke softly.

Sara Stanhope shook her head. 'That is kind. But I think it is too late.'

She stopped and looked down at her hands. For a moment or two the only noise was the faint sound of traffic from the world outside.

'When I arrived in Bangkok there was a group of about ten of us, all poor girls, all told we were going to Australia to work as au pairs, waitresses, cleaners, cooks. We were all young, all excited.'

'Where did you learn to speak English? You're very fluent.'

'When my mother was alive, she made sure we went to school every day. It was just a village school, nothing special, but it had a good English language teacher. He was very kind to me. Told me I was his prize pupil—and I did win some prizes. I wanted to be an English language teacher just like him when I grew up. That was one of the things my dad said to me as he put me on the bus to Bangkok. I was upset, you see, saying goodbye to my siblings. Maybe he felt guilty. Anyway, he said something about how I would improve my English living in Australia and how that would help me achieve my ambitions. It comforted me then, but it makes me sick to think about it now.'

'Speaking English as well as you do may be what saved your life.'

Siriporn—that was how Megan thought of her—nodded. 'I thank my mother and my teacher for that.'

Such little things that mean the difference between life and death, Megan thought. A mother who cared was one thing, but the presence of a skilled teacher in a remote little school quite another. Her heart went out to the girl Siriporn had been and to all the other girls, traded like so much wool or iron ore.

'What happened when you arrived in Australia?'

'We had a chaperone. She was also Thai. She had our passports and all our travel documents. She said she was from the employment agency, and she could speak English. It was her job to help us get through customs and immigration. I nearly told her that I could speak English too, but something stopped me. I don't know what. Part of it was not wanting to be a show-off; I had learnt at school that nobody likes a girl who knows things.

I didn't intend to keep my skill a secret forever, not then, but after only a day or two I decided not to tell anyone.'

'But you did tell Coco.'

'That was some time into the future, and I had come to trust her.'

'Do you still trust her?'

'Yes. I do.'

'When did you realise the situation you were in?'

Siriporn looked stricken. 'As soon as we arrived at the brothel. The men who ran the place grabbed two of the girls—not me, thank God—and beat and raped them in front of our eyes. We screamed and sobbed. We were terrified they would do the same to us. That's how they wanted us to feel, of course. They used those girls and their suffering as a warning. We were told that if we tried to run they would kill us. They told us we owed them a debt for bringing us to Sydney and that we would work there as prostitutes until it was paid. I wanted to believe that they meant what they said and that we would not have to endure the situation for long, but I knew they were lying.'

'You were raped nightly?' Megan kept her voice gentle.

Siriporn nodded. 'Multiple times. It was a living hell.'

The four people in the room sat in silence. The big-city lawyer looked distressed. This was not his usual gig.

'The only thing that made it bearable was the other girls. They were from all over the world. From Thailand, of course, the Philippines, South America.'

'And you met Gloria Ramos there?'

'Yes, and Concepcion. They were inseparable.'

'But you all spoke different languages. How did you communicate?'

'With gestures, snatches of broken English. We had to be discreet about it; they did not like to see us talking to one another.'

'Did you know Yulia?'

'I knew her but I wasn't able to talk to her. She was from some place in Europe—Albania, Ukraine, Belarus, somewhere like that. She seemed very young, very frightened. No one could speak her language.'

'And Coco Potts?'

'She was in charge. She was the only person who was kind, but she was off her face a lot of the time.'

'She got some of you out.'

'Sort of.'

'What do you mean by that?'

'She sent four of us to live with the Egg Man—usually one at a time, though Gloria and Concepcion overlapped. To help care for his disabled sister, Coco said.'

Megan heard Phil's intake of breath.

'So the Egg Man was Trevor Farrow?' she said. 'And Nan Farrow was his twin sister?'

'I did not know they were twins.'

'Did Trevor Farrow rape you? Do you think he killed the girls who had gone to his farm before you—like Gloria and Concepcion?'

'No. Trevor liked to watch and to film. I don't know if he killed anyone. I didn't know anything about who did what to the other girls, just what they did to me. I hoped the girls had been moved on, but after a while, I began to suspect they'd been killed. No one ever told me anything and I knew better than to ask.'

'Did they know you spoke English?' Megan prodded gently.

'No. I kept that to myself. They were still careful, though. Didn't talk much in front of me, but it was a few things they said—I can't remember what exactly—that made me start to suspect that the other three girls were not just gone but dead.'

'You can't remember exactly? But generally?'

'It was when they talked about the *special* films. That's what they called them. And the way they complained about only having three. I started to get a feeling . . . I suppose I was lucky they said that much, even though it made me want to vomit. That's what made me so determined to get away, first chance I got.'

Megan felt a bit queasy herself, and desperately sad for the teenaged Siriporn who had found herself in such a horrifying place. Nevertheless, she pressed on. 'You said Trevor liked to watch. Who did he watch?'

'Sammy Lee and the other man.'

'The other man who looked a bit like the photofit of Zorro?'

Siriporn nodded. She looked exhausted. Megan sympathised. She felt a bit shattered herself, as well as confused.

Sammy Lee's involvement made little sense. Why take the girls to the boondocks to abuse them? Why involve Trevor Farrow and the other man? Although Farrow was how he got them out of the brothel. Farrow and Coco, of course. Was she involved? What was Coco not telling them?

'What did they do with the films?' Phil asked.

Siriporn shrugged. Her eyes were wet with tears. She dashed them away. 'Sold them, I suppose. I have lived in dread of one of them turning up on the internet.'

They'll be there, thought Megan, *but on the dark web*. She'd have to get the federal police involved to track them down. Fortunately the dark web was not a place Sara Stanhope was likely to visit. The films explained why Sammy Lee was killed. He was stealing girls from the traffickers; they'd never let that go unpunished. But why kill the girls? Surely they could have kept them alive and made endless videos? Or was murdering them the thrill?

How much of this did Coco know? Was she aware her half-brother was a serial killer? Was that why she had led them up the garden path? And how exactly did she put a stop to it? Megan took a breath, preparing to ask these questions aloud, when the door behind them opened. Samira Kumar was there, pulling an apologetic face.

'Sorry, Sarge, but can I talk to you for a moment?'

TWENTY

'I'm sorry to interrupt,' Kumar said when Megan had joined her in the corridor, 'but it's urgent. They've found another body.'

'*What?*'

Megan stared at her, trying to take it in. Another body? But if Coco's and Siriporn's accounts were true, only three girls were murdered. And hadn't Siriporn just told them that Coco had put a stop to the killing? So who the hell had they found?

'Another body?' she repeated incredulously.

Kumar nodded. 'But it's not like the others.'

'What do you mean?'

'Forensics is yet to confirm, but they think it's a man.'

'A *man*?' Megan was blindsided. 'Without forensics, why do they think that?'

'He's carrying ID.'

'And . . . ?'

'It's Sammy Lee.'

If there had been a chair handy, Megan would have sat down. She'd just been told Lee might be the killer, and now he was a victim. She'd known he'd been murdered, she'd been told that multiple times, but by the triad he worked for. Why would a crime syndicate mess around with burying him all the way up in Burraga Swamp? It made no sense.

'Are you sure? Ms Stanhope has just ID'd Sammy Lee as one of her abusers, and likely as one of the men who killed Gloria Ramos, Concepcion and Yulia.'

'Maybe it's not him, but whoever it is has been buried with his ID. How would someone else have that?'

Good question. Megan had no idea. 'Any clue yet as to how he died?'

'Josh said his skull was stoved in.'

'Different MO from the women.'

Megan was still trying to make sense of what she was hearing.

'A different killer?' she suggested.

'Or a different motive.'

Kumar made a very interesting point.

'Is Scotty on her way up to the SOC?'

Kumar nodded. 'Josh is up there already.'

'Can you get up there too?'

Kumar looked out the window and Megan followed her gaze. The sun was burning bright in the hazy sky. 'There's something else,' she said. 'A fire—in the Barringtons. It's a long way from Burraga Swamp, but . . .' She swallowed and straightened. 'Of course, Sarge,' she said.

'Detective Senior Sergeant Blaxland re-entered the room. Interview with Sara Siriporn Stanhope recommenced at eleven forty-two a.m.' Phil flicked record.

Megan had drunk a glass of cold water before she returned to the interview room. Despite the bombshell Kumar had dropped, she needed to stay calm and focused. She wanted to bombard Siriporn with questions, but Ms Stanhope was understandably shaky. She was a witness, but also a sexual assault victim—and hers was a particularly harrowing story, amounting to torture. Siriporn was traumatised and just hanging on emotionally. Hers was a past she had worked hard to bury and here they were, asking her to dig it all up again. She must proceed at Siriporn's pace, however impatient she might be.

'You are aware Sammy Lee is dead?' she said.

'Yes.'

'Are you aware how he died?'

'I just heard what everyone else heard, that it was a mob hit.'

'How did you feel when you heard he was dead?'

Siriporn looked at Megan. 'I felt . . . numb. I tried never to think about him or Coco or anything to do with that place or any of the people in it. It has always felt as if . . . as if it happened to another person.'

'Did you see the stories about the lyrebird and the discovery of the bodies in the Barringtons?'

Siriporn nodded.

'Did you see the shoelace and the photofits when they were publicised?'

Again, she nodded.

'You did not come forward?'

Siriporn shook her head.

'Did you think about coming forward?'

Another shake.

'How did you feel?'

'I was afraid. I worried that it would open it all up again—as it has. I was afraid I would get dragged back into a past I hoped I'd left behind—as I have been.'

'Yet you were the only person who survived. The only person who could tell the tale.'

'What good would that do? They were all dead. How would digging it all up again help anyone? And I knew it could badly hurt me.' Siriporn's voice was wobbly.

'It would help Luna Ramos, Gloria's daughter, and any relatives we may find of the other victims.'

Siriporn slumped in her chair.

'We need to find who the killer or killers are, if there was anyone else involved and if there were any further victims. It isn't up to one person—you or anyone—to decide that justice has been done. That's not the way the law works.' Phil was impassioned. It seemed to do the trick.

'I am not the only person who knows what happened. Coco Potts knows. After I told her everything, she told me she would put an end to it, and she did.'

'Do you know how?'

'No. I didn't care. I just wanted to leave all that behind and never think about it again. I'd done what I could. I couldn't bring back the women who were already dead. I just tried to prevent anyone else from dying.'

'Do you know who the other man who abused you was? Did he have a name?' Phil asked.

'Not that I knew.'

'Why were you wearing shoes that were too big for you when you escaped the Farrow farm and Mrs Lewis picked you up?' Megan asked.

'I nicked a pair of Nan's. They took my shoes as soon as I arrived. It was freezing at that time of year in that godforsaken place, and the road was stony and the bush terrifying. Trevor freaked me out about the snakes and spiders. He talked about them all the time. Keeping us barefoot was a very effective way to stop us running.'

'Who took your shoes?'

'Trevor.'

'Do you know what he did with them?'

'No. Once he had them, I never saw them again.'

'What about Nan? Do you think she knew what was going on? Was she an accomplice?'

Siriporn leant back in her chair and frowned. 'I don't know. Nan was always kind. When I cried she brought me tea and homemade biscuits and patted my hand. So I think she knew the men were being cruel to us, but how much she knew?' Siriporn opened her hands and shrugged.

'Was she afraid of the three men?'

'I think so. She avoided them.'

'Farrow too?'

'When the others were there, yes. When they weren't, no.'

'Do you think he hurt her or mistreated her in anyway?' Megan was frightened for Nan.

'I never saw any sign. They were close. It almost seemed as if he spoke her language. She fussed over him, almost mothered him, and he was very gentle with her. The way they were together made me feel almost crazy, given how brutal and indifferent he was with us. It was as if he was two people—good Trevor and bad Trevor—the Egg Man. It made it seem worse in a way—as if, because he could be so kind to his sister, it must be my fault when he tortured me.'

Samira and Josh were standing behind Scotty inside the tent that had been erected to protect the body. Scotty got up from her haunches with difficulty. Josh took a step towards her, but she waved him away.

'It's a man, all right. We'll need to get a DNA match before I can definitively ID him as Sammy Lee, but I'd say the chances are good.'

She arched her back. 'Sciatica giving me curry.'

Samira liked the seventies slang. It made the forensic expert seem less intimidating.

'I can smell bushfire,' Scotty said as she pulled off her gloves and wiped her sweaty hands on her overalls.

Samira looked up at the pink sky uneasily. She turned to Josh. 'How far away did you say that fire was again?'

'It's two valleys away to the west and the wind has dropped. The fireys are hoping they can head it off with some backburning and by bulldozing a few firebreaks between it and us, especially now it's getting dark.'

Josh is trying to sound confident, Samira thought, *but we are all jittery.* This was rainforest, he'd told her. It wasn't meant to burn, but it had been dry for weeks—for months, if you didn't count the one decent downfall that had revealed the grave. The unseasonal hot winds had sucked every drop of moisture out of the ground. The flooding rains from last year had turbocharged the undergrowth and litter on the forest floor.

Josh looked westwards and wiped his brow. 'Even so,' he said, 'they're worried. Nicko was telling us over dinner that they've never seen it like this before.'

Nicko was the brother who was a firey, Samira remembered.

'He told Mum to pack a bag and make sure she put all the insurance documents in it. He said that if the wind changes she might have to get out in a hurry.'

Samira looked at the rainforest around them. The understorey was thick with weeds. The ground was covered in dead leaves, fallen trees, bark and sticks. The decades of neglect were showing. There was one road into this place and one road out and it wound through the forest, lined with trees without a break, even once you got into the farmland. A raging inferno like the ones she'd seen on TV from 2019 didn't bear thinking about. *The powers that he had been worried enough then*, Samira thought. *They must be even more worried now.* That's why they'd sent those helicopters in a few weeks ago to put out the candles. In the past they'd just have left them to burn themselves out, Josh had told her. Not anymore. Too risky.

Scotty looked to the west and shrugged. 'No point in worrying about that now. I'll head back with the body, but I'll leave my team here to collect any evidence and clean up. Would you two mind giving them a hand?'

Samira knew they had to do as they were asked, but she didn't like it.

—

'Thank you, Ms Stanhope. We really appreciate you coming in, and we especially appreciate your candour. We know how difficult it must have been to revisit those days.'

'When will you want my client to return to do the photofit?' Siriporn and her solicitor were standing up, gathering their belongings.

'Could you return tomorrow?' Megan had asked Constable Kumar to make an urgent request for Bob. She'd sent a text to Megan telling her that he could manage to squeeze them in the next day, otherwise they'd have to wait a week.

'That's very inconvenient,' Siriporn said.

Megan could insist, of course, because it was a murder investigation, but she didn't like to—Siriporn had been through enough. 'I can imagine,' she said, 'but it would be very helpful.'

'What time would you need her?' asked the solicitor.

'Is after lunch manageable? Say two p.m.?'

Siriporn nodded and sighed. Perhaps she'd hoped the ordeal was finally over.

'Thank you for making the time.'

Megan received a wan smile by way of reply.

'We'll walk you out.' Megan and Phil didn't do that for every witness, but Megan felt Siriporn deserved that courtesy.

When they stepped outside into the car park, the hot air was heavy with smoke.

'Bushfire,' Siriporn said.

'Inevitable in this weather,' Megan replied.

They all stood and looked into the middle distance for a moment, breathing the heavy air.

'Thank you for your kindness,' Siriporn said, holding out her hand.

Had they been kind? Megan hoped they had. This woman had suffered. The way she had turned her life around was admirable. Megan grasped the proffered hand. 'It was a pleasure to meet you.' A cliché, but she meant it.

The car they drove away in was a top-of-the-line Beemer. Phil eyed it with ill-disguised envy.

'Nice,' he said.

'She's done well.'

'Should we arrest Trevor Farrow now?'

'I want to talk to Coco Potts again first. Check her evidence against what Siriporn has just told us. I don't want to arrest anyone until I have dotted every i and crossed every t.'

'You're not worried he might do a runner?'

'No. He doesn't know what we know.'

'But he'll know the case is live again. He'll know we've found the bodies. And he'll know the case is making national—and international—news . . . thanks to Professor Weston.'

'If he does do a runner, he'll be doing us a favour by confirming his guilt. No, I want to get the story straight in my head before we bring him in.'

'And you need Ms Potts to do that.'

'Yes.'

'But what about the third man? We still don't know who he is.'

Megan nodded. 'I don't understand why she tells us some things and not others,' she said as they walked back into the station.

'Don't you?' said Phil. 'I reckon it's obvious—she's got something to hide.'

TWENTY-ONE

The bar was noisy, but at least the air-conditioning was icy. Megan and Phil had found a booth at the back, where it was a bit quieter and they could thrash out their next steps without being overheard.

Megan had stopped Phil on impulse as he'd walked past her office. It had been a long day and she was tired, but she was also excited. They were closing in on the killers, of that she was certain. She was also worried about Phil and worried about the loose ends she was still unable to tie. One in particular—Coco Potts.

'Phil?' she'd called after him, slinging her bag over her shoulder. He'd stopped and turned.

'I know it's late, but do you want to grab a quick drink somewhere that's air-conditioned?'

It was 8 p.m. and dark, but still very hot.

'Great idea,' Phil said, grinning. It was touching to see him respond so eagerly but also disconcerting. His need for company was palpable.

Now Megan shuffled her bottom along the padded vinyl of the banquette, her sweaty legs sticking to the upholstery. She put her bag down beside her and looked at her old friend and colleague opposite. There were circles under his eyes, she noticed, and his hair needed a good trim.

'Is Clare expecting you home?' she asked.

It was as if a cloud had crossed his face.

'Clare's left me.'

Megan stared at him in shock. Phil and Clare had always seemed so solid. The sort of couple everyone envied—tight, jocular, no dramas, no histrionics.

'I am so sorry,' she said.

Phil nodded and looked down at his hands, palms flat on the table. 'A year ago now, but I'm still not used to it. Every time I go home I expect her to be there. Every time I get a shock when I realise she isn't. I hate going home.'

'Where has she gone? Is she really at her mum's?'

'She's moved to Sydney, near Judith. She needs some space, she told me. She wants to find out who she is.' Phil said the last few words in a high-pitched, whiny voice that made Megan uncomfortable. It sounded as if he was mocking his wife. A nasty little thought: *No wonder she left.*

'And how have Judith and Leila taken it?'

Judith and Leila were Phil's and Clare's grown daughters.

Phil shrugged. 'Okay, I guess. They're tight with their mother.'

Now Megan felt irritated. Phil sounded so sorry for himself.

'The unwooded chardonnay and the Heaps Normal?'

The waitress had brought their drinks. Megan took her chardonnay and raised her eyebrows at Phil's non-alcoholic beer.

'Once I start, I can't stop,' he explained. 'So I don't start. Not when I'm out, anyway.'

He's drinking alone at home, thought Megan. *Poor bugger.*

'No one else at the station knows,' he said. 'Can you keep it under your hat?'

'Of course, but you'll have to tell people eventually.'

'I'm still hoping she'll come back.'

Megan took a large swig of the chardonnay. Thank God they had the case to talk about, otherwise this evening would be heavy going. It was much easier to stick to the serial killer—or killers.

'Speaking of coming back . . .' Megan almost winced at her own segue. 'I want to interview Coco Potts again first thing. There's so much she's not telling us and I want to know what and I want to know why.'

'Like I said before, she's got something to hide.'

You'd know, thought Megan, realising she was being unkind.

'Do you think she's involved in the murders?' she asked. 'That she wasn't sending the girls to the back of beyond to help them, but knew what was going on? Perhaps she was getting a cut from the films they were making.'

Phil tilted his head to the side, considering. 'It's possible,' he said, 'but I don't think so. Something else is going on, something less obvious. If she was up to her neck in it, she wouldn't have told us as much as she has; she risked incriminating herself by putting us on to Sammy. And Siriporn has told us she trusted Coco. That means she never saw any sign that Coco was involved.'

Megan nodded at her partner. She liked this Phil much better than the sad sack from a few moments ago.

'Do you think Trevor Farrow killed Sammy Lee?'

'I don't know. I don't even know if Trevor Farrow killed Gloria, Concepcion and Yulia. Maybe Sammy Lee did. Or the third man. According to Siriporn, Trevor preferred to watch rather than participate. He doesn't sound like the ringleader, more like a dupe.' Phil's analysis was sound.

'What about Nan? She can't have been oblivious to what was going on. All those women coming and then disappearing, and Sammy and the other one.'

'Even Siriporn was confused about the part she played.'

Megan felt sad about Nan. This was not going to end well for her, and Megan couldn't help thinking she was more a victim than a perpetrator. 'What chance had she ever had, up there in the boondocks, with a psycho for a twin brother and no opportunity to escape or make a life for herself?' asked Megan.

'You've got to be able to speak to escape,' Phil said. 'Siriporn got away because she could speak English . . .'

'Nan was trapped from the very beginning because she could not,' Megan said.

'Why can't she speak?' asked Phil.

'I don't know; some kind of brain damage at birth, apparently. Perhaps a stroke that affected the part of her brain that controls speech.'

Phil nodded but said nothing. What was there to say? Instead, he returned to the matter at hand. 'All right, so our plan for tomorrow is to interview Coco Potts and find out what she's hiding.'

'What about Ms Stanhope and the photofit?'

'Hopefully we'll be back by then but, if not, Bob can take care of it. He's the expert.'

'It'd be good to be there. Even if just to say hello and goodbye and thank her for her time. This must be an ordeal.'

Megan had been unsettled by Siriporn's interview. It had been gruelling. And if she felt bad just listening to Siriporn's story, she couldn't imagine what it must be like for the woman herself having to relive it. She could understand why she'd tried to avoid getting involved again.

'She is very brave,' Phil said.

'When we talk to Coco tomorrow, we can check her story against Siriporn's. Then, we should have enough to arrest Farrow.'

'And he can tell us who the third man is, so we may not need the third photofit at all.'

'And then our work will be done.'

Megan felt a sudden wave of sadness. She thought about how Phil had livened up when they stopped talking about his marriage problems and went back to discussing the case. That was how it was for her too. She'd felt like herself again since returning to the job and she did not want to go back to being the half-alive person she had been ever since Guido died. She would miss all this more than she could say.

As if reading her mind, Phil said, 'I reckon Lisa would have you back in a heartbeat, Megsy.'

Megsy? Phil hadn't called her that since she'd returned. It cheered her. It was that feeling again, the one she'd lost when she'd left. That feeling of belonging.

'Do you think?'

'We're always understaffed and good detectives are hard to find.'

'Pie in the sky at the moment. We've got to put the case to bed first, and this one has a habit of blowing up in all directions. Let's wait to see what Coco Potts has got to say for herself.'

'I'll ask her to come in first thing tomorrow,' Phil said.

'You told us that you didn't know Siriporn is now Ms Sara Stanhope. Even though she is one of Australia's most sought-after corporate caterers, and her photo appears often in the media. You also admit you have been at many of the same events and may even have been introduced.'

Megan looked at Coco. Coco looked straight back. She did not even blink.

Coco looks as if she has dressed even more carefully than usual, Megan thought. Clothes as a weapon. She wore a sleeveless white linen dress. It was nothing like the floaty, vaguely alternative linen layers Siriporn favoured. Her dress was crisp and tailored and—despite its simplicity—looked like it had cost a fortune. Her only accessory was a long necklace of orange, red and pink beads. She looked spectacular, even though she must have risen at the crack of dawn to be here. Despite the heat, and the smell of smoke that had everyone in the station on edge, she looked both cool and composed.

Megan judged Coco to be about her own age and she had given up sleeveless dresses years ago, self-conscious about what her long-dead mother had always referred to as her cheerios. Coco's shoulders and upper arms were toned, hairless and honey-coloured. *How does she manage that?* Megan wondered. Money and time, she supposed, both of which Megan lacked.

'I did. And it's true.'

'She said she knew who you were.'

'Well, she would. I wasn't pretending to be someone else. I assume she was careful to keep her distance from anyone who might blow her cover.'

That made sense.

'She said she told you what was happening to the women you sent to the farm.'

'I told you that too.'

'She also said that Zorro—whom the girls nicknamed the Egg Man—is Trevor Farrow and that you knew who he was all along.'

'She did, did she?'

'She said she told you who he was and what he was doing, and that you promised to put a stop to it.'

'And I did. No more women were sent there from Pitt Street after Siriporn got away.'

'But that's because the brothel was raided soon afterwards and the girls who were still there were freed—'

'Then deported,' Phil interjected.

'—and you were arrested and eventually convicted for human trafficking. You spent the next couple of years behind bars.'

Coco said nothing but continued to meet Megan's gaze.

'Why didn't you tell us about Trevor Farrow when we first spoke to you?'

'Honour among thieves.'

'What?'

'I am Leonard Potts's child. It was drummed into me to keep schtum, never to name names. And I had left that life behind. I'd kicked my habit. Got a legit job. I didn't want any of it coming back to haunt me.'

'Bullshit.' Phil wasn't buying it.

'Believe what you want. I wanted you to catch them, sure, but I was worried that if I told you everything, I'd be putting myself in the shit.'

'It was not telling us everything that did that.' Phil was aggressive.

'You protected a serial killer.' Megan was calm, the good cop to Phil's bad cop. 'Three serial killers.'

'I'd stopped it. I knew he wouldn't kill again.'

'And the others?'

'I knew they wouldn't either.'

'How can you be so sure?'

'I said I'd put the triad onto them if they continued. That fixed it.'

'We could charge you with impeding a police investigation. You are legally obliged to tell us everything you know.' Phil played bad cop brilliantly.

'Do your worst. I told you everything I thought you needed to know.'

'It's not up to you to decide that.'

Coco shrugged.

Megan changed tack. 'Where was Sammy Lee when the police raided the brothel in Pitt Street?'

'I don't recall. I don't think he was there. He was probably tipped off. Half the police were being paid by the people who ran the place.'

'Why did the bribes stop working?'

'No idea. All that stuff went on behind closed doors.'

'Did you know that Gloria, Concepcion and Yulia had been murdered?'

Coco lowered her eyes. 'Only after Siriporn told me.'

'So you were lying when you pretended to be so shocked by their murders when I first told you about them?' Megan felt like a fool. What with the fudged photofit and now this.

'Only about the fact that I didn't know. Everything else about my reaction was very real.'

'Why did you lie?'

'I was afraid. I didn't want to implicate myself. Whether you think I am guilty of anything or not is immaterial. I feel guilty. Very guilty.'

'It is an offence to lie to the police.' Phil was angry.

'Charge me if you like.'

'Are you lying to us now?'

'No.'

But Megan no longer knew whether she could believe this woman or not. 'Were there any other girls sent to the farm who have not been seen since?'

Coco shook her head. 'Gloria, Concepcion and Yulia, that's all. I swear that's all.'

'All?' Phil's hand slapped the table.

Coco's head shot up. 'I don't mean it like that. I mean there was no one after Siriporn. No one.'

Megan put the hot-pink high heel on the table between them.

'You have already identified this shoe found on Boot Hill as yours.'

Coco nodded.

'You also told us you had no idea how it got there.'

She nodded again.

'You took it there, didn't you?'

Coco said nothing.

'If you didn't take it to Boot Hill, who did?'

She shook her head.

'You implied your half-brother, Sammy Lee, may have taken it. Siriporn has already told us that he visited the Farrow farm regularly.'

'I didn't imply that! You did.'

'Did you know that Sammy Lee was involved in abusing the women at Farrow's farm and filming them, we assume for pornographic purposes?'

Coco said nothing.

'Siriporn told you, and you told her you would put a stop to it.'

'And I did.'

'How did you put a stop to it?'

'I told you: I threatened to tell the Chinese—and then the raid closed the place down.'

The two women looked at each other. The tension between them was icy. Phil broke the impasse.

'We've found another body in Burraga Swamp.'

'Not possible!' Coco sounded genuinely shocked.

'It's a man's body this time.'

'A man? Do you know who?'

Sammy Lee was Coco's half-brother, Megan reminded herself. He might have been a sadistic criminal, but she could not assume that the news would not be a blow. She softened her tone.

'Coco, we think it is Sammy Lee.'

Coco jerked back in her chair as if she'd been punched. 'What makes you think that?'

'He was carrying Sammy's ID—but we'd like a sample of your DNA to make sure.'

'It can't be! Sammy was murdered in a gangland hit!'

'In Burraga Swamp?' Phil said. 'Very unlikely.'

'Maybe it's not him.'

'So how did he come by Sammy Lee's ID? Can you suggest another explanation?'

'No.'

'Hence the DNA.'

Coco held out her arm to Phil. 'Do you want to take a sample now?'

'No, before you leave is fine.'

'There are only three plausible suspects for Sammy Lee's murder. Trevor Farrow, the third man and you,' Megan said.

'Siriporn has told us a third man, whose name she did not know, was involved. Did you know about him?'

'It must have been Trev's friend. The one he said he was getting the other girls for.'

'Do you know who he was?'

Coco ignored the question. 'Or Siriporn,' she said. 'It could have been Siriporn who killed Sammy.'

That was a new theory.

'How would she have got rid of the body? She had no car. She didn't even have any shoes,' Phil said.

Megan, Phil and Coco all looked at the pink heel. Its flash looked garish beneath the harsh white light of the fluoro tube above their heads.

Coco reached towards her shoe. Megan caught her by the wrist. 'It's evidence.'

Coco put her hand on the table and stretched her perfectly manicured fingers. Her hands were large, but elegant. 'I hung it on Boot Hill,' she said.

'Why?'

'As a reminder to them that I knew what they were doing and that they had to stop it, or else.'

'Or else what?'

'Like I told you: I'd tell the higher-ups.'

'Not the cops?'

'No. They weren't afraid of the cops, but they were terrified of the triad. Sammy especially.'

'Why would the triad care?'

'They were stealing from them; they had bought the girls and therefore they owned them. They might not have minded a bit of porno on the side—as long as they got a cut, of course—but murder? Nah. Those girls were nice little earners. If someone wanted to murder them, they'd have to pay, and pay more than their so-called debt.'

'Did you tell the higher-ups?'

'No need. They didn't do it again and that's all I wanted to achieve.'

'Who was killing them? Was it Sammy? Trevor? Or the third man?'

'Could have been all three, for all I know. May as well have been.'

'Who was the third man?' Megan asked again.

'I don't know.'

'How could you not know? Didn't you speak to them all?'

'Yes. But I had never seen the third man before and I have never seen him since. No one told me his name and I didn't ask.'

'What did he look like?'

'A bit like Trevor. He was shorter and darker, but just as unkempt.'

'He didn't come to the brothel then, with Trevor?'

Coco shook her head.

'Was Sammy the ringleader?'

'You'd think he would be, wouldn't you, but I'm not sure.'

'Who was then?'

'The other guy. He thought he was the cat's pyjamas. All schmooze and greasy compliments. Maybe it was him.'

'Maybe?'

'Look, I didn't ask questions. I just went up there wearing my fuck-off-pink heels and read them the riot act. I didn't hang about to apportion blame. They were all a bunch of murdering psychos as far as I was concerned.'

'Why didn't they just kill you too?'

'I was armed. I'm not a complete fool. And Sammy knew I was a crack shot. Our dad taught us together. It was about the only time he paid us any attention. I had my gun trained on them the whole time. I scared the shit out of Trev and the other guy. Sammy didn't really believe I'd shoot him, perhaps, but he was crapping himself about his bosses.'

'And Nan?'

Coco leant back in her chair. 'That was weird. Here was this fucking sadist looking after his disabled sister. I mean, she made great cover. Who would ever suspect such a saintly, caring brother of being a sexually deviant serial killer? When I arrived at that house of horrors and she opened the door, sitting in her wheelchair looking like your aunty, I wondered if Siriporn had made the whole thing up.'

'Do you think Nan was involved?'

'I doubt it.'

'Do you think she was afraid too?'

'Yes, but not in the way you mean. She was completely dependent on her brother for everything and always had been. If she shopped him, what would happen to her?'

'So she just turned a blind eye?'

'I guess. But how could anyone know for sure? According to Siriporn she could understand but she couldn't speak.'

'Did you try to speak to her yourself?'

'I never got near her. Trev made sure of that. He wheeled her to the back of the house as soon as I arrived.'

'What else stood out to you?'

'Just how creepy it was. I spoke to them in the front room of the house. It was old but very neat. The furniture was ancient. All brown and murky, with faded floral patterns and greyish antimacassars. There was an old radiogram—pre-war, I reckon—and, I kid you not, a wind-up gramophone. The twins' parents' stuff, I suppose. The two of them had just left everything exactly as it was. There was a TV set on top of the radiogram but it looked pretty ancient too. God knows if it worked, way out there. It was like time had frozen.'

'You knew Trevor and Nan were twins?'

'Yeah. I can't remember how. I just did. Maybe Sammy told me.'

'Do you have any idea what happened to the films the men made?'

'No. I didn't go looking for them either. Once you see stuff like that, it sticks in your head.' Then Coco remembered who she was talking to. 'But you'd know that better than me.'

'Do you think they filmed the murders?'

'God! I hope not! That makes me feel sick.' Coco had gone pale.

'Then why kill them?'

'Got what they needed from each one and then got someone new. That market clamours for new girls. They couldn't let them go once they were done with them, so . . .' Coco ran her finger across her neck.

'They killed them to stop them talking?'

'It worked.'

'They could've just sent them back to the brothel.'

'No, they'd have warned the other girls. We'd have had a riot on our hands.'

'But one of the murders *was* recorded—just not by technology.'

'What do you mean?'

'Here . . .'

Megan had uploaded Jessica Weston's original video onto her phone. She wanted to see Coco's reaction.

Coco gasped when she watched the lyrebird throw back its head and mimic the woman's screams. She covered her eyes and gestured at Megan to stop the recording. Her distress was enough to convince Megan to hit pause.

'That was Gloria! Her voice, her accent, everything. I'd recognise it anywhere. It's as if she's speaking to me from the grave.'

'And what is she saying?'

But Coco just shook her head.

'Is she asking you to tell us the whole truth?' Phil leant forward, slapping his hand on the table again.

'I am!'

'I don't think you are. Just like you weren't before. You're holding something back.'

'No. Why would I do that?'

'Did you kill Sammy Lee?'

Coco gasped for a second time. 'No, of course I didn't. He was my baby brother. I loved that little boy. I hated the adult Sammy most of the time, but I could never harm him.'

'Yet he harmed you. He got you addicted to heroin, then made sure you stayed addicted and would commit crimes for him and keep quiet about his activities in exchange for your next fix.'

'I played my part in becoming an addict. I wasn't exactly unwilling. And he gave me good stuff. By doing that he kept me alive.'

'The better to do his bidding.'

'He may have lived to regret that.'

'Or died regretting it.'

'I didn't kill him. I have never killed anyone.'

'You certainly helped feed him victims that he then killed. That might make you want to kill him.'

'I didn't know what they were doing. I thought I was helping those girls. As soon as I found out what was really going on, I put a stop to it.'

'There'd have been no more effective way to stop it than kill the ringleader.'

'As I've already told you, I don't think Sammy was the ringleader. And I didn't need to kill anyone to put the fear of God into them, so why would I? I'm not a psycho!'

The atmosphere in the room was palpable. Coco was breathing hard, her hands gripping the edge of the table. She made an effort to calm down.

'Anyway, if I had killed him, I'd have shot him in the back of the head, execution-style, to make sure it looked like a gangland hit.'

'How do you know that's not how he was killed?'

'I don't. I didn't kill him, so how could I know? But as you haven't shown any interest in the fact that I had a gun, I gathered that was not how he died.'

'What else don't you know?'

'Lots of things. I was wasted most of the time. But I'd have remembered if I killed someone, especially my last living blood relative.'

—※—

'Thank you again, Ms Stanhope. We realise how difficult this must be for you.'

Megan was walking Siriporn to the car park for the second time in two days. Their star witness had spent the last hour or so working with Bob, putting together the third and final—Megan hoped—photofit. Megan also hoped it would prove unnecessary and that Trevor Farrow would identify his accomplice when they arrested him in the morning, as they planned to do.

As Sara Stanhope's BMW disappeared out of the car park, Megan looked down at the photofit in her hand. *Fingers crossed Farrow spilled the beans,* she thought. The photofit Siriporn and Bob had created looked to be about as useful as the one Coco and Bob had made of Zorro.

She walked back into the station and made her way to Kumar's cubicle. It was empty, so she put the flyer on her desk and scrawled a quick note on a post it: *This is the photofit of the third man care of Siriporn. Not sure how helpful it will be but hopefully we'll crack the case tomorrow without it. I'll also email you the soft copy. Send it around anyway. Thanks.*

Megan went back into her own office and logged on to her computer. She had a lot of paperwork to do before the morning.

An hour later, after Samira had returned from the canteen, she looked up and watched as Megan turned out the light in her office and closed the door behind her. It wasn't that late, but the older woman looked tired. The interview with Coco Potts had been lengthy and, Samira imagined, intense. She'd looked at the new photofit when she'd returned to her desk from the canteen, and she'd felt her boss's pain. They were all still wondering who the third man could be. They'd had a great result with the photofit of Siriporn but not a single hit for the hairy bloke, and now they had another hairy bloke. It could be anybody. Haircuts and beards were the easiest things to change.

'Goodnight,' Megan said from the door onto the corridor. 'Don't stay back too late. It's going to be a big day tomorrow.'

Samira nodded and waved. Then she went back to the photofit she had now uploaded onto her screen. She took a long hard look at the face of the man behind the heavy beard, zooming in and out, closely examining his features. She had an inkling that there was something familiar about them, but she could not put her finger on it. Then, a thought struck her. She stared intently at the man's eyes. Was there a resemblance? Or was it just wishful thinking? She ran her hands through her own thick, dark hair. An idea. What if? It was a long shot, but she emailed Bob. After she'd identified herself and the case she was working on, she wrote the following: *I know it's late, but I wonder if you could do me a real favour. Could you adjust the attached photofit, the one you did for us today, by removing every skerrick of hair from his face? Not just hair and beard, but eyebrows and eyelashes, the lot, and then send it back to me. I need it tonight, if at all possible. I'll be waiting by my computer, no matter how late. So sorry to spring this on you at such short notice, but I reckon it might be the key to the whole case. Thank you in advance, etc.*

To her astonishment and relief, she received a reply almost immediately.

Sure, that shouldn't take long. It's an interesting case.

Samira could not believe her luck.

I owe you a very expensive bottle of your favourite tipple! she replied.

She was tempted to kiss Bob's email on the screen, but restrained herself, not that there was anyone around to see. They'd all gone home. She knew she might be in for a very long wait, but she didn't care. She was elated. This was the kind of police work she had always wanted to do, and relying on a suspect to identify another suspect felt a bit dodgy to her.

Samira waited for an hour or so, drinking coke and eating chips and lollies from the vending machine. The canteen had long closed. She scrolled through Facebook and played endless games of solitaire on her computer. She was weary and bored and had begun to wonder whether she was on a wild goose chase. She was sick of sitting over a silent inbox, hoping Bob was a man of his word.

Ping! went her computer: *You have one new message.*

She opened it and saw a face in front of her that was unmistakeable. She emailed it immediately to Josh Baker. *Do you see what I see?* she wrote.

—

Coco sat on her balcony, a glass of wine in her hand. It was evening and as she had driven home she had noticed the brilliant orange sun hanging low over the sprawling suburbs to the west. Now, the last of its pink and orange rays stretched out in front of her. The glowing colours were reflected by the harbour, inflaming the east all the way to the horizon. To the north was another sunset, a strip of shimmering light illuminating the darkening sky. It reminded Coco of a movie she'd seen once. One of those movies where they want to tell you fast that you are on another planet. Two sunsets will do that.

But Coco was not on another planet. Everyone in Sydney, everyone in the world, knew what the strip of shimmering light to the north was. It was bushfire.

A pigeon flew onto her railing and scratched under its wing with its beak. Many of the residents hated the pigeons roosting on their balconies, because of the poo and because they were believed to carry lice. Coco liked the birds; she liked all birds, even the bin chickens that scattered rubbish all over the streets as they dug around for food. She liked how they survived in a man-made environment that should've been hostile to them. Maybe she had a sense of fellow feeling.

The pigeon hopped onto the rock in the birdbath that she kept in the corner of her small slice of city skyline. With a quick, smooth movement the bird immersed its head, chest and wings in the water, fluffing its feathers. She sympathised. It was still hot, oppressively hot, and many Sydneysiders were seeking relief with a quick dip, so why not the pigeon? It hopped back onto the rock and preened itself. Then the bird flew away, silhouetted against the fading light.

Coco got up and walked to the birdbath and reached into the water. It was warm, having been in full sun all afternoon. She turned the rock over to cool it. She did not want the birds to burn their feet. It was a black river rock and it held the heat. It was smooth and heavy. Very heavy. She'd found it at Burraga Swamp but now it lived here and provided a landing place for the feral city birds. Coco smiled to herself. It had always been a useful rock, wherever it had lain. She wiped her wet hands on the front of her jeans. What was it her father had always told her? Never leave any incriminating evidence.

She sat back down on her comfortable chair and drained her glass. However slow and sleepy her movements, however still she sat, however she tried to distract herself with thoughts of birds, sci-fi movies and lessons from childhood, it was an act. Coco was tired. It had been a long day. She'd stopped off at the brothel for a few hours on her way home from Maitland. Saturday nights were busy. She couldn't just not show. She was also agitated. All of Sydney was agitated. Not only did the smell of bushfires permeate every building, no matter how hermetically sealed, but burnt gum leaves were everywhere, even here in deepest Potts Point. They fluttered like black snow onto every surface.

But her agitation was caused by more than the fires. The police interview had been an ordeal, worse than she'd expected. She had experienced emotions she'd not felt for a long time and had kidded herself she was immune to—shame, fear, guilt, humiliation. She was ashamed of her association with a knuckle-dragging low-life like Trev Farrow. She felt besmirched, as if his blackness and sleaze had rubbed off on her, leaving a filthy residue, like the burnt leaves. It was as if by speaking of them, she had breathed them in. But it was worse than that. It had been a real shock to discover that Sammy's body had been found at Burraga Swamp. Bloody Trev; she'd relied on him to handle the business discreetly. All he'd had to do was get rid of the body. He didn't have the brains he was born with.

Alone on her balcony in the gathering dark, Coco let herself cry.

A splashing in the birdbath. Coco turned to see a sparrow waggling its wings in the water, the drops falling on its little, wriggly, urgent body. A vivid image of small Sammy giggling and tumbling in the bath almost made her cry out in pain. It was dark now. The glow to the north was intense and sinister. A siren in the street below pulled her back into the present. She got up and went inside.

TWENTY-TWO

Jessica's phone buzzed. It was Sunday morning and she was luxuriating in the lovely liminal state between waking and sleep. Who would call her at this hour? She rolled over, intending to ignore it, then started to worry that it might be Sheridan. She'd called her daughter a few times over the weekend but Sheridan hadn't picked up. She did that sometimes, when she was mad with her mother. Jessica was sick of it and had stopped calling. Two could play at that game, and perhaps not being so needy had paid off. Jessica unplugged her phone from the charger beside her bed with a small feeling of triumph. Maybe she was learning how to manage her difficult daughter at last.

She looked at the caller ID. Not Sheridan. It was a message from *Hazards Near Me*. She opened it. Fires had been popping up all over the Hunter and Central Coast over the last few days. Things had calmed down a bit since the wind dropped last night and most were now 'being controlled' according to the app, but there was a new one near Cessnock, not far from where Sheridan's dad, Steve, lived. Then she heard the wind rattle the old window; it must have picked up again. She checked the weather. Another scorcher and the fire danger classified as catastrophic for the third day in a row. Maybe she'd better give Steve a call, just to make sure he was aware and prepared.

'Have you seen there's a fire up past Kurri Kurri?' Jessica asked him, when he answered.

'Yeah. Just popped up on the app. It's a fair way away yet.'

'Just thought I'd let you know.'

'You're not usually so concerned about my welfare.'

They'd divorced amicably enough, a long time ago, but they didn't have a lot to do with each other. Steve was a viticulturist for one of the posher vineyards in the Hunter, she always forgot which one, and a nice enough guy. They just didn't have much in common except Sheridan.

'Don't get any ideas. It's because you've got Sheridan with you.'

'I don't have Sheridan.'

Jessica felt her stomach drop through the floor.

'What do you mean? She left me a note Friday afternoon saying she was coming to your house for a few days. She said she needed a break.'

'I'm sorry, Jess, but she's not here. I haven't seen her for at least a couple of weeks.'

'Where the fuck is she then?'

Jessica's stomach returned to its usual spot. Now she felt furious. What stupid game was her wayward daughter playing this time?

'Don't panic. Maybe she's at a friend's house.'

'I'm not panicking—I'm ropeable. Why do I keep falling for her bullshit?'

'Mind you, with all these fires, I don't like not knowing where she is.'

Steve had a point. Jessica didn't like it either.

—

Sheridan woke in the semi-dark. There was no window in the cellar, but light came through the gaps in the floorboards overhead. Either someone had a light on, or it was morning. For a minute, she forgot where she was. The realisation, when it came, was sickening. She felt the fear rise in her gut. For a moment or two she thought she might vomit. There was a disgusting smelly toilet with no seat in the cellar, directly in the line of sight of the camera, but she was busting, and fear had turned her bowels to liquid. She had to go. She grabbed the stiff and scratchy blanket off the bed and used it to cover herself as she sat on the loo, draping it over her head, slumping forward so it covered her knees. She could not bear the thought of the gravelly voiced man and whoever else was up there watching her.

Her parents would be looking for her. She was certain of that. Her mum was a panic merchant; she'd call the cops for sure. Sheridan felt a rush of love and gratitude for her mother. Her father was great fun, but not much use in a crisis. It was her mum she could rely on to come and get her. All she had to do was keep her head, be brave and wait.

There was no toilet paper to wipe her bum. She looked around for something—anything. There were some newspaper clippings on the noticeboard, but they were too far away. And she'd have to walk past the camera to get to them. In the end, she tore the cuffs off her shirt. Disgusting but necessary. She tucked them in behind the base. She might need them again. The toilet flushed, thank God. She waited till she heard the cistern fill, then lifted the lid and swished her hands about in the water. As she went back to the mattress, she noticed a smell, and it wasn't anything to do with the nasty toilet. It was a familiar summer smell. She sniffed. Bushfire. Fear rose again in her gut. She was locked in.

She walked over to read the clippings on the noticeboard. What she saw made her cry out. Every clipping was about the lyrebird murders. Story after story. There was the photo of her mother at Burraga Swamp, looking stiff and uncomfortable. Next to it the one of that policewoman and her mum at the bar with their mouths hanging open. There was even the photo of her from the School Students 4 Climate Action demonstration. Her name was circled in the caption underneath. That made her stomach lurch. She took them down and stuffed them in her pocket. Evidence, she told herself. Sheridan meant to survive.

—

Jessica spent the morning calling all of Sheridan's friends whose numbers she knew, then got them to give her the numbers of other friends. She even called School Students 4 Climate Action, wondering if they'd cooked up some foolhardy stunt to take advantage of the fire crisis. Nobody knew anything. Jessica was aware that teenagers lied easily to cover for one another, and she tried to comfort herself with that thought, but she didn't like the concern she heard in their voices. She didn't think they could fake that. There was a tight, gassy feeling of fear in her belly that she was finding hard to reason away.

Instead, she sat by the TV, watching the ABC report on the increasingly disastrous situation as the hot wind changed direction, flinging the huge and catastrophic fires back towards the villages and townships of the valleys that ran like splayed fingers from the Barrington Tops. She kept trying to tell herself that Sheridan could not possibly be in the vicinity. That she was much more likely in Sydney, hanging out in a squat or something. Did they still have squats? Jessica had no idea. But no matter how much common-sense self-talk she did, her anxiety would not be quelled. She knew Sheridan would have rung her when she saw the news about the fires. Sheridan was a pain in the arse, but she was fundamentally a good person. Her rebellion wasn't about drugs or sex or anything like that. It was about fighting for action on climate change! By that measure, the kid was a saint, not to mention a chip off the old block.

By early afternoon, as reports of evacuations and properties being threatened intensified, Jessica could sit still no longer. She decided to call Megan.

'*Hello, you've called Megan Blaxland. I can't come to the phone right now. You can leave a message after the tone or, if it's an urgent police matter, call Maitland Police on . . .*'

Was it an urgent police matter? Or just a bolshie teen off with her mates on the weekend? Jessica wasn't sure. She left a message.

'Sheridan is missing, Megan. I thought she was at Steve's, but she isn't. We don't know where she is. I'm frightened.'

Megan had driven into work that morning with a clear plan of action. She and Phil would go and arrest Trevor Farrow and bring Nan in for questioning, though what they'd get out of her was hard to say. Megan felt genuinely concerned for Nan. The identity of the third man still nagged at her, but she comforted herself knowing that Trevor Farrow would give him up and then the case would be closed.

As she got closer to the station, however, she began to worry that her nice plan was about to be derailed. ABC Local Radio was wall-to-wall fire emergency. The wind had picked up overnight and the day was going to be another scorcher. Evacuation notifications were going out everywhere, including in the Barringtons. She had a feeling every available copper was going to have their hands full getting people out rather than bringing anyone in.

As she walked through the glass doors, her fears were confirmed. The foyer was full of uniforms pulling on their high-vis and grabbing patrol car keys. She spotted Kumar and Baker and made a beeline for them.

'What's happening?'

'The whole shift has been seconded for fire evacuations and road closures. Josh and I are headed up to Gresford. That fire in Mount Royal is looking seriously scary.'

Kumar sounded breathless. Megan could see she was pumped on adrenaline. Judging by the racket around them, it seemed everyone was.

'We've got to make sure everybody gets out. Traffic control will be the main job.' Baker was calm. 'It shouldn't take long. Most of the locals are either members of the Rural Fire Service and out cutting firebreaks or they're well aware of the need to get the hell out. Mum's already evacuated. She had everything packed days ago and she's just rung me from my aunty's in Maitland. That's what most people will be doing.'

'We still have to make sure.' Kumar's voice sounded less certain.

Baker shrugged. 'We can't force them out and there are always a few die-hards.'

Bad choice of words, Megan thought.

'If you come across Trevor and Nan Farrow take note of where they go,' she interjected. 'I'm just finishing the paperwork on the warrants for their arrest.'

'Nan too?'

Megan nodded. 'Bring her in for her own safety.'

'What about him?' Kumar thrust the new photofit at her boss. Megan looked at it, puzzled.

'Who is this?'

'It's Siriporn's photofit with all the hair removed.'

'It's Leo Blake to the life!' Baker said. 'Samira is a genius!'

'Bob did it for me yesterday. I hope that's okay.' Kumar was suddenly worried she'd gone over her boss's head.

'Alopecia . . .' Megan said, the light finally dawning.

'That's my hunch,' Kumar said.

'Bring him in too.'

'For questioning?' Kumar asked.

Before Megan had time to reply, the shift sergeant called for everyone's attention. The uniforms had to go, and they had to go now. Megan nodded furiously at the two young coppers, hoping they would get the message. Kumar was swept out with the crowd, but Megan could see her looking back, her face a picture of fear, confusion, but also excitement. Megan felt a pang of anxiety. Fires were dangerous and she knew Kumar was afraid of them. But she'd be okay, she assured herself. *She's a good cop. A brilliant cop*, she thought, as she looked down at the revised photofit she held in her hands. *We've got you. Job done.* Then she was jostled by the phalanx of coppers heading out into the car park. She'd lost sight of Kumar and Baker.

There was traffic everywhere. People who had been evacuated but had no friends or family to shelter with were streaming into Maitland. They'd be looked after in school halls, sports centres and other public buildings. Jessica didn't envy them. It'd be hot and tedious and who knew when they could return home or what they might find when they did? *We are all at the mercy of a vengeful climate*, she thought, then a picture of a terrified Sheridan filled her mind's eye and she had to bite her lip hard to make the vision fade. Too impatient to wait for Megan to call back, she'd decided to go to the police station herself. If the mountain would not come to Mohammed . . .

A police car screaming past pulled her back into the present. She had lost count of the number of cop cars and fire trucks she'd pulled over to let pass, their sirens turbocharging her already jangling nerves. She'd seen fire seasons before, but nothing like this. How was she going to get anyone to pay attention to a missing fifteen-year-old, and how was anyone going to find her? She was very afraid now. Sheridan would have called her with all this going on. She wasn't heartless. She would have called—if she could. And there was something else, a thought niggling at the back of her mind. She had lost her mother, suddenly and violently. She was not going to lose her daughter in the same way. Then a further chilling thought. It wasn't just the fires that threatened. There was a serial killer on the loose out there too. A serial killer who probably knew who she was and who Sheridan was.

A car stopped suddenly in front of her. Jessica slammed on the brakes and leant on her horn. She had to get to the police. She had to get to Megan. If anyone could save Sheridan, it was her. The traffic in front was at a standstill. She couldn't see what was causing the problem. She dialled Steve and, this time, she was in a panic.

'Any news?' he asked.

'Meet me at Maitland police station.'

'Is that really necessary?'

'Have you seen what's going on? It's chaos. There's no way Sheridan wouldn't have contacted us to let us know she was safe.'

'Or maybe she thinks we're both still blissfully ignorant that she's missing at all? Maybe she thinks her ruse has worked.'

But Jessica wasn't buying it.

'Either our daughter is a cold-hearted bitch who would let her parents go through hell while the world is burning down, or she . . . or she . . .' Jessica could not form the words.

'Or she what?'

'It's just . . . my name has been in the papers . . . they call me the Lyrebird Lady . . .'

'I saw.'

'And Sheridan's name has been mentioned too. The killer is still out there as far as we know, and maybe he's put two and two together . . .'

'Calm down! The serial killer thing is just silly. The case is twenty years old! Whoever the killer was is either dead or long gone.'

'The cops think he's still out there, and with my face and name all over the papers . . .'

'It's a cold case. Cold. They call it that for a reason.'

'I'm not going to waste time arguing with you. Meet me at the cop station.'

Steve had hung up. Jessica dialled her daughter for the hundredth time.

'Hey, this is Sheridan. Don't leave a message. That's sooo boooring. I'll call you back when I see the missed call. If I want to talk to you, that is. BYEEEEEE!'

'Sheridan, where are you? Your father and I are frantic and I'm on my way to the police. If you are at a friend's or something, don't worry, you're not in trouble, just call me. I just want to know you're okay . . .'

Jessica stared at her phone, willing it to ring, willing Sheridan's familiar number to pop up on the screen. Nothing happened.

The traffic in front of her was still stationary. She could not put up with it any longer. She wrenched the steering wheel to the left and mounted the kerb. Then she slammed the car into reverse, did a U-turn, and screeched off in the opposite direction. She'd find another way.

Sheridan continued to walk around the cellar. She needed to act normal. There was one spot where the lens of the camera could not follow. She upended one of the packing cases and sat on it. It was a relief to know she could not be seen.

A squeak of the floorboards above her head froze her blood. Was someone coming down? Were they intending to do something to her? Something awful? Her blood started pumping and her heart raced. She was glad she was invisible to the camera as she fought to gain control. Panic was not helpful. She needed her wits about her. She followed the sound of the weight on the floor above as it moved. But it wasn't footsteps she could hear. It was wheels. There was someone up there wheeling something about—was it a suitcase, a wheelbarrow? Was that where they intended to hide her body? She put her hands across her mouth to stifle the scream that was bubbling up from her guts. Then the wheels moved away. They were no longer above her. They had moved deeper into the old house. Maybe there was someone in a wheelchair up there. That thought creeped her out even more.

Jessica ran into the police station. Steve was already standing at the counter talking to the cop behind the screen. He turned as she came through the automatic doors. All around them was bedlam. People in high-vis coming and going; dirty, exhausted, sobbing people reporting someone missing.

'Any word?' Steve asked. 'Anything from Sheridan—her friends?'

Jessica shook her head and burst into tears. The rush of fear was so great she could not speak. She had to struggle to hold herself together.

'Is Megan Blaxland here? I want to speak to her. She's . . . she's . . . we know each other . . .'

'She's here,' said the cop, 'but she's asked not to be disturbed.'

'Tell her Jessica Weston is here and that Sheridan is missing. Tell her I think the lyrebird killer has got her.'

She didn't care if they all thought she was a lunatic. If sheer force of emotion was what it took to get Megan out here, then she had more than enough. Why she had suddenly been gripped by the dread that the lyrebird killer had Sheridan, she did not know—but no matter how hard she tried, she could not let the idea go.

—

Megan was busy sending pictures of Leo Blake and Trevor Farrow out to police around the state, when the constable on the front desk called through to say that Jessica was in reception and why. Megan hesitated. She was flat out. They had serial killers to catch. She turned towards Phil, who was ploughing his way through a pile of paperwork.

'Jessica Weston is in reception. Her daughter is missing.'

'Tell her to file a missing person's report,' Phil said, not taking his eyes off his screen.

According to the rules, Phil was right, but still Megan hesitated. Instinct told her otherwise.

'The last time we ignored Jessica Weston, it didn't turn out well,' she reminded him.

Phil shrugged. 'On your head be it.'

'I'll listen to what she has to say. You stay here and finish all this.' With a sweep of her arm Megan encompassed the paperwork they needed to complete before making the arrests, and the evidence they were compiling for the DPP.

Megan hurried to reception. She felt torn, but she ushered Jessica and Steve to an interview room away from the chaos, reminding herself of how worried she would have been if Jason had ever gone AWOL. 'How long has Sheridan been missing?' she asked, once they'd all sat down.

'Almost two days, but we only realised this morning,' Jessica replied. 'She told me she was going to Steve's, and I thought she was there.'

'So the last time you saw her was when she told you she was going to her father's?'

Jessica shook her head. 'The last time I saw her was when she left for school that morning. When I got home that afternoon I found a note.'

Jessica scrabbled in her tote and pulled out a crumpled bit of paper. It looked like it had been torn from a school exercise book.

Megan smoothed it out. 'Did you check if she really had gone to her dad's?'

Jessica flushed. 'I know I should have, but I was so angry with her. We'd been fighting for days—weeks! I was glad she'd gone to Steve's, glad to see the back of her—but only for a few days. She's gone to stay with him heaps of times before. I never dreamt that she might be . . . might be . . .' But Jessica could not finish the thought. 'I spoke to her on the phone that afternoon and she said she was at the bus stop.'

'Do you know which one?'

Jessica told her.

'We'll send someone to take a look,' Megan said, but how she would find anyone—and when—she wasn't sure.

'I tried to ring her again a few times, but she never picked up. She's done that before and it infuriates me. I decided two could play at that game. I know I should have kept trying. I know I should. I wish I had . . .' She was wailing now.

'What makes you think the lyrebird killer took her?'

Megan reminded herself that Jessica had no idea who their suspects were. Why would Trevor Farrow or Leo Blake want to snatch Sheridan Weston? It made no sense.

'He's out there, isn't he?' Jessica said. 'Still on the loose? And our names and faces have been all over the news, all over the papers about these murders. Hardly a day goes by without another story. And Sheridan's name is out there too because of that fucking climate demonstration. Who else would it be?' Jessica leant forward. 'She'd have rung me, if she could, with all these awful fires. She'd know I'd be frantic. She'd have rung me . . .'

'You were angry with your daughter. Was she angry with you?'

'Of course. Almost constantly.'

'Maybe she's run away? That seems a likelier explanation than . . . the lyrebird killer.'

'Could he have her?' Steve asked.

'I still can't see why he would snatch Sheridan, even if he knew who she was.'

'He's a fucking serial killer! Does he need a reason?' Jessica was frantic.

'I don't know. But if he did, what would it be?'

'Revenge. He'd got away with it, hadn't he? Killed them all two decades ago and no one had even missed them, until me and my bloody lyrebird.'

Megan took her point, but it seemed like a long bow.

Jessica put her hand on Steve's shoulder. 'I'm so sorry, Steve,' she said. 'This is all my fault.'

'What do you mean?'

'I should have given her your surname when she was born, like you wanted. That way he'd never have known—she could have had her picture plastered all over the place and he'd never have known she was anything to do with me.'

'Now you're being silly. How were you supposed to know this might happen?'

'I think you're both getting ahead of yourselves,' Megan said. 'We don't know what's happened to Sheridan. I still think it's most likely she's run off somewhere and will reappear once she's cooled down.'

'Can we do an appeal?' Steve leant forward. 'Ask Sheridan to get in touch and let us know she's okay, or ask if anyone saw anything or knows where she is? If she was kidnapped'—Steve swallowed hard, as if the word was stuck in his throat—'somebody must have seen something.'

Megan felt stricken. Ordinarily an appeal would be a great idea, but in the middle of a fire emergency? With all this drama and people missing all over the place?

'I'll let all the police who are out doing evacuations and traffic control know to keep their eyes open,' Megan said. 'I'll text them her photo. Have you brought one?'

Jessica opened the photo app on her phone. 'How many do you want?'

TWENTY-THREE

Sheridan had stopped trying to be brave. She was terrified. She sat huddled on the sticky mattress, her legs pulled up to her chest, and rested her head on her knees. The cellar was heavy with smoke. She'd taken her shirt off, dunked it in the cistern and—after putting it back on—pulled it up over her face. The moist cloth acted like a filter, which helped her to breathe a little easier. Above her head she could hear the wheelchair squeaking backwards and forwards across the old floorboards. She could also hear whoever it was—a woman, she thought, and that was comforting—coughing. The smoke was getting to her too. *Why won't the woman let me out?* Sheridan wondered. Surely they hadn't brought her here to let her burn in the fire or choke to death on the smoke? And if it was a bushfire, surely the firefighters would come to try to save the house, and then they'd find her and save her too.

And—another hope—maybe there was a storm coming. She could hear the almost continuous rumble of thunder. A storm meant rain, and rain would put the fire out. All she had to do was wait, she reassured herself, just keep breathing and wait. But no matter how sensible she tried to be, every time she thought about being locked in, she was hit with a wave of black panic. If the fireys didn't come, if the person upstairs didn't unlock the door, if it didn't rain in time, if her mum didn't come . . . That was when she began to scream.

Sadie Lewis was locking up the East Gresford post office when Josh and Samira pulled up outside.

'They've told us to get out,' she said unnecessarily.

Samira nodded. They'd passed a steady stream of traffic heading towards Maitland since they'd left Bolwarra. They'd had to pull over as the occasional fire truck roared past with its siren blaring, but no ambulances, thank God. All she and Josh had to do, according to their briefing, was check on any people who had decided to stay and fight or who, for some reason, had not been able to evacuate.

Sadie looked over her shoulder towards the Barringtons. The sky was black above the Tops, except for a huge orange-and-red glow ringing the distant forest. The postmistress turned back to the two young coppers. She seemed suddenly small and uncertain.

'I've never seen it like this,' she said. 'We've had fires before, of course we have, but never like this. It's the noise . . .' She stopped and they all listened. It was a low rumble, a sort of steady, menacing bass, like a lion preparing to roar. 'Can you hear it?'

'Never heard anything like that before,' Josh said. 'It's . . . creepy.'

'Do you have somewhere to go?' Samira asked.

Sadie gestured towards her car. They could see it was stuffed with belongings, like so many of those they had passed on the way.

We've become refugees in our own country, thought Samira.

'I'll go to my sister's in Newcastle,' the postmistress said. 'Surely we'll be safe enough there?' It was a question, not a statement.

Josh smiled. 'If Newcastle burns,' he said, 'it really is Armageddon.'

For some reason—perhaps it was that low roar—his remark was not as reassuring as it ought to be.

'Do you know if there's anyone staying behind?' Samira asked.

Sadie shook her head as she opened her car door. 'I don't know. From the look of the cars going past, everyone that wanted to get out has done.'

'What about Nan Farrow?' Samira asked. 'Do you know if she got out?'

Sadie looked stricken. 'I don't know. I can't remember seeing her—and Trev will be out fighting the fires with all the other volunteers. I don't think anyone expected the wind to change the way it has . . .'

'We'll check,' Josh said, closing the driver's door behind her. 'You don't need to worry.'

Sadie wound down the window. 'Be careful,' she said. 'Your mother would never forgive me if anything happened to you.'

'We won't do anything stupid. Tell Mum I'm okay.'

The postmistress nodded and waggled her fingers at them through the driver's window as she accelerated away.

Of course we will check, Samira thought. It was what they were here for. It was their job. But she suddenly felt nauseated. She swallowed hard, determined not to let Josh see how shit scared she was. No use looking for Trevor, he was out there somewhere. Samira looked back up at the ring of fire. She didn't envy anyone up there, no matter what they had done.

'Should we tell a firey where we're going?' she asked.

'Bugger just telling them. We'll get some of them to come with us. It's their job as much as ours to make sure everyone's accounted for. Lives first, properties second.'

Another fire engine rounded the corner at speed, its siren blaring. Samira almost jumped out of her skin.

—

The smell of smoke on Masseys Creek Road was so pungent it brought tears to Samira's eyes and scoured her throat. The heat would have been unbearable if she'd had the time to notice it. Her police shirt and high-vis were soaked with sweat and covered in black marks; it was raining burnt and burning gum leaves.

'The fire is heading this way,' said the firey behind the wheel. 'The Eccleston blokes were out all last night bulldozing containment lines. Usually that'd hold it, but with this bastard . . .' The man shrugged.

'Do you know if all the houses got checked?' Josh asked.

He was sitting in the front seat of the fire truck while Samira sat behind him with the other firefighters. Samira was glad they were there—she felt safer in this vehicle, surrounded by these men and women—but she still didn't feel remotely comfortable. Every burning gum leaf freaked her out, and there were hundreds of them, especially as they got closer to the fire front. Even though it was not yet midday, it was so dark that the rig had its headlights on.

'They should've been,' said the woman sitting next to Samira, 'but it's impossible to know for sure. No one told us there was a disabled woman living way out here, otherwise we'd have made her a priority.'

'Her brother probably got her out. He's her carer,' Samira said.

'He's also a volunteer firefighter, so he might not have been able to get to her. Most of the Gresford fireys have been out all night too.'

A suspected serial killer and a volunteer firefighter: Trevor Farrow was a mystery wrapped in an enigma. It was on the tip of Samira's tongue to tell them that he was the main suspect in the lyrebird killer case, but she stopped herself. He hadn't been charged.

'How many houses down this road?' asked the driver as he turned from the bitumen onto the dirt.

'Five or six,' Josh said.

'We'd better check them all. We've brought some equipment for anyone who has decided to defend their home.'

Stay and defend their home against this? Samira thought. The low rumble had grown to a full-throated growl.

But the place seemed deserted. House after house was empty, with sheds and outbuildings closed and locked up, but front gates, fence gates and paddock gates all open so stock were able to roam. A cow loomed up at them through the heavy smoke. The firey behind the wheel pulled the rig sharply to one side, ramming into a ditch. The cow looked at Samira through the window, its eyes shining in the dark, then lumbered off into the gloom.

'Everyone okay?' asked the driver.

They were, and after a couple of spins of its back wheels, the rig reversed smoothly onto the road.

'One good thing about this weather,' Josh said with grim humour. 'No chance of getting bogged.'

—

A loud bang on the cellar door. Then another and another. Sheridan jumped at the sound. She heard a voice, a woman's voice, calling out. Sheridan couldn't understand what she was saying. Maybe she was speaking another language. 'IBID! IBID! IBID!' was what it sounded like. Nevertheless, the words galvanised her. Coughing through the smoke, her lungs feeling like they would burst, she ran up the stairs and banged on the door in reply.

'Let me out! Let me out!'

The woman banged back, softer this time, mimicking Sheridan's rhythm. Sheridan replied—call and response using fists. They repeated the action. It was comforting for a few moments, then Sheridan lost patience. Why didn't the woman open the door and let her out? She hammered on the door again and screamed.

'Open the door! Open it now!'

'Ibid, ibid!' the woman on the other side said.

Then Sheridan heard the rattle of a bolt and chain and the door shaking. Sheridan understood. The woman could not open the door. They were stuck here together. Sheridan slumped onto the top step. It was harder to breathe now. She could see the smoke curling through the floorboards, but she could not bear to go back down into the cellar. She wanted to be near the woman on the other side of the door. If she was to die that day, she would not die alone.

TWENTY-FOUR

Maitland police station was shut tighter than a drum and the air-conditioning was labouring manfully. Megan looked up at the outlet above her desk. They still had power, thank God. It'd be like an oven in here if they lost it. The smell of smoke clung to everything. She swivelled in her office chair and looked through the window across the car park. On a clear day, she could see the dark blue of the Barringtons in the distance. Now she could just make out the top of the office buildings a couple of streets away. She felt anxious, especially about her colleagues who were out there. She knew Kumar and Baker would be heading right into the thick of it to do their job, and she was worried for them. Cops didn't usually die in fires, a distinction that belonged to firefighters, but that didn't mean they couldn't. And these fires, as every radio announcer and TV commentator kept repeating, were unprecedented. Megan was sick of the word.

Jessica and Steve had refused to go home. They were sitting in the tearoom. At least it kept them out of harm's way. Megan still felt it was unlikely that Trevor Farrow or Leo Blake had snatched the girl—after all, why would they?—but a missing teenager in the middle of this chaos? The fire made finding anyone daunting. She had put out an all-points bulletin with a photo of Sheridan throughout New South Wales and was still hopeful that it would bear fruit. She'd had a lot of luck finding people via images recently.

Mostly, however, she was frustrated. Yesterday they'd cracked this cold case wide open, and she'd been all stirred up, ready to make arrests, but the fire emergency had put paid to that. She'd asked Phil to find out where Farrow and Blake were likely to be during a bushfire. His last update had been over an hour ago. He'd told her that Farrow was a long-time member of the Gresford Rural Fire Brigade. Apparently, they'd been out all night bulldozing containment lines to try to protect property and livestock. They weren't due to be relieved for a couple of hours.

'Couldn't you get in touch with them?' she had asked him.

'No, they're out of radio range. The one black spot in all of New South Wales during these fires. The fireys are spewing. Until they come back, no one knows what's going on up there.'

'Or even if they're alive.'

'Exactly.'

'I wouldn't put it past Farrow to die fighting a fire and be hailed as a bloody hero!'

Phil snorted. 'That'd be just our luck.'

'When they do get relieved, where will they go?'

'They'll head to their fire station.'

'Is that where we'll find him?'

Phil had shrugged. 'Maybe.'

'And Blake?'

'Who knows, in this chaos? He's not a volunteer firefighter, apparently, so he's probably been evacuated with everyone else.'

'Where would he go? To a relative? A friend?'

'No idea. He could also have gone to any number of evacuee stations. Looking at his social media and searching his profile, he doesn't appear to have many relatives or friends. He's going to be harder to find.'

'Bloody hell, as if this investigation wasn't complicated enough.'

And that was the last she'd heard. Megan got up off her chair. She'd make a cup of tea. Nothing else to do.

Jessica sat forward on her chair as Megan entered. 'Any news?'

'Not yet.'

'Do you have people looking?'

'I've sent the photos around.'

'Why aren't you out there?'

'I wouldn't know where to start.'

'Find the lyrebird killer and you'll find her.'

'You don't know that.'

'Do you know who he is yet?'

Megan did not know how to answer the question.

'You do, don't you?'

'We have a suspect, yes.'

'Let's go then. Let's go get him.'

'You can't come.'

'There's no way you're leaving me behind,' Jessica said, standing up.

'Or me.' Steve stood up too.

Megan gestured for them both to sit down. 'At the moment, we're not going anywhere.'

'We?'

'Senior Sergeant Arlott will come with me . . . when the time comes.'

'And if you find Sheridan?'

'We will bring her back to you. I promise.'

'You still think she'll come back on her own steam after having had a wild weekend in the big smoke.' Jessica sounded teary.

'I hope so.' But Megan was no longer certain. Why was she expecting a serial killer to act rationally? Jessica's point about him seeking revenge because she'd blown his perfect crime apart had unsettled her. And the fire gave Farrow or Blake—or both of them—the perfect alibi. They could do what they wanted with Sheridan, then toss her body into the flames and no one would ever be any the wiser. The thought made her feel ill. She looked at the clock on the wall. She couldn't sit around drinking tea any longer. She'd get Phil and the two of them would head up to the Gresford fire station to await their suspect.

'Go home, Jessica. I promise I'll let you know as soon as there is any news.'

—

As the fire rig lurched up the rutted driveway to the old weatherboard house, Samira looked at her phone. *SOS only*, it said. There was never much reception out here, she knew that, but the electricity must also be down. The time was 12.30 p.m. yet it could easily be midnight. The sky had gone from a whitish grey to a dirty brown and now it was going black. Without her torch and the fire rig's headlights, she couldn't see an inch in front of her.

The fire truck pulled up outside Farrow's, but the driver kept the engine running. The only thing Samira could see was the line of fire up above them, deep in the hills, glowing red and orange against the black. Above it was a swarm of helicopters, identifiable only by the lights that blinked on their fuselage and tails. It was a scene from a movie, not real life.

'Here,' said the woman who had been sitting next to Samira. 'Put these on.'

She handed Samira a breathing apparatus, which Samira had only ever seen in American disaster movies. This was serious.

A plane flew low above their heads. They could just see its lights through the gloom. A huge gush of water, like a dam releasing its spillway, fell onto the fire front. The flames shrank under the onslaught, then sprang up again as tall as skyscrapers. The wind in front of the line of fire was blowing burning embers towards them—sticks, leaves, evil red lumps of God-knew-what. Samira was relieved to have her rubber mask, but Christ, it was hot.

The woman handed her a protective jacket. It was heavy and far too big, but Samira had never felt more grateful for anything.

'This way,' Josh said, leading them through the dark, past the rusted gate. His voice was muffled by his heavy mask.

Josh banged on the front door. 'Nan! Nan! Are you in there?'

How they could have heard any kind of answer over the howling and roaring of the fire, Samira could not imagine. Terror made her push past Josh and wrench open the door. It was not locked. Inside it appeared empty. Samira stood still for a moment and listened, sweeping her torch from side to side. Nothing. Everything was still. Had it been a wild-goose chase? Had they risked their lives for no reason? As embers blew through the open door, the woman firey slammed it shut and stomped on anything that glowed. The rest of the crew had stayed outside. Samira could hear them hosing the house down already. Once the door was shut, she could hear a faint sound from the back of the house, almost like a cat mewling. That's when Samira realised she had not heard the chained dog barking. Was it dead or had it gone?

'Hear that?' she said to Josh and the firefighter.

She didn't wait for an answer but took off down the hall in the direction of the sound. Even if it was just a cat, at least they could rescue that poor creature.

The house was bigger than she'd realised. It rambled along corridors and through room after room, as if it had been added on to at a whim. Samira came to a fork in the narrow corridor. She stopped, wondering which way to go. It felt like she was in a nightmare. Pitch black, the way lit only by torchlight, with smoke swirling about choking them all—and it was her job, her responsibility, to find the right path.

Then she heard it.

'Ibid, ibid.'

It was hardly more than a whisper, but it was enough to guide her. She rounded a corner and there was Nan, slumped over in her wheelchair, her head resting on a small door. A door that was bolted and padlocked. *She must have got confused trying to get out*, Samira thought immediately. Samira gestured for Josh and the others to stay where they were. Fire or no fire, she would walk up to the older woman quietly. She pushed her mask onto the top of her head so Nan would know who she was. She squatted down and put her hand on the older woman's spindly wrist.

'Nan,' she said, smiling, 'we've come to get you out of here.'

Nan blinked, as if waking from sleep. *Smoke inhalation*, Samira thought. *We arrived just in time.*

Then the woman shook herself free and began to bang loudly on the door. 'Ibid! Ibid! Ibid!' Her voice was whispery and croaky from the smoke but there was no mistaking her terror.

'It's okay, Nan, it's okay. We're here to get you out and take you to safety.'

Her words made no difference. Nan was still babbling frantically and reaching beseechingly towards the locked door.

'No, no, you're confused,' Samira said soothingly. 'That's not the way out.'

Josh stepped forward and took over, wheeling Nan back the way they had come.

'See, here's Josh. You remember Josh? He's here to help get you out.'

But Nan was not to be placated. She was sobbing now and pointing frantically back into the bowels of the house. *She's completely lost it*, Samira thought.

'She seems very upset about something,' Josh said, looking over his shoulder. 'Are you sure we shouldn't go back and check? Maybe there's a cat or something back there.'

Samira stopped and hesitated. She'd wondered about a cat . . . And where had the dog gone?

But there was no time to think.

'We've got to get out of here fast!' the firey yelled. She grabbed the wheelchair from Josh and began to run out the front door, towards the rig, Samira and Josh running along behind; Nan was still screaming and crying and reaching back towards the house.

―

Sheridan banged on the door hopelessly. She knew that the people had gone. She knew they could not hear her due to the fearsome roar of the approaching fire. She did not know why the woman in the wheelchair had not told them she was there. She coughed. It was harder to breathe at the top of the stairs. She looked down into the cellar, but she could not bear to go back there. She put her head in her hands and closed her eyes. She had done all she could do. What happened next was not up to her.

―

'It's going to be bloody awful at Gresford,' Phil said, looking out of the window as Megan backed the police four-wheel drive from of its parking space.

'Probably, but what else can we do?'

Phil said nothing and began flicking through the paperwork they had brought with them, making sure for the tenth time that everything was in order. Neither of them noticed the car parked on the side of the road as they exited the gates. Neither of them noticed when it pulled out and began following them down the road.

TWENTY-FIVE

In the foyer, people were yelling and arguing and jostling one another, demanding attention. Samira was doing her best to reassure Nan, who was still weeping. She had probably never been in a place like this in her whole life. No wonder the poor woman was bewildered. She was a bit quieter now though. Perhaps she'd worn herself out. She was probably in shock.

'Karen will look after you,' Samira said. She scanned the crowded foyer looking for the social worker they had called as soon as they had signal. All she could see was cops.

Josh came up to them. He had a copy of the revised photofit in his hands. 'Nan,' he said gently, crouching down beside her, 'was this one of the men who did bad things to your carers?' He held it in front of her.

She looked at it, her eyes wide. Then she looked back at Josh and nodded furiously. She stabbed at the picture with her finger, over and over, as if she wanted to stab it to pieces.

'Thank you,' Josh said. 'Leo Blake?'

She nodded again, and made a noise, halfway between a snarl and a growl. It was an expression of disgust. Then she touched Josh's hand and reached up to do the same to Samira's. Once she had their full attention, she gestured over her shoulder again, as she'd done in the burning house. Now she was motioning towards the car park, in the direction from which they had just come. She put her hands together as if she was praying, beseeching them.

For what? Samira wondered. Forgiveness?

'It's okay. We know you could not do anything,' said Josh. 'And we are going to catch them. Thanks, in large part, to you.'

This did not seem to comfort Nan at all. She groaned and shook her head, over and over, as if they were refusing to understand her.

'Here she is,' said Samira as a smiling woman came up to them.

'You must be Nan. I'm Karen,' the woman said as she grasped the back of the wheelchair.

'Ms Nan Farrow,' corrected Samira.

The social worker ignored her. 'I'll make sure you see a doctor, and get a good hot shower and anything else you may need.'

Samira hoped that Nan would be all right for now, though she did not like to think about what might happen to her next. She wasn't going back to her old life, that was for certain.

Nan looked up at the woman bending over her with the kindly smile and closed her eyes. Then she cried out. A sound so desolate it made Samira want to cry too. Maybe she was suffering from shock herself.

'Baker! Kumar!' The duty sergeant was barking at them from the desk behind the screen. Such was the shortage of available cops he was manning reception.

Exhausted as she was, Samira felt the adrenaline surge. As long as they didn't have to go back towards that monstrous fire, she didn't mind what they were asked to do.

—

She couldn't sweat. It was the first thing Megan noticed. It was incredibly hot, but the humidity was non-existent. She'd heard people talking about nostril hairs freezing instantly in extreme cold. This felt similar but at the other end of the temperature spectrum. Whatever it was, it felt weird—but then, everything about heading towards a bushfire, when every instinct told you to turn and run, was weird. The road and the farms were devoid of people, sure enough, but the birds and animals had gone too. Everything that could escape had escaped.

But it wasn't silent. It was the opposite of silent. The fire created its own hellscape of noise. The wind was howling around them, seeming to gust from every direction. With it came waves of sparks, spiralling orange against the dark. They had parked the car outside the Gresford fire station, but neither Megan nor Phil made a move to get out. Out meant all that. Megan looked at Phil and he looked at her. Then he undid his seatbelt. Nothing for it then but to plunge into hell and make for the safety of the station.

The RFS knew they were coming. Megan had made the required phone calls to the Gresford chiefs as a courtesy but also because she thought they might need help taking their man into custody. He'd been fighting this fire for who knew how long. It would be understandable if his comrades didn't take kindly to one of their own being arrested.

Just as Megan took hold of the doorhandle, the car radio crackled. None of their phones worked anymore—power out and Telstra down, no doubt; it was a miracle the police radio was still operational. Megan gestured for Phil to stay put, then she grasped the handset.

Lisa George was on the other end. All hands at the pump.

'Can you hear me, Megan?'

'I can hear you!'

'Baker and Kumar have got Nan Farrow out. She's on her way to Maitland hospital.'

'Is she all right?'

'She's in a state. Hardly surprising, given she must have thought she was trapped and abandoned in that fire.'

'Was there anyone else in the house?'

'Do you mean her brother? He's out fighting the fires apparently.'

'No one else? Leo Blake?'

'No sign of him yet. He's probably in an evac centre somewhere. According to Baker and Kumar, it's apocalyptic out there. No one in their right mind would stay a second longer than they had to.'

Megan looked around her at the smoke, the dark and the flying embers. Were they in their right minds?

'One good thing,' the inspector continued, 'Nan has positively identified Blake. We have enough to arrest him.'

'And Nan's all right?'

'Physically, yeah—a bit of smoke inhalation, that's all.'

'We're about to arrest Farrow.'

'Take care of yourselves. The fire is a monster.'

'We're at the Gresford fire station. We'll be right.'

'Good. But no heroics.'

'It's me you're talking to.' And Megan ended the call.

'Sarge?' Phil sounded alarmed.

Megan looked up. A man was emerging from the smoke. It was Trevor Farrow, walking towards them in his firefighter's kit. He was filthy and covered in smut and soot. She opened her door. The heat smacked her in the face so hard it took her breath away.

'Trevor Farrow?'

The man stopped and stared at them as if he had only just noticed the police car. His face looked peculiar. He had a towel or an old-fashioned cloth nappy tied around his neck. He picked it up and wiped at the muck coating his features. All he managed to do was smear the grime even further. His eyes were red-rimmed and sore-looking.

'What do you want?'

'Trevor Farrow?' Megan repeated. She was out of the car, standing in front of him. 'You are under arrest for the murder of Gloria Ramos and two other as yet unidentified women. You are also under arrest for the murder of Sammy Lee. You do not have to do or say anything . . .'

As Megan cautioned him, the man continued to stare at them blankly, as if trying to make sense of what was happening. Phil walked towards him with handcuffs. The sight of them seemed to bring Farrow back to life. He began to back away.

'I can't waste time with this bullshit. I have to get Nan! She's still at the house.'

Before Phil could take a step, Farrow took off at a run and disappeared into the smoky dark.

'She's not there! We've got her!' Megan shouted. But she couldn't see the man at all and didn't know if he had heard her. Then she heard a car door slam. It could only be Farrow's.

'Fuck!' She wrenched open her own door. 'Get in!' she yelled at Phil.

—

The hall at Maitland Grossmann High was packed with people. Josh and Samira's job was to keep order. Many of the refugees from the fire knew each other and they sat in ragged clumps, villagers with villagers, farmers with farmers and valley-dwellers with valley-dwellers. Josh seemed to know everyone sitting in the Gresford group. They bombarded him with questions. Mostly they wanted to know about their neighbours and their homes. Samira hung back, feeling oddly shy. She didn't know these people, not the way Josh did. She envied him his sense of belonging. Instead, she looked at the assortment of people sitting around them. Families clutching dogs, cats and kittens sat on school chairs eating the sandwiches being handed around by volunteers. One boy was guarding a fish tank holding a huge diamond python; a girl clutched a struggling chicken. Mothers soothed babies and an older couple in the corner sniped at each other in whispers while they drank coffee from a thermos. Everyone seemed grumpy. *And who can blame them?* Samira thought. They were uncomfortable, exposed and anxious. A man moving through the crowd caught her eye. There was something familiar about him, something about the way he wore his hat. She wondered who it was, then he turned, and she saw his face.

'Josh, Leo Blake is over there.'

He looked in the direction she was pointing.

Blake turned and saw them. He stood still, then acknowledged them with a nod.

'He doesn't know there's a warrant out for his arrest,' Samira said.

'Good. It'll make it all the easier then.'

They walked towards their suspect, taking their time, smiling back at him as if all they intended was to shoot the breeze.

'Hello, Mr Blake,' Samira said.

He examined her from top to bottom. Especially bottom.

'How's my house?' he asked.

Samira was taken aback. 'I don't know.'

Josh stepped forward. 'Leo Blake, you are under arrest for the murders of Gloria Ramos and two other as yet unidentified women.' Josh snapped a pair of handcuffs on him.

People nearby began to mutter. Someone picked up their phone and took a photo—or maybe a video, Samira couldn't be sure.

The smile dropped from Blake's face as if Josh had slapped it.

'What . . . but . . . no . . . I . . .'

Josh expertly steered the man towards the exit. People moved aside to let them through.

'Maybe he's the arsonist,' Samira heard someone say.

The crowd suddenly buzzed with anger and tension. Samira could almost see the rumour fly around the room. They needed to get Blake out of there fast, but she did not want to leave an angry crowd unsupervised. They were desperate for someone to blame. The arrest in such circumstances gave them that someone.

'String the bastard up!' A voice from the back of the crowd.

As angry people pressed in around them, blocking their passage to the door, she saw panic on Blake's face. Samira stepped forward, putting herself between him and the crowd. It was their duty to protect him, no matter what he had done. She moved forcefully towards the main protestors. It was a strange feeling to watch them drop back.

'Let us do our job,' she said to them.

Josh took his baton out.

'I'll call for replacements,' Samira said to him, reaching for her radio and speaking into it urgently. They couldn't leave all these people here unattended. She could feel the increased tension crackling around them like an electrical storm.

Her radio buzzed. To her relief, she heard the despatcher.

'Urgent assistance required at Maitland Grossmann school hall. All units in the vicinity, assistance required.'

As if in answer, she heard a police siren. Relief flooded through her. The crowd turned their heads towards the sound. She could almost feel the tension begin to recede.

'Throw the book at him!' a red-faced bloke yelled at her as the crowd parted to let them through.

We intend to, thought Samira, *but not for arson*.

'There's someone behind us.'

'Good,' said Phil. 'It'll be the fireys. We need all the help we can get.'

The drive was hellish. The wind was tearing branches, sticks and whole boughs from the trees that lined the road. The heavier ones thumped onto the police car's roof. Some sounded so loud they made Megan and Phil duck instinctively. They could not see the potholes but did not dare to slow down, so the car lurched and shuddered and bashed its way north. Megan turned on the siren to let Farrow know he had no hope of getting away, but also to warn any fire trucks or people attempting to flee (surely there was no one left now) that they were coming. The siren was as good as useless, she knew that, but it was the best they could do. Burning embers kept hitting the windscreen. It was like driving through the worst hailstorm, except the projectiles were made of fire, not ice.

When they turned into Farrow's rutted drive, they caught a glimpse of his car's tail-lights ahead of them and accelerated.

'SHIT!'

Megan slammed on the brakes. A huge tree had come crashing down across the driveway, missing them by inches. Smoking leaves were touching the front of their bonnet.

'We'll have to go after him on foot!' she yelled, breathing hard.

'Are you sure?'

'We can't just leave him, whatever he's done. He can't get out now. He's trapped. Forget about arresting him, we're rescuing him.'

'A fucking serial killer!'

Phil was right. Megan knew he was right, but this serial killer thought he was rescuing his disabled sister. Regardless, she had a duty of care for anyone in her custody and he was under caution. On top of that, sheer humanity meant you didn't leave anyone out and unprotected in a bushfire, no matter who they were. And if the fireys were behind them they'd be here any minute to help.

'He's under arrest. We have no choice.'

'He fucking escaped! His responsibility!'

'We need to hear his story. We need to be certain about the facts.'

Megan got out of the car and so did Phil. It was even more chaotic and terrifying than the scene at the fire station. The sky had turned black, and the fire seemed demonic, bellowing at them across the narrow valley behind the house.

'Pull your shirt over your mouth and nose!' she yelled, as she did the same. God knew if it made any difference.

They inched their way around the fallen tree by torchlight. Flying embers were smouldering on the tree but it wasn't alight, thank God. The smoke was tearing at their throats and their voices were hoarse from both breathing and yelling. In seconds, Megan's eyes were watering copiously, but it felt as if her tears were made of acid. Sparks and embers rained down on them, stinging like needles.

They pushed through the rusty gate and saw that the front door of the house was wide open. Farrow must have gone in. The house had not yet gone up but there were spot fires in the grass and bushes around it. It looked to Megan's inexpert eye as if it might ignite at any moment. Both Phil and Megan stopped, uncertain about what to do next. Neither of them wanted to go in. Then, to their considerable relief, Farrow emerged from the dark of the hallway. He was carrying someone in his arms. A girl by the look of her. He looked at the two cops, then put her down. *Jesus Christ*, thought Megan. *Nan's gone, so who is this?*

'It's the Weston girl!' Farrow yelled.

Fuck, thought Megan. *Jessica was right.*

'Leo Michael Blake, you are under arrest for the trafficking and murder of Gloria Ramos and two other women. You are also charged with the trafficking and rape of Sara Siriporn Stanhope and the murder of Sammy Leonard Lee.'

Josh was reading the charge sheet. Arlott and Blaxland were both still out, chasing Farrow up in the Barringtons, so Samira and Josh had to do the interview. Samira was nervous. Ordinarily, interviewing a suspect accused of a crime this serious would have been way above their pay grade, hers in particular. Samira had hoped they could put him in a holding cell and wait until the others returned, but the cells were already full. Police had been arresting looters, suspected arsonists and those who in their fear and frustration had let fly with a punch or two. Inspector George had told them to interview him.

'Just a formality,' she'd said. 'But no bloody defence lawyer can fault us for interviewing him after his arrest when his alleged accomplice and two of our officers are still out there, in the fire.

We need to know what he knows.' The Inspector had begun to walk away. Then she'd turned and smiled at Samira. 'And, as it was your excellent police work that identified Mr Blake, I reckon you've earnt first crack at him.'

Josh gave his partner a gentle congratulatory punch on the arm, but Samira just looked at the floor. She hoped she was up to it.

It's an opportunity, Samira told herself, *not a threat*. She looked at the man across the table. He was smallish, wrinkled, brown and almost completely hairless. He looked like a walnut. A sinister, hostile walnut. The lack of eyelashes and eyebrows made him look almost otherworldly. Or was that just her anxiety playing tricks?

He seemed smug now rather than panic-stricken, but at the mention of Sammy Lee, Blake lost his cool. 'Sammy Lee! What the fuck? I didn't murder Sammy Lee!' He caught himself. 'Or anyone else. You've got the wrong bloke.'

He sat back and folded his arms across his chest. The duty lawyer whispered something in his ear.

Not the sharpest tool in the shed, Samira thought, feeling a little better.

'You've got me mixed up with Trevor Farrow. He's the man you want.'

'Trevor Farrow is currently being arrested,' Josh said.

We hope, Samira added silently. They had not heard anything from the two sergeants. Samira felt a little tick of fear for their safety at the back of her skull. She pushed it away. Formality or not, what she and Josh were about to do required all her concentration.

The man sitting opposite stared at them defiantly. 'Trev's out fighting the fires,' he said.

'We had to rescue his sister,' Samira said. 'He'd left her alone in the house.'

Blake showed no emotion. His eyes were flat and blank, like a reptile's. 'What's that got to do with me?'

'Nan's a witness. She has already identified you.'

'She's retarded! Can't say a word that anyone can understand.'

'She can still nod and point,' Josh said. 'That's enough for identification and a line-up.'

'And Nan's not retarded,' Samira said hotly. 'She's just as smart as anyone.' *Smarter than you*, she thought, but held her tongue.

'We know that you, Farrow and Lee filmed the abuse you inflicted on the women you trafficked,' Josh said.

'I don't know what you are talking about.'

'We have found some of those films already. We will find more. You will be identified.' Samira looked at Josh. She was unaware that they'd actually found any footage yet. Was Josh trying it on? If so, it was working.

Blake shifted in his chair. 'You can't prove it was me.'

'I am sure that we can, but we don't have to. One of the women you kidnapped and abused escaped. She has also identified you as one of the men involved.' Josh was emphatic.

'She's lying!'

Another warning look from his solicitor. 'Or mistaken.'

'We can put you in more than one line-up. Our witness has already agreed to participate.' Samira was all business.

'We also have the testimony of the manager of the brothel where you sourced the women, who, when she realised what you were up to, put a stop to it.'

'That drug-addled ladyboy! I wouldn't believe a word that pervert says. I bet she—he—whatever was up to her fake tits in it.'

'We have a very strong case. A victim who can positively identify you, film evidence and an eyewitness who is happy to testify. I would advise you to tell us everything you know. I can't promise you any kind of leniency. Given the seriousness of the charges, you are facing a long jail sentence. However, judges tend to look favourably on offenders who cooperate. Frankly, Mr Blake, it's the only hope you've got.' Josh sounded as if he interviewed serial killers daily.

Blake snorted in disbelief. Reality had not hit him yet, but it had hit the lawyer.

'Could we take a break? I'd like to have a private word with my client.'

—

Megan ran to the verandah. It was Sheridan all right. Megan checked for vital signs. Unconscious, but still alive. Phil was beside her, trying to get signal on his radio. Farrow stepped back into the dark hallway.

'What the fuck is she doing here?' Megan shouted at the man disappearing into the house, but he ignored her.

'Nan!' he cried out. 'Nan!' He sounded as if he was choking on tears, but maybe it was the smoke.

'She's not in there!' Megan yelled. 'She's safe. My officers took her away an hour ago.' *And missed the girl*, she couldn't help thinking. She looked up at the man hesitating on the threshold. Farrow had kidnapped Sheridan, but Farrow had also saved her.

Despite the deafening roar of the fire, Farrow had heard her. She saw him turn. *Thank God*, she thought. *We have to get out of here, and now.*

'I don't believe you!'

'Why would I lie? She's safe. I promise.'

Farrow hesitated. Phil stepped towards him. Megan just had to hold Farrow's attention for a few more seconds . . . Then Sheridan groaned and her eyelids fluttered. Megan broke eye contact with the man and looked at the crumpled girl she was half-cradling in her lap. Sheridan had to be her first priority. She owed Jessica that. Phil could deal with her kidnapper.

Megan stood and pulled Sheridan's arm across her shoulders. The girl coughed and muttered something. She must have been half-conscious because she wasn't a dead weight, thank God. They began to move slowly away from the house, avoiding the spot fires that were already taking hold in the unkempt grass.

A sound of smashing glass drew Megan's attention back to the house. The heat was causing the windows to explode. Farrow was standing in the doorway. Phil had hit the deck and covered his head. Farrow didn't so much as flinch.

'My house!' he wailed. 'My parents' house. My father built this house with his bare hands. We've lived here all our lives. Nan! Nan!' Then he ran through the front door.

Phil sprang up and ran in after him.

Shit! thought Megan. She couldn't help him, not with Sheridan. What the fuck would she do if he didn't come out?

'Phil!' she yelled, as loudly as she could.

Should she put the girl down and go back? She looked around for a safe place to leave a semi-conscious fifteen-year-old. Everything around them was either burning or looked like it was about to.

'Give her to me!'

Like an apparition, Jessica appeared out of the black and the smoke. She took her daughter into her arms and hoisted her into a standing position. Megan was struck dumb. She could not believe what she was seeing.

'Jessica?' she said stupidly.

'It's all right,' Jessica was saying as she began to walk her daughter away from the fire. 'I've got you.'

'I knew you'd come, Mum. I knew you would.'

'Get Arlott!' Jessica yelled over her shoulder, and her command shook Megan out of her stupor. She did as she was told, running towards the burning house as fast as she could.

To her profound relief, Phil appeared in the doorway, gasping but still clutching his shirt over his mouth and nose.

'I lost him. The back of the house is on fire. You can't see an inch in front of you, and I can't get a breath!' His skin was white below the grime, and he was breathing in great wheezy gulps.

Megan hesitated. Should she go in after Farrow?

The duty solicitor looked up as Samira and Josh re-entered the interview room. 'My client has agreed to answer all your questions, however, he wants to make it clear that he has lived a blameless life for the past twenty years and he knows nothing at all about the murder of Sammy Lee.'

Josh nodded. Samira looked at the man they had arrested. He still radiated hostility. But he was also afraid. The lawyer had done his job.

'Mr Blake, you admit you were involved in the trafficking of Gloria Ramos, Sara Siriporn Stanhope and the other two women, who we believe were known as Yulia and Concepcion?' Josh said.

Blake gave a stiff nod.

'Can you say "yes" for the benefit of the tape?'

'Yes.' His response was almost inaudible.

'Louder, please.'

'*Yes!*'

'You admit you raped them multiple times and filmed those rapes?'

'I admit nothing. I want to plead the fifth.'

His lawyer nudged him.

'You are not in the USA, Mr Blake. There is no fifth amendment. You do have the right to remain silent, as I explained when I cautioned you. However, your lawyer has just told us you intend to answer our questions.'

'I've changed my mind.'

'You admit you were involved in their eventual murders?'

'I didn't kill them. Trev did that. He took them off to that mosquito-infested swamp and did them in. Then he buried them. That was his job.'

'Why did he kill them? Why didn't he send them back to the brothel?' Samira asked.

'They'd talk, that's why. Plus you get big bucks for . . .' Blake stopped.

'For what, Mr Blake?'

'Snuff films. There are some real psychos out there.'

And in here, thought Samira, as nausea rose.

'But I had nothing to do with any of that and you can't prove that I did.'

'As long as you don't appear in any of the films, of course.'

Was it Samira's imagination, or had Blake gone a little pale under his tan?

'The films gave you something of value but the gangsters who had trafficked the women originally didn't like losing their merchandise, did they?' Josh leant forward.

'Merchandise?' Samira hadn't meant to say anything, but the word had shocked her.

Blake didn't flinch. 'Yeah, that's how triads think of them.'

Not just the triads, she thought.

'Did you share in the profits?'

Blake shrugged. 'I was only in it for the money. I'm not a weirdo. Not like Trev.'

Samira remembered Leo Blake's palatial riverside house and gardens on the tongue of land, and how it was the first thing he'd asked about when they saw him at the school hall. Was that how he'd paid for it? If they could prove that, maybe Luna and Siriporn could get some compensation.

'Did you watch those films?' she asked.

Blake shook his head, indignant. 'I told you: I'm not a weirdo.'

'So why did you stop buying, abusing, filming and killing the girls? You had a nice little business going.' Josh pushed the point.

'Like I said, I didn't get involved in any of that stuff.'

'Nevertheless, you had a nice little earner.'

'When Trev let that Thai girl escape, it all went tits up.'

'How do you mean?'

'Within days, Sammy Lee's sister or brother or whatever was on Trev's doorstep reading us the riot act.'

'What did she say?'

Blake shrugged. 'It was a long time ago. I can't remember it word for word.'

'Give us the gist, Mr Blake,' Josh said drily.

'She said she'd tell Sammy Lee's bosses what we were doing. That put the frighteners on Sammy all right.'

'But not you?'

'I didn't care about them.'

'But you all stopped, not just Lee.'

'Yeah, but then he wound up dead a few weeks later.'

'Do you know who killed him?'

'His bosses. The ones the ladyboy threatened him with.'

'And Farrow?'

'She put the fear of God into him too.'

'But you weren't scared?' Josh sounded sceptical.

Blake flushed. 'Why push our luck? If the girl told the madam, who else might she tell? After Sammy Lee died, we backed off.'

'Ms Potts left a warning, didn't she? On Boot Hill,' Samira asked.

'Yeah. Weird. That whole place is weird, if you ask me. I suppose it's burnt to the ground now.'

'A pink high heel.'

'Bloody great big feet she had. Made me feel sick.'

He was making Samira feel sick.

'What was the deal with the shoes, anyway? Were they some kind of trophy?' Josh continued.

Blake folded his arms across his chest. 'What are you talking about? Only shoe I know about is the ladyboy's.'

'We found one of Gloria Ramos's shoes hanging on Boot Hill. We suspect there were shoes from other victims there too.'

Blake's grey eyes were wary. 'Nothing to do with me. Trev took the women's shoes away when they first arrived. He said it'd stop them running. I dunno what he did with them after that.'

'Why would he hang them on Boot Hill?'

'I told you: he's nuts. Maybe they *were* a trophy or something. If he'd told me, I'd have stopped him. Shit like that is how you get caught.'

'Were you friends with Trevor Farrow?' Josh had moved on.

'Nah. It was a professional relationship. We were just doing business.'

'How did you meet him?'

'He sold me eggs and chooks.'

'How did you get from eggs and chooks to rape and murder?'

'I didn't do any rape or murder.'

'Nevertheless.' Josh was not about to be deflected.

'I saw one of the girls looking after Nan one day—the one called Gloria, I think—and she was sweet and juicy. I said something about her to Trev; you know, locker room talk.'

'What did you say?'

'I can't remember—probably something about how she could park her shoes under my bed any time. Then Trev said he owned her.'

'He owned her?' Samira was shocked.

'Yeah. He said she was bought and paid for, and he could do anything he liked with her. He was boasting, I knew that, but it sort of went from there.'

'How do you mean?'

'What he said gave me ideas. Trev didn't have ideas, but he liked mine.'

—

A huge explosion. Debris flew out of the front door. Megan ducked, but something hard and sharp caught her on the shoulder.

'Gas bottle, probably. Farrow's a goner.' Phil wheezed out the words. He started to limp towards her. She grabbed him and put his arm over her good shoulder.

'Lean on me.'

His breathing worried her. It was noisy and harsh.

'Where's the girl?' he managed.

'She's okay.' She would explain the miraculous appearance of Jessica later.

'Can you make it?' she asked.

Phil nodded.

'We're too old for this shit,' she said as they started moving. She saw a flash of his teeth through the dark. That grin.

She was half-pulling, half-dragging Phil towards the car. Behind them she could hear more explosions and the crashing of what she could only assume were beams and wall braces. They had to get out of there. Fast. She looked at Phil.

'I'm okay,' he said.

She wasn't sure she believed him.

'The tree is here. We have to go around it.'

She sensed him nodding. It was now so black she could not see him at all. She couldn't see any sign of Sheridan or Jessica either. Had it been a hallucination?

Megan had her torch, and its feeble yellow light was the only guide they had. Phil was a dead weight. *Has he passed out?* she wondered. Then, suddenly, Jessica was beside them, taking Phil's other arm.

'Sheridan's in my car,' she said.

Megan had no idea how her friend had managed to be in this place at this time, but she'd never been more grateful to anyone in her life.

'Thank you,' she said.

After a step or two, made easier because they were sharing Phil's weight, Megan's torchlight reflected on the police car's metal door. She wrenched it open and together they hauled the unconscious man onto the back seat. Megan even managed to get the seatbelt around him and fastened. God knew what the drive was going to be like.

'Are you all right?' Jessica asked.

Megan nodded, but she felt dreadful.

A terrible crash. They turned to look. The roof of the old house had caved in. Trevor Farrow had died as he had lived: in the house his parents had built.

'Let's get out of here,' Jessica said.

—

'How did Sammy Lee get involved?'

'The girls went missing and he came to find out what was going on. That bitch probably told him.'

'What bitch?'

'His half-sister, brother, whatever she was. Anyway, when he realised what a good thing we had going, he wanted in. He said he could keep the triad off our backs.'

'You said you saw Gloria Ramos caring for Nan. So the girls were also used as carers?'

Blake shrugged. 'I guess. I didn't pay much attention to that side of things.'

'How much do you think Nan knew?'

'I don't know, but she must have had her suspicions. Not a lot she could do about it, though.'

'What made you decide when a girl's time was up?'

'Like I keep telling you, I didn't decide anything. I wanted a bit of fun and I didn't mind making a buck out of it, but I never wanted to do anything weird.'

'Let's assume what you are telling me is correct; what made Lee and Farrow decide a girl's time was up?'

'When sales began to drop, and the customers started demanding something new. As far as I was concerned it was business.'

'Is there anything else you want to add to your statement, Mr Blake?' Josh sat up straight.

'I didn't kill anybody, all right? It was Trev. All Trev.'

—

Phil was silent all the way back to the Gresford fire station. Megan just hoped he was still alive. She hoped Sheridan was too. She clung to the lifeline of Jessica's twin red tail-lights as they drove through the chaotic dark. The journey back was even worse, as the fire was getting closer. Burning debris was falling all around them and littering their path. Twice Megan had to reverse to drive around a branch that fell in front of her. When they finally got back to the fire station, her relief was tempered by horror at seeing the car park almost empty. Even the fireys were evacuating. She saw Jessica's car had pulled up outside the door. She watched as her friend got out of the car, scooped Sheridan into her arms and was inside the fire station in seconds. Only then did Megan park the four-wheel drive in the middle of the driveway to stop anyone else leaving. She knew Sheridan and Phil needed urgent attention, and she wouldn't move her car until they were receiving it. Only then did she sprint after her friend.

'Help!' she cried, to the handful of people packing up inside the fire shed. 'I have an unconscious police officer in the car, suffering from smoke inhalation—like her.' Megan pointed to Sheridan, relieved to see someone already bending over her with an oxygen mask.

One of the fireys ripped open the box he'd just sealed and pulled out another oxygen cylinder. 'Righto,' he said cheerfully.

Two more ran out into the car park with a stretcher.

'Where's Farrow?' the RFS chief asked Megan as he held the mask to Phil's face. He knew they had come to make the arrest.

Megan shook her head. 'Roof fell in. This guy and the girl nearly got caught under it with him.' Megan gestured towards Phil.

'Fuck. I thought we hadn't lost anyone.' The man looked gutted. Killer or not, Farrow had been one of his crew.

'We did what we could.'

'You shouldn't have gone after him alone. You may be cops, but in a fire you're amateurs.'

'Just as well we did. He had the girl locked up in his cellar.'

She looked over at Sheridan, who was being expertly tended to. Jessica was sitting beside her daughter, holding her hand.

A bloke came over and handed Megan a cup of tea. It was a tea bag with water from the instant hot-water tap above the sink, no milk but lots of sugar. Ordinarily, Megan would have turned her nose up at it; now she grabbed it with both hands and drank it down. It tasted like nectar.

'How are you doing?' the man asked, putting a gentle hand on her uninjured shoulder.

'I'm okay,' she said, but was suddenly aware of how wobbly she felt. She was done in. She hadn't let herself think about how close they had come to a horrible death. She swallowed hard. No time for self-pity. They needed to get Phil and Sheridan to hospital.

Jessica turned and looked at her. Megan smiled, but the effort was too great and to her horror she found she was crying. Jessica reached across the space between them and took her hand.

TWENTY-SIX

They had left the fire behind them. Once they got to Paterson, Megan's phone pinged loudly. *You are entering a 4G area.* She had been in a half-sleep, her head thrumming against the passenger window of the fire rig. Ahead, its siren blaring, was the ambulance carrying Phil, Sheridan and Jessica, who had refused to leave her daughter's side. Megan had always liked Jessica; now she admired her. What she had done was totally against the rules, and Megan letting her do it went against all police protocols—Inspector George would have a fit when she found out—but Megan just felt grateful.

As they had sipped their scalding tea while waiting for the ambulance to reach the Gresford fire station, Jessica had explained how she came to be on Masseys Creek Road.

'I know you told me to go home, but I couldn't do it. I lied to Steve and told him we should both return to our respective places in case Sheridan turned up at one of them, but I knew she wasn't going to do that. I was certain that if she knew about the fires—and there was no way she wouldn't have—she'd have contacted us. If she didn't, it was because she couldn't. I was not going to sit by and let something horrible happen to my daughter without at least trying to find her.

'After I left you, I was sitting in my car, wondering what I should do, then I saw you and Phil drive out of the car park. So I just followed you. I had no idea where you were going, or why, but I knew you were doing something and that's what I needed to do too.'

'How did you get through the police cordon?' Megan finished the delicious tea. She felt a bit woozy. As if she might have to put her head between her knees. She resisted the impulse.

'I just gave them your names and ranks and said that I was with you, and they waved me through.'

'You could have been killed.'

'So could you.'

'It's our job. We're cops.'

'It's my job. She's my daughter.'

Megan looked at her friend. She thought about what she might have done if Jason had ever been in that sort of danger. Would she have been as brave? She didn't know.

'I was wondering how I would explain my presence at the Gresford fire station, when I saw that man's car drive out—he's the lyrebird killer, isn't he? And then I saw you take off after him. I just tucked myself in behind you.'

'It was a terrifying drive.'

'The thought that Sheridan might be trapped somewhere in the middle of that inferno made me even more determined to keep going. You were on the tail of the man who I believed might have my daughter. What would you have done?'

Megan put her mug down and looked at Jessica's filthy, ash-smeared face. She supposed she must look like that too. 'I don't know what I would have done. I am both appalled by the risks you took and so fucking grateful that you did.'

'And I was right.'

'Again.'

A wave of white exhaustion broke over Megan as she thought about what might have happened if Jessica hadn't appeared when she did. She doubted very much that she could have got both Sheridan and Phil to the car on her own. She didn't like to think about who she might have left behind. Thank God Jessica had appeared through the smoke, so she didn't have to make such a choice.

'I think we should take you to the hospital to get checked out too.' A firey was beside her.

Megan shook her head emphatically. It wasn't that she was against the idea of seeing a doctor. Her shoulder was killing her, and it felt as if her shirt had stuck to the wound, but the press would be at the hospital, desperate for details, and she'd have to deal with her colleagues asking what had happened and wanting answers. She couldn't take that. She just wanted to have a hot shower and crawl into bed.

'No,' she croaked. 'I want to go home.'

'That was . . . intense!'

Samira leant back in her chair in the tearoom. Blake was being processed by the duty sergeant. When Megan and Phil returned with Farrow—Samira glanced in the direction of the fire in the hills; *if they come back at all*, an interior voice whispered—the case would be cracked, apart from the paperwork. She felt elated and impatient to tell Megan about their triumph. She and Josh had been an integral part of bringing these evil bastards to justice. Her hunch about the photofit had paid off in spades, and, if she did say so herself, their interrogation of Blake had been very productive. She almost looked forward to helping prepare the brief of evidence for the DPP.

Josh felt the same. He raised his mug. 'To us!' he said. 'You've got what it takes, Samira. Don't let anyone tell you different.'

They clinked mugs. It wasn't champagne, but it still felt celebratory.

The door to the tearoom opened, and Inspector George appeared.

'Well done, you two,' she said, as she sat down beside them. 'Solving this case is a real feather in both your caps, especially so early in your careers.'

'Thank you, ma'am,' said Samira, thrilled by the compliment. 'We were just part of the team.'

'We were lucky to be working with Senior Sergeants Blaxland and Arlott,' said Josh.

That brought Samira back down to earth. Had they returned? Had they arrested Farrow? Would they have to do another interview?

'Are the sergeants all right, ma'am? Have you heard anything?'

'They're not back yet, but Megan . . . Senior Sergeant Blaxland . . . has just radioed in.'

'Have they got Farrow?'

'He died in the fire while they were trying to arrest him. He'd returned to the farm to rescue his sister.'

'We'd already got her out,' Samira protested.

'Yes. Good job. Instead, he brought Sheridan Weston out of the house. He'd had her imprisoned in the cellar. She and Senior Sergeant Arlott are on their way to hospital now.'

'Are they okay?' Josh asked.

Samira was too shocked to say anything. There was a buzzing in her ears. Sheridan Weston? What was she doing there? A vivid image of Nan reaching back to the locked door, banging on it, crying and beseeching them as they wheeled her away filled her brain. She went cold all over.

'That's what Nan was so upset about. She was trying to tell us that Sheridan was in that cellar!' Samira thought she might throw up.

'Shit,' said Josh. He looked a bit pale too.

'It's okay. The girl's out of danger now. She's on her way to hospital.' The Inspector was trying to be reassuring, but Samira was not able to think about anything except how they had ignored

Nan and so almost condemned a fifteen-year-old girl to a fiery death. She moaned out loud.

Inspector George gave her a worried look. 'Are you all right? You've had a hell of a day.'

Samira nodded, but she didn't trust herself to speak.

'Look, I can understand why you're upset,' the Inspector said, 'but don't be too hard on yourself. None of us knew she was out there.' Her voice softened. 'Do you want to go home? Your shift's nearly over anyway.'

Samira shook her head. What would she do alone in her little flat other than beat herself up? She wanted to be with Josh.

'Don't worry, Inspector,' said Josh. 'Samira will be fine. She always is.'

—

Megan had been right about the shirt. The blood from the shoulder wound had dried and stuck the cotton fast to her back. The pain when she tried to peel it off was excruciating. Instead, she just got into the shower shirt and all, letting the warm water dissolve the blood until she could—slowly, painfully—extricate her arm. Then she let the ripped and bloodied shirt fall onto the tiles and watched the reddish water swirl down the drain. It was comforting to see it wash away.

It hadn't just been her shirt that was ruined. As she undressed, she discovered that her suit, shirt, even her underclothes were covered in tiny burn holes, as if someone had methodically poked her with a lit cigarette from top to toe. Her skin was burnt too. She couldn't remember feeling anything much at the time.

Despite the burns, the worst was the exhaustion. When she climbed out of the shower, she wrapped the towel around her as best she could—her left arm was now so painful she could only move it with great care—then sat on the toilet seat, mustering the energy to dry herself and climb into bed. She stared at the medicine cabinet above the sink. She probably needed to put something on her shoulder wound. It was painful enough now; she couldn't bear to contemplate how it might feel if it got infected. She yearned for Guido. He would have brought her tea, wrapped her in his arms, dried her aching and burnt flesh tenderly and dressed her wounds. But there was no Guido. There was no one. Just her.

She got up off the toilet seat, found the betadine and, looking backwards into the mirror, managed to squirt some of the yellow disinfectant over the nasty-looking cut on her shoulder. *It probably needs stitches*, she thought. She'd do something about that tomorrow. She couldn't manoeuvre her usual t-shirt over her head, but she managed to get into one of Guido's pyjama tops. The worn, familiar softness of the old flannelette was comforting. Next, she took two of the Panadeine Forte she kept in the drawer by her bed, left over from the period before Guido graduated to morphine, then she crawled under the covers and pulled her knees up to her chest, just as she had when she'd been ill as a little girl.

Samira and Josh had finally got something stronger than tea, but they no longer felt like celebrating. Samira could not get the image of Nan, babbling and reaching back to the locked door, out of her mind. Why had she ignored her? Terror at the fire and her desire to get the hell out of there? Or had she also failed to take Nan seriously?

Samira's shame was overwhelming. Maybe she should resign. If not for her colleagues, that poor girl could have burnt to death, and it would have been her fault. Samira wanted to cry, but she was sitting at the bar in the pub, surrounded by people, so she took a sip of her beer instead. Josh looked over and gave her another gentle punch on the arm.

'Snap out of it, Samira. It was Farrow who went back to the house. Probably to get Nan, but it was him who brought the girl out and saved her life. If he hadn't done that, Phil and Megan probably wouldn't have found her either.' Was Josh trying to reassure himself, or her? They both felt bad.

'Her mother would have gone in after her.'

He frowned. 'That was bizarre—Professor Weston turning up out of the blue.'

'She's a very gutsy woman.'

'More stupid than gutsy, if you ask me. We're lucky she didn't get killed.'

'We're all lucky she was there.' Samira picked some peanuts from the dish on the bar, then put them on the dark, sticky wood.

'Why would Farrow kidnap someone and then save their life?'

'He was always a strange man,' Josh said. 'Creepy and gruff, often nasty. Us kids used to give him a wide berth. Mum said he wasn't right in the head, but he looked after Nan, so it was hard to just straight up hate him. He was a vengeful bastard, though. If anyone ever wronged him or Nan, he made sure he got back at them. Even if it took years.'

'Do you think that's why he kidnapped Sheridan? To get back at Professor Weston for opening the whole case up in the first place? After twenty years he must have thought he'd pulled off the perfect crime.'

Josh shrugged. 'That's what Blake thought, but who knows what goes on inside that nutter's head? I'd rather not think about it.'

'Nothing is going on in it anymore.' Samira stared at the peanuts.

'I feel sorry for Nan, though. What will she do without him?'

'Do you think he abused her too? Was she afraid of him?'

'She always did what he told her to, but she was completely dependent on him for everything. Was she scared? I dunno.'

'Will she go to jail? It'd be awful if she was the only person who ended up paying for the murders of those women.'

'Thanks to you, Leo Blake is going down for a very long time. And Sammy Lee was murdered. She's not the only one who will pay. And she'll inherit the Farrow land. That'll fetch enough to afford proper carers and assisted living.'

Samira drained her beer. She still had not said what she wanted to say.

'I am so sorry.'

'What for?' he said.

'For missing Sheridan.'

'You didn't miss her on your own. It never crossed my mind she'd be in that house.'

Samira put the peanuts in her mouth.

'Another?' asked the bartender.

Josh nodded. 'And it was fucking terrifying in that place,' he went on. 'I thought you were amazing, charging down that corridor. It was only because you did that I dared to follow; if it had been up to me, we might not have got either of them out.'

—

Megan woke in broad daylight to find her son leaning over her with a cup of tea.

'Jason?' she said, wondering if he, like Jessica, was another apparition.

'Lisa George rang me yesterday. She told me a little about what you had been through and I got on the first available flight.'

'You didn't need to do that...'

Megan tried to pull herself upright, but her head spun, and she felt like she might be about to black out. She slumped back against the pillows. 'Ow!' Her shoulder still felt like it was on fire.

'It's either me or hospital,' Jason said, tucking the blankets in around her. 'And the doctor will be here in a few minutes to look at that shoulder.'

Jason sat down on the bed and helped Megan to sit up against the pillows. He was as gentle and tender as his father would have been.

'You are very like your dad.'

'I hope so.'

He held the teacup to her lips, but she would not be fed like an infant. With the hand of her good arm she took the tea from him and drank it thirstily. It was the second-best cup of tea she had ever tasted; she doubted the one she'd had at the Gresford fire station could ever be surpassed.

Over the next few days, she had reason to be even more grateful for that delicious cuppa. The shoulder was bad, but once it had been stitched and dressed painkillers kept it bearable. The worst was the dehydration. She had to spend two days in bed drinking water and bloody herbal tea. Doctor's orders; otherwise, her GP threatened, hospital and intravenous fluids. Jason stayed and looked after her.

'You're very like your dad,' she said as they sat in front of the TV watching *Vera*.

'You've told me that already.'

Had she? Megan didn't remember much about the first twenty-four hours after she got home.

'You look after me the way your dad would have.'

Her son flashed a smile at her.

'I think I'll go back to work tomorrow,' she said.

His smile disappeared.

She held up her hand to stifle any protest. 'I'll come home as soon as I feel wobbly, but this case has to be finalised, and I have not gone through all this only to let someone else cross the finish line.'

TWENTY-SEVEN

A week passed, and apart from the bandage on her shoulder most of Megan's wounds were healing, though she still struggled with a feeling of unreality. Work helped keep her grounded. Wrapping up the case was deeply satisfying. But since Jason had gone back to Melbourne, going home was hard. Going to sleep was harder. Closing her eyes meant replaying what had happened in the fire like a movie projected against her eyelids.

But at least I am alive to tell the tale, she thought, glancing at Phil, Kumar and Baker sitting further along the church pew. The two constables and Phil wore their dress uniforms and held their hats to their chests respectfully. Megan wore her best black suit, and she'd had her hair cut and blow-dried for the occasion. It had needed to be. A lot of it had been singed in the fire. Fortunately, the hairdresser had worked miracles and she didn't look too peculiar.

Phil had just been released from hospital. Megan was pleased to see him.

'Are you okay?' she whispered.

Phil shrugged. 'I still feel a bit spacey—like the ground beneath my feet isn't quite solid or something.'

'I feel weird too. Shock perhaps . . . Do you have someone to look after you? Jason came up from Melbourne for a few days. I don't know what I would have done without him.'

'Judith's moved in, and Clare comes round most days.'

'Clare?'

'Yeah, don't get excited. She's only being kind.'

'It's good you can be friends. You were together a long time.'

Phil looked stricken for a moment, then he gathered himself. 'I'm okay. I've managed by myself for a year now. I'm used to it.'

A year! Shit. Megan had forgotten they'd been apart for so long.

'I'm glad Judith's with you. What about Leila?'

'She's got her hands full with a newborn.'

'You're a grandpa! That's wonderful news.'

Phil flashed his trademark grin. 'Yeah. Time something went right.'

―

The priest was waiting to start the funeral mass as mourners continued to straggle into St Helen's. It was a pretty pink-brick Catholic church, built at a time when the pews were packed every Sunday. Now, the congregation was so small the priest commuted. He didn't even live in Gresford anymore. Luna and Bridie had chosen St Helen's because it was close to where Gloria had lain, forgotten, for all those years. Now, it was where she would be remembered.

'I can't think of a place where it would feel right to bury her,' Luna had said to Bridie.

'Not in Manila? Or Zamboanga City?'

'No. Nothing good ever happened to her there.'

The fires were almost all out. It had rained in the early morning after that terrible day. A good thirty millimetres had fallen hard in a great drenching downfall. The fire, no matter how fearsome and huge it had become, was no match for the water. Within half an hour the fires were mostly doused. It had drizzled ever since.

The rain was a godsend, but the damage the fire had done was apocalyptic. Ten houses had gone, including Farrow's farm, and countless outbuildings had been lost along with machinery and equipment, endless kilometres of fences and too many animals—wild, domestic and livestock—to comprehend. Worst of all, three human lives had been taken: Trevor Farrow; a woman who'd had a heart attack while being evacuated; and a man who had stayed to fight for his home. The fires had made headlines around the world, and the political argument continued about whether the devastation was due to arson or climate change.

The church they were sitting in had escaped the flames, but the lawn around it was scorched to a crisp. Everything smelt burnt. The once-beautiful green hills of pasture and woodland behind the little town had been decimated. Everything was black and brown, not a soft surface anywhere. The ground looked as if it had been scoured. Only stones and clay remained. There were no insects, no birds. Just the occasional crash as a burnt-out tree on the hillside gave up its hold on the earth.

The priest cleared his throat. 'Welcome, friends, to the funeral of Gloria Maria Ramos. Welcome especially to her daughter Luna, who has travelled here from Manila, and to Gloria's and Luna's close friend Bridie Turner. They have taken great pains over this funeral. You will find the order of service in the funeral booklet. We will begin by rising and singing Gloria's favourite hymn, "Amazing Grace".'

Megan rose with the rest of the congregation, holding the leaflet with its fuzzy photo of Gloria that she recognised from the incident room. Kumar jostled her left arm as they got up and the pain that shot through Megan's injured limb was so excruciating she couldn't repress a gasp.

'God! Sorry!'

Kumar had been tiptoeing around her for days now. It could have been irritating, but Megan understood why the new constable was mortified by her failure to rescue Sheridan Weston. Her remorse was what would make her a good cop. She cared about people. She wanted to do what was right.

'No problem,' she said, but she moved a step or two away.

Megan was pleased with the choice of hymn. *I once was lost but now am found*: what could be more appropriate?

Megan had watched the video of Leo Blake's interrogation as soon as she returned to work. The two uniforms had done a good job, and she'd made sure to congratulate them. They had risen to the challenge. But she suspected that Kumar could not bear to hear any praise yet. Her failing—as she saw it—was too raw. Megan remembered what that felt like. Now, listening to the hymn, she could not help thinking about the callous way Blake had spoken about the women he had brutally raped and helped to murder. The thought of their vulnerability and terror, caught so brilliantly by the lyrebird, made Megan's chest ache. Her only consolation was that they had arrested Blake and she had every confidence that, given the strength of the case they had put together for the DPP, he would die in jail. Farrow and Lee were already dead.

She felt little emotion about Lee's demise, as she had never met him, but her feelings about Farrow were complicated. He was a brutal and sadistic killer, but he had rescued Sheridan. It had taken courage to do that. She could not reconcile the man lugging the girl's body onto the verandah, the man who cared for his disabled sister so tenderly, the man who spent countless hours voluntarily fighting catastrophic fires, with the man who had committed such terrible crimes. No one was born a monster, she reminded herself. They were made one. Even Blake. For a moment she wondered what his back story was, but she pushed the thought aside. It seemed disrespectful to be thinking about him at Gloria's funeral. And they had solved the case. They had fulfilled their obligation to the women who'd died. They could not save them or bring them back, but they could bring their story into the court, and they could bring at least one of their killers to justice.

Solving the case wasn't her only consolation. Luna Ramos and Bridie Turner sat side by side in the front pew. *The one good thing to come out of all this horror*, Megan thought, as she looked at the backs of their heads, *is the relationship that has developed between those two*. Gloria had mothered them both, in different ways, and now they really were like sisters.

When the congregation resumed their seats, Luna and Bridie rose together and went to the pulpit.

'Gloria was my mother,' Luna began, 'but I hardly knew her. She spent all of my early years working in foreign countries, sending her pay back to me and my grandmother. But even when she was so far away, she always stayed in touch. When the money stopped coming, when she stopped writing us letters, we knew something terrible had happened to her. We knew she would never abandon us of her own doing.' Luna's voice cracked, and Sara Stanhope, sitting in the second row, heaved a sob. Sara was catering the funeral. Amanda had offered to pay. Sara had refused the money at first, but Bridie had persuaded her that treating the catering as a professional transaction would keep any interest from the press at bay. Megan could only imagine how much Sara was dreading Blake's court case. She was pleased that Brian Stanhope AC sat beside his wife, and hoped that maybe Blake would see sense and plead guilty.

Bridie, standing beside Luna at the pulpit, took up where her friend had left off. 'I knew and loved Gloria. She was as much a mother to me as my own mother . . .'

More of a mother, thought Megan, watching them from the back. Amanda, seated next to the Stanhopes, was holding a white handkerchief to her eyes. Megan did not like Amanda

Turner, she never had, but she was supporting her daughter by being here, and supporting Sara by paying for the catering, so maybe she should cut the woman some slack.

The person whose presence at the funeral really surprised Megan was Ian Turner. He sat right up the back, handcuffed to a corrections officer. His head was bowed as if in prayer. Megan had been astonished when the prison had rung to ask if she had any objections to him attending the funeral.

'As long as Bridie Turner and Luna Ramos have no objections,' Megan had replied.

Clearly, they had not.

Coco Potts sat a row or two in front of Turner. She showed no sign of knowing him. Megan studied Coco. She still had her doubts about Coco's story. Had she told them the whole truth?

'Do you think Coco told us everything?' she whispered to Phil.

He shook his head.

'Do you think she killed Sammy Lee?'

He looked at her. 'It's possible.'

'But we have no evidence.'

'Nothing to justify ongoing investigation, certainly.'

Good, thought Megan, but she did not say so out loud.

The two young women returned to their seats and the priest took his place at the pulpit. Megan returned her attention to the service.

Coco sat on her own. She preferred it that way. She felt terrible about Gloria—and Concepcion, Yulia and Siriporn—and she supposed that she always would. The least she could do was come and pay her respects. She felt a little cheered by the number of people in the church. *Gloria would have been astonished at the turnout*, she thought. She knew Ian Turner was sitting behind her. She had never met him, glimpsed him once or twice, perhaps, but who else would be at the funeral in handcuffs, flanked by corrections officers? *It was brave of him to come*, she thought.

Bang!

Coco turned to the back of the church, and so did everyone else. A middle-aged woman stood in the doorway dressed in her Sunday best. The wooden door had been caught by the wind just as she had edged it open, hoping to sneak in quietly.

'Sorry,' she said. 'The wind.'

Wind still makes everyone nervous, thought Coco. *Even though there is nothing left to burn.*

The woman slid in next to Coco, up the back of the church. Coco scooted over. The newcomer nodded at her. Coco wondered who she was and what she had to do with this tragic story.

'I've been helping with the wake,' the woman whispered. 'That's why I'm late. Gorgeous food. She catered it.' She pointed at Sara Stanhope.

Coco raised her eyebrows. So Sara Stanhope had catered Gloria Ramos's funeral. It made a funny kind of sense, when she thought about it. They'd been friends and they'd been fellow victims. Coco hadn't intended to go to the wake, but she wouldn't miss it now. Nan wasn't in the congregation, Coco noticed. Just as well. She was an accessory to all that horror. Unwilling, perhaps, but she'd never tried to do anything to stop it, as far as anyone knew. Coco wondered what would happen to Nan. Would she be charged? Tried? Would she go to jail? It hardly seemed likely. She'd end up in some sort of institution. She felt pity for Nan. She still grieved for the little Sammy Lee she had loved when they were both children. She felt nothing but contempt for the other two, Trevor Farrow and Leo Blake. *One died in the fire—burnt in hell*, she thought to herself, as he so richly deserved. *And the other will rot in jail.* Good. Justice had been served.

'I feel really awful about poor Gloria Ramos,' the woman beside her was saying. 'My name is Sadie Lewis. I was the postmistress the whole time she lived here, the whole time all those poor women did, and I never even noticed any of them, except Siriporn . . . I mean Ms Stanhope.'

Amanda Turner shot them a look.

'We'd better be quiet,' Coco said.

Sadie nodded and smiled. 'I've never been much good at that.'

Lucky you, thought Coco. *There's no lesson I've learnt more thoroughly than how to hold my tongue.*

—

When the service ended, the mourners rose to leave. The priest suggested those in the front pews lead the way. As Megan stood and walked past the last pew, where Ian Turner still sat hunched over, trying to make himself as small as possible, she stopped.

'Mr Turner?'

He looked up at her, eyes red from crying.

'It was the least I could do,' he said.

—

It was a four-minute walk from the little brick church to the School of Arts where Gloria Ramos's wake was to be held. The small group of mourners walked through the scorched landscape in a ragtag assortment. All the houses in East Gresford were still standing, but the blackened and burnt gardens stood testament to how hard the fire crews had worked to save them.

'I had no idea the fires had been this bad,' Amanda Turner said to Megan as she picked her way carefully among the ash in her bright, white sneakers. 'I mean, I saw on the news, but it brings it home to you, getting this close.'

You don't know the half of it, thought Megan.

'How is Bridie doing?' she asked.

'Good, I think. She and Luna are sharing her flat now, and Luna is applying for permanent residency. I'm doing what I can to help. Seems the least I can do.'

That turn of phrase again. Amanda and Ian Turner had more in common than they knew.

'Excuse me,' Megan said. 'I just need to make sure my colleague is okay. He had quite a time of it during the fires.' She turned and waited for Phil to catch up.

'No sign of Jessica or Sheridan Weston.' Phil's voice was still a bit hoarse.

'I think Sheridan may still be in hospital. She went through a hell of an ordeal.'

'So did Jessica.'

Megan nodded. They walked on a few more paces in silence.

'How are Kumar and Baker doing?' he asked.

Phil had not returned to duty yet. Megan had taken the opportunity to recommend him for a bravery award. He'd have been furious if he'd caught wind of it.

'Baker has taken it on the chin. He's got such a good temperament for this job. He'll go far, I think. Kumar is still beating herself up.'

'Who can blame her?'

'Not me. I beat myself up for weeks when I first came back to this case. I was mortified that I'd ever let it go cold.'

'You and me both.'

'But you have to forgive yourself, especially if it turns out okay in the end. You're no use to yourself, or to the job, if you don't.'

'Kumar will sort herself out. She's emotional, but she's smart too.'

Phil Arlott has changed, Megan thought, as they walked side by side through the blackened landscape. He was softer, kinder more open to people's failings. Megan had always liked her old partner. She liked him even more now.

'Sheridan Weston is a smart girl too,' he said, as he pushed open the gate leading to the School of Arts. 'Kumar told me about the clippings Farrow had on his wall, which the girl had the presence of mind to stuff into her pocket. The coroner is going to find them very helpful.'

The food at the wake was not just good, but among the best Megan had ever tasted. She loaded her plate with curry puffs and money bags and duck pancakes and all manner of delicacies she did not recognise and could not put a name to.

'I imagine this is the first and last time this little hall will see food of this quality.' Coco was standing beside Megan.

'Not just this little hall; I reckon anywhere for hundreds of ks around. I intend to make the most of it.'

'Me too.' Coco had loaded her plate.

They took two of the seats that ringed the hall. Megan had not expected to sit with Coco, but it felt rude to walk away. Sadie Lewis took the empty seat on Megan's other side. Megan introduced them to one another.

'We've already met,' Coco said.

Bridie and Luna walked up to them. They were doing the rounds of the guests.

'Thank you so much for coming,' Bridie said.

'And thank you, Mrs Lewis, for helping Ms Stanhope with the food,' Luna added.

'My pleasure, love. I am so sorry for your loss. I wish—'

'Can I offer you some pad see ew?' Sara Stanhope was holding a tray of white cartons.

'Yes, please!' said Sadie Lewis, reaching for one.

Bridie and Luna took one each.

'How are you two doing?' asked Megan.

'Okay,' said Bridie. 'Sara, Luna and I have decided to set up a foundation for trafficked women. Mum and Brian—Mr Stanhope—are going to fund it.'

'And we're going to run it,' Luna finished. 'It feels good to do something useful. Something positive. I don't want Mum and the others to have died for nothing.'

'That's a great idea. I should put you in touch with a cop I know who has retired from the sex trafficking squad. I reckon he could be really helpful.'

'And your husband is helping too?' Coco also took one of the delicious-smelling cartons from Sara's tray.

'He is a good man. I am very lucky.'

'Yes,' said Coco. 'You are.'

The last thing Megan would ever have called Siriporn was lucky, but, she had to agree, Sara she had made her own luck. At least one of the women from that horrible place had found their way. Then Megan thought about Coco's life now. Maybe there were two.

Megan watched as Sara and Coco looked at each other and smiled. There were things they knew that no one else ever would or ever could, no matter how much of their story they told.

Once everyone had taken a container, Sara moved on to the group sitting nearby. Luna and Bridie followed her.

'Would you like a drink?' Coco asked. 'I brought a case of champagne. It should have chilled by now.'

Megan nodded; she was off duty. Sadie Lewis held out her glass. 'Don't mind if I do.'

Coco grinned and took their glasses to the kitchen at the back of the hall.

'Trevor Farrow, eh?' Sadie said, exhaling heavily. Farrow's name had been everywhere. ALLEGED LYREBIRD SERIAL KILLER

ARRESTED WHILE FIGHTING THE FIRES, screamed the headlines, THEN KILLED SAVING THE TEEN HE KIDNAPPED. What a story. People were already talking about film rights.

'That's for the inquest to decide, but we think so, yeah. He certainly kidnapped Sheridan Weston.'

'Poor little mite. He was always a strange fellow. I've known the Farrow twins all my life. We went to school together.'

Coco returned with the champagne. They took their glasses.

'I'm just telling the sergeant here about how I've known Trev and Nan all my life,' Sadie said.

'Do go on,' Coco said, sipping on her drink.

'Well, I wouldn't have picked him as a serial killer or a sexual pervert, but he was always a bully. You had to walk on eggshells around him . . .'

'That was the nickname the girls—Gloria—had for him,' Coco broke in. 'The Egg Man.'

'He sold them, of course,' Sadie said. 'Eggs, I mean. So did his parents before him. Nice little farm and business they had back in the day, but my mum said that the birth of the twins really destroyed that family. Trev was normal weight—he got all the nutrients, and Nan was born half-starved and with all sorts of issues. Then she had some sort of stroke. That's why she couldn't speak or write. Their mother never forgave Trev, or so my mother said. Made him look after Nan twenty-four-seven. He was a good brother, it has to be said. He certainly didn't take anything out on her, and he might have, given how nasty his mum was to him.'

'Maybe he took it out on other women,' Coco suggested.

'Maybe,' said Sadie. 'When his mother died, she made him swear to look after Nan, or so the story went. And to his credit, he did. He didn't look after anything else, though. After she'd gone, he just let everything go to rack and ruin. God knows how they paid the bills. Maybe their mum left them some money.'

'And their dad?' Megan asked.

'He shot through not long after the twins were born. No one knows what happened to him. Poor Mrs Farrow had her hands full, but she kept things going and then when Trev got old enough—not so very old; eight or nine, something like that—she put him to work. The welfare people used to go round to check up on them, I remember that. But Liz Farrow was always able to put on a good show—house spick and span, kids washed and in nice clean clothes, farm spruce, chickens well fed, and the twins turning up often enough at school that no one bothered them. Nan was sick a lot, but people didn't care so much back then. You couldn't get away with it now, of course.'

Megan almost felt sorry for Trevor Farrow; small Trevor Farrow anyway.

'Remember that poem?' Coco asked. 'The one about how your parents fuck you up, even though they don't mean to?'

'Sounds like a funny kind of poem,' said Sadie, giving Coco a disapproving look.

'Did you know Leo Blake too?' Megan asked.

'Not really. He didn't grow up here. A Johnny-come-lately and a piece of work. Never passed the time of day, ordered me about like I was his servant or something. I'm not at all surprised he was a sadistic, murdering prick.'

'Why, Mrs Lewis!' said Coco.

Sadie giggled and finished her champagne. 'Sorry, I am a one-pot screamer. Always have been.'

'In that case, let me get you another.' And Coco took her glass.

TWENTY-EIGHT

Although they had driven through countless kilometres of burnt-out forest, Jessica was still shocked when they pulled into the car park of Burraga Swamp. The beautiful place she remembered was devastated. It was a desecration.

'Jesus Christ!' she whispered.

'Will it recover?' Sheridan whispered back. It seemed wrong to speak at a normal volume.

'I don't know. This is temperate rainforest, not eucalypt. It's not meant to burn. I don't know how it will come back or if it even will.'

Sheridan burst into tears. She cried easily these days. She was still wobbly from her ordeal. Trauma response, the doctor had called it, telling Jessica to go gently. They'd fussed over Jessica too, examining her for burns and testing her lungs. But she was fine. A bit singed here and there, but she had her daughter back. That was all she cared about.

Jessica had not wanted to come here at all, but Sheridan had insisted, even bought the three huge bunches of native flowers sitting on the back seat.

'I could easily have ended up just like Gloria Ramos and the other women, if not for you,' her daughter had said. 'I just want to pay my respects.'

Jessica had tried to persuade her to lay her flowers on the grave at St Helen's Catholic Church in Gresford, but Sheridan had been insistent.

'I want to pay my respects where they died. I don't care where their bodies are.'

And so they were here, in the continuing drizzle, walking through the blasted and blackened remnants of the once-magnificent Barringtons. The forest floor crackled underfoot—not with fallen leaf litter and twigs as it once had, but with burnt-out embers and lumps of stuff that was no longer recognisable. There was hardly a leaf to be seen. It was as if they had all been vaporised. The canopy had gone, and with it the miniature ecosystems of staghorns, bird's-nest ferns, orchids and air ferns suspended in the clefts of branches. And the forest was still and silent. They could hear nothing but the sound of their own feet and the whisper of rain falling on the broken and brittle remains. No birds sang, no insects buzzed or whirred, no frogs chirruped, no small creatures or reptiles crashed through the undergrowth as they approached. The forest seemed lifeless. Sheridan was weeping quietly as they walked, her tears falling on the flowers along with the misty rain.

Jessica was not sure where the first grave had been. Nothing looked as it had. The cluster of tree ferns had gone, and only the twisted trunks of the magnificent strangler figs remained. They looked agonised, as if they had died writhing in pain. Occasionally she caught a glimpse of a green shoot, a tiny unfurling of a new leaf on a blackened stump, a spike pushing up through the ground. When she saw them, she stopped and pointed them out to Sheridan.

'Maybe it will recover. Life is tenacious.'

In the end she picked a place that looked as if it could have been the spot, although there were many of those.

'I think it was here.'

Sheridan sobbed as she surveyed their surroundings. 'What a terrible place to die.'

'It was beautiful once.'

Sheridan and Jessica laid the flowers down gently, as if they might bruise the ground. Then the two of them stood back and stared at the bouquets. Jessica felt awkward, she felt they needed to perform a ritual, say a prayer, something to mark the moment. She could not think of anything that didn't feel fake and performative. She looked at Sheridan, who had stopped crying. They were lucky to still have each other, Jessica knew that, but she didn't feel lucky. The flowers were so colourful against the bleak remains of the forest they wrenched her heart. They were symbols of the women who had been killed. Bright and beautiful against the dark.

'Shall we go to the swamp?' she asked her daughter after they had stood in silence for a few minutes. She needed to move. Even the weather seemed to be mourning.

Sheridan nodded and then reached out and took her mother's hand. She hadn't done that since she was a little girl. Jessica felt suddenly overwhelmed by the desire to protect her child and the impossibility of doing so. Why were they here, in this desolate place? Why had they come? She wanted to turn and run back to their car and then drive to the safety of their house on its nice green suburban street, with its newly mown lawns and neatly trimmed hedges, and never ever let Sheridan leave. Instead, she led her daughter towards the next killing field.

They reached the entrance to the swamp. The rotting log had gone; only the indentation it had made in the ground remained. Jessica bent and put her hand on the bare earth. It should have taken a century for that great tree to return to the ground. In that fire, it had probably taken minutes. But the swamp was not as desolate as the rest of the forest. Perhaps the water in the bog had saved it from the worst. Yes, the sedges and grasses had gone, but there were green shoots everywhere, covering the circumference. Jessica sighed and let her shoulders relax. Sheridan noticed the movement, caught her mother's eye, and smiled.

'Look,' she breathed.

Hand in hand, mother and daughter stood at the entrance. The hills still rose in a perfect circle around the flat hanging peat bog, but they were starkly changed. They were covered in the broken and burnt remnants of the once-great forest, poking like dead fingers towards the sky. Nothing moved.

Then, a sound, a bell-like sound, carrying across the bowl of the swamp, echoing from one hillside to another. There could be no mistaking it. It was melancholic to hear it, yet joyous. A phoenix rising from the ashes.

'Listen,' Jessica said. 'It's a lyrebird.'

Then an answering call, from the hills behind them.

The bird began its repertoire. Mimicking other birds at first, making the forest sound the way it used to for a few moments. Then, suddenly, a siren rent the air followed by a chainsaw and the sound of men yelling. As the bird demonstrated its artistry, the other joined in with the sound of a helicopter. It sounded so close, Jessica and Sheridan both looked up. Next it was as if a water bomber had released its load. The swoosh and splash of it so vivid, the two women almost expected to be drenched. The first bird again, mimicking the growl and the roar of the fire itself.

'I heard that,' Sheridan whispered. 'That's what it sounded like while I was locked in that cellar.'

Mother and daughter stood and listened to the two birds replaying the terrible cacophony of destruction. When they stopped, their calls echoed for a moment, then silence.

'Will you come with me to the next anti-coal blockade?' Sheridan asked.

Jessica squeezed her hand. 'I'll be there.'

ACKNOWLEDGEMENTS

There are so many people who helped me write this book. Some helped me with the research, which was extensive and, at times, confronting. Some helped me keep going, particularly when I made a false start. Some helped me solve what I call the puzzle of the book. All books are a puzzle, or they are to me anyway. I start with an idea and then find myself getting deeper into an ever more complicated labyrinth, which twists and turns and leads me to many dead ends and a few productive ones. Maybe some authors can find their way to the story they are telling alone, but I need guiding hands. Others just encouraged me and believed in my idea. Everyone who helped was equally important to the creation of this book, and all of them deserve a formal and heartfelt thank you. So, here goes.

The idea for *Lyrebird* came to me on a walk through the Barrington Tops with my husband. I was struggling with writing a quite different novel and was deep in my own head as we walked along the dirt road through the forest. My husband stopped me suddenly because a lyrebird had stepped out of the undergrowth a few feet in front of us and begun walking along the road ahead. We followed slowly, hardly daring to breathe, aware of what a privilege it is to see such a magnificent, wild creature up close. The bird seemed blithely unaware of our presence. It was while we were following behind that the idea for this book came to me. I knew immediately that it was an idea I had to pursue. The first acknowledgment, therefore, must be to that bird, who entered my life for a minute or two and then scurried away, leaving behind the beginning of an entirely new story.

Next are Caroline Baum and David Roach, who were the first people I confided in about the idea, and whose unbridled enthusiasm and encouragement gave me the confidence I needed to begin. Clever, creative, generous-hearted friends are the very best kind.

I also owe the brilliant Kathryn Heyman, who would not let me wallow in self-pity as I struggled with my first idea, but gently, kindly and determinedly made me do her wonderful writing course and so keep the faith, if not in that book, at least in my right to write. She also put me in touch with a writing mentor, Malcolm Knox. I simply could not have asked for a better, kinder, more skilled guide through the thickets of this complex story than Malcolm. I have something he said to me at the forefront of everything I write now. 'Not all economical writing is good writing,' he said. 'But all good writing is economical.' For a chronic over-writer like me, that was the single best piece of advice I could have received. I tried very hard (and it was hard) to stick to it.

My dear friend Terry Ryan, who I met doing the outrageously politically incorrect but very funny Ancient History Reviews when we were both students at Macquarie Uni in the seventies, has always been a brilliant creative muse, generous with ideas and suggestions as well as kind but firm criticism when required. If he likes something, I know he means it.

The research required for this novel was extensive and specialised. I am very glad to say that human trafficking, organised crime and sexual slavery are not things I have experienced, and I understood I needed to find people who could talk to me honestly and expertly about that dark world. My friend, the legendary investigative journalist Kate McClymont, had lunch with me one day, giving me the benefit of her extensive knowledge of the dark side of Sydney and New South Wales, and also access to her contact list. She put me on to Detective Sergeant Rob Guilder, AFP Organised Crime, who had worked to combat human trafficking and organised crime. He was generous with his expertise and his experiences. He suggested I also contact Andy Warton, a former federal agent with the Australian Federal Police, who was equally as expert and told me many stories which really helped me imaginatively enter the murky world that he and Rob had spent their careers trying to fight. I am indebted to them.

Crime novels need a lot of hard information, not least forensic science. All I knew about forensics was gleaned from *Silent Witness* and, much as I enjoy the show, I was nervous that it wasn't the most reliable of sources. One evening, at a fund raiser, someone foolishly asked me what I was up to, and

I told them. I soon found myself lamenting my lack of forensic knowledge. 'I'm a retired forensic scientist,' the bloke sitting opposite me suddenly said, and that's how I found the highly experienced and always obliging Andrew Sparks. I asked him so many questions I am sure he regretted outing himself at that function, but I am eternally grateful he did. Serendipity is a wonderful thing.

Huge appreciation must also go to my publisher at Allen & Unwin, Cate Paterson, my editor Christa Munns, my copyeditor Ali Lavau and my proofreader Greer Gamble. They saved me from myself so many times I basically lost count. I also owe my literary agent, Jacinta di Mase, a debt of gratitude. It was she who bluntly told me that the novel I was struggling with wasn't up to scratch and so forced me to reconsider and come up with a better idea. Given her enthusiastic support of *Lyrebird*, it seems I did. Had she been less honest, maybe this novel would never have existed.

I also want to thank Hannah Diviney, disability and women's rights advocate, author, actor, speaker and commentator, who very kindly agreed to read the manuscript to make sure I had not been inadvertently insensitive or clumsy in my depiction of Nan Farrow. I owe the same debt to my old Senate running mate, Hannah Maher, who is also an incredible activist and advocate. She is a policy writer and LGBTQ inclusive practice trainer and will be a sensational addition to our parliament one day. She read the manuscript to make sure Coco Potts was portrayed with respect and dignity. The wise and empathic counsel of the two Hannahs was very important.

Award-winning journalist and author Margaret Simons kindly put me in touch with two Filipina social workers working at Angeles Relief Inc, an Australian charity that helps abandoned children of sex tourists in the Philippines. Margaret is the President of the charity. Pam Yangco and Charlene Patungan generously read the manuscript and helped me to ensure that, again, my portrayals of Gloria and Luna, and of sex-trafficked women in general, are respectful, empathic and, above all, accurate. If you would care to donate to their work, as I have done, here is their website: www.angelesrelief.org.

I am also lucky enough that an old school friend (hello, Forest High), Greg Mullins AO AFSM, is a former Commissioner of Fire and Rescue, NSW, as well as an internationally acknowledged expert on climate change and its effect on fires. We shared a memorable coffee as he told me what it is like to face a catastrophic bushfire. He also gave me a copy of his excellent book *Firestorm*. Who knew the boy with the afro at the back of the bus would become such an internationally renowned expert and advocate? If the bushfire scenes in this book achieve any authenticity, it is thanks to Greg.

If like me, you are concerned about climate change and want to do something about it, I recommend donating to Rising Tide, who organise an annual anti-coal blockade at Newcastle Harbour, rather like the one mentioned in the book. Their website is risingtide.org.au.

My final thanks, as always, must go to my family, especially my husband Ralph, who allows me to read my work to him most evenings. This is an act of true love, especially in the early drafts. My daughters, Polly and Charlotte, are always enthusiastic, encouraging and genuinely excited about my writing. I did not realise how much I would enjoy having adult daughters who occasionally parent me, especially when my self-doubt gets out of control.

Lastly, I want to acknowledge you—the reader. Every one of you makes a new *Lyrebird* through the act of reading and imagining the story I tell in your own way. Thank you all for making that effort. Without readers there can be no literature.